Pride Publishing books by Gareth Chris

All on the Line
Brought by the Storm
Saved by the Pitcher
Found by Chance

Collections
Oh, Baby!: He Doesn't Know Jack

All on the Line

FOUND BY CHANCE

GARETH CHRIS

Found by Chance
ISBN # 978-1-80250-747-8

Interior text design by Claire Siemaszkiewicz
Pride Publishing

Published in 2024 by Pride Publishing, United Kingdom.

Pride Publishing is an imprint of Totally Entwined Group Limited.

FOUND BY CHANCE

Dedication

I'd like to thank my editor, Anna Olson, as well as Rebecca Scott from Totally Entwined. Both continue to provide terrific support and the *All on the Line* series wouldn't have been possible without them.

Chapter One

Chance accepted the good-luck wishes from his assistant Aurora with a slight frown, wondering if her uncharacteristic encouragement meant she perceived just how screwed he felt. He was about to make a marketing pitch to the top physician group in the Bay Area, and he wasn't as prepared as he would have liked to have been. Having recently won prestigious industry awards and even being dubbed the 'Marketing Boy Wonder' by the *San Francisco Business Monthly* magazine, he had lofty expectations to meet. Chance knew that today, however, it wasn't whether he'd fall short—it was a question of the degree to which he'd disappoint.

The head of Marketing, Maria, had given him three potential clients in as many weeks, and all had anticipated proposals within unreasonable time frames. He had landed the first two accounts, but he had felt confident about those. Chance had been able to give them decent attention, but that had been at the expense of focus on the physicians' group campaign. Exacerbating the problem, he had just moved into a new house, and the little bit of oversight he'd provided the moving company had sucked up valuable time from his work.

Now as he walked to the boardroom, he felt like a man stumbling to a lethal injection. Maria had reminded him of the importance of this potential client when he had arrived to work. Knowing she would be furious if he failed to seal the deal with the prospect wasn't bolstering his confidence any.

When he entered the meeting room, the only individual behaving like they were excited was Maria. She affected the charm and suck-up demeanor that she always had when potential clients were present. His boss shot him a proud smile, and Chance knew it was for the benefit of the physicians' group members—not him.

"Gentlemen, this is our finest Marketing Campaign Manager, Chance Findley." She beamed, pointing to Chance as if he would be invisible otherwise. "Or, as the *San Francisco Business Monthly* refers to him, the 'Marketing Boy Wonder.'"

Chance grimaced. He had hoped the clients were unaware as it was not the time to set expectations even higher.

Chance employed a Maria tactic, attempting to turn on the charm to distract them from anything meaningful. He rushed to the two men who rose to shake hands, offering them his megawatt smile and effusive compliments about the work they did on the board.

Even before the introductions were made, Chance figured out which of the two men was the decision-maker—the doctor who towered at a few inches over six feet and was built like a linebacker. The man had neatly groomed jet-black hair, a head that was more squared than most and a suit that screamed custom-made. Maria introduced him as Dr. Kendall. Kendall squeezed Chance's hand firmly enough that Chance knew it was more a gesture of dominance than cordiality. Dr. Kendall didn't offer a smile, and his piercing gray-blue eyes added to his intimidating presence.

Chance was happy to turn his attention to the second man who also remained straight-faced, but at least appeared as nervous as Chance. He was introduced as Dr. Yeon.

Maria jumped into the conversation to babble more about the Marketing firm's accomplishments and awards, but she began to falter when her boasting was met with Dr. Kendall's disinterest and finger-tapping against the conference room table. She pivoted to a briefer, less demonstrative overview of Chance's resume before handing the meeting to him.

Chance had been hoping the doctors would be professionals who knew little about the creative aspects of attracting donors, employees and patients. Maybe then, his less-than-stellar campaign would appeal to them enough that, given a little more time, he could enhance it to delight them with a final proposal. Instead, Kendall was eyeing Chance like he was the guy who'd walked into a formal gala wearing a sweatshirt and jeans. Yeon sat like a child at a dining table full of adult strangers, which Chance took as a sign that the doctor sensed his partner's impatience.

Chance turned to his marketing display board, inhaling a deep breath when his back was turned to the group. He unveiled the unimpressive contents of his work, trying to add vibrance with his tone and on-the-fly commentary. As he continued speaking, flat-sides were becoming more apparent to him than when he had last reviewed the pitch in his overly tired state. He presented alternatives as he proceeded, as if that had been his intent all along—to give a base campaign and customize it as the doctors saw fit. Each time Chance looked back to the physicians, they had the same expressions and movements. Kendall appeared to be annoyed and Yeon fidgeted. Maria's gaze signaled that Chance needed to right the ship, but he knew that was impossible since the campaign hadn't been seaworthy to start.

When Chance finished, even he couldn't pretend the presentation was satisfactory. He closed with a comment that it was customary for him to show a prospective client the bare bones of what was possible and that with a little more time, he would spin his magic to make the physician practice stand out in the marketplace.

Maria glared at him, messaging that she didn't appreciate Chance's lie about how they did business, but she played along. Donning a smile, she turned to the doctors and emphasized that Chance had wanted to get reactions to better understand what would meet their needs.

Dr. Kendall looked to his watch with irritation, then locked eyes with Maria. "My reaction is that I've wasted my morning, not to mention the money we put forward for this...presentation. I'm sure I was clear that I wanted to review a *final* proposal today." He turned an icy stare to Chance. "If I wanted something *bare bones*, I would have said so. Unlike this firm, I mean what I say and I deliver accordingly."

He rose from the table and Dr. Yeon stood, as well, casting apologetic glances to Maria and Chance.

"Dr. Kendall, you're right," Chance interjected. "I promise you that I can do better. In fact, just as I was speaking, I was formulating new ideas that I think would resonate very well in the marketplace. If you could give me a couple of additional days…"

Dr. Kendall shook his head. "There's a conference I'll be leaving the state for this afternoon. I won't have time to give you a second chance." He turned to Maria. "Your firm, and Mr. Findley in particular, came highly recommended. I will be honest with you. I cannot fathom why. To say that I'm unimpressed would be an understatement. Dr. Yeon and I met with one of your competitors yesterday to review their proposal. It wasn't wonderful, but it was far better than this. It appears we'll have to settle for it. You should know that I will suggest to others on the commerce board that they do business elsewhere."

The doctors began to walk around the conference table, ignoring Chance and making their way to the door.

Maria scurried to their sides before they could exit. "I understand your disappointment. We have a strong reputation for a reason. This was unacceptable, and you have my deepest apologies. Of course, we'll refund the money."

Dr. Kendall looked down on her like she was an irritating dog that had just lifted its leg in the doctor's direction. "That is the least you can do. I appreciate the apology, but it doesn't change the fact that you wasted my valuable time." He shot a disapproving look back at Chance, then returned his gaze to Maria. "Perhaps you shouldn't rely on a 'boy wonder' to do an adult's job. Thank you for informing me of the magazine's misplaced accolades. I'll make it a point to write a rebuttal opinion detailing my experience. I'm quite sure, with my prominence in the community, the *Business Monthly* will provide space for it on their comments-to-the-editor page. We'll see ourselves out."

Maria turned to stare down Chance once the doctors filed out.

"Maria, I'm so sorry," Chance mumbled. "I know this account was important to you…"

"It was important to *the firm*, Chance," she snapped. "Dr. Kendall was not overstating his importance. We would have been better off never making a pitch to him than the garbage you slung this morning. Now he'll tear us apart with the community. What were you thinking? This wasn't anywhere near ready to present."

Chance sighed, scratching his neck with nervous energy. "I know it wasn't my usual quality. Maria, you gave me too much to do in a short period of time."

"Great accountability," Maria barked back. "When it comes to annual compensation, you point out that you're my top producer. If you want the money, then don't complain when you have tight deadlines and blame me for your failure. When I was in your shoes, I had time pressures far more aggressive than this. And you know what, Chance? I delivered."

Chance refrained from rolling his eyes. He had heard from several colleagues that had worked with Maria through the years that she was far less accomplished than she bragged. She had risen to her level because what she lacked in talent she made up for with hard work, tenacity and an abundance of ass-kissing.

"I won us the other two accounts," Chance reminded her sheepishly.

Instead of pacifying Maria, Chance's comment inflamed her. "So what? You think that means you can just blow off the third one? I don't pay you to work two-thirds of a week, Chance."

Chance started to anger. "Maria, I've always put in far more hours than a standard work week. You know that. I've been busting my butt for this firm for the last two years. You knew I was moving this past week, too. I told you in advance that I would need some time and you still saddled me with three prospects."

Maria was unmoved. "So, what you're confessing is that your personal life interfered with your obligations to the firm. Noted, Chance."

Chance wiped a hand over his face, beginning to sweat. He wished his boss didn't see that. "Maria, with all due respect, I think you're being unfair. Despite the move, I still put in well over seventy hours this past week. I do have matters that need attention, too. I'm human. And unlike my peers, I don't have a partner at home to help me with those personal needs."

"That's not my problem," Maria snipped. "Did you think the job came with a mail-order bride? It's up to you to find a way. I always did and I've never married." Chance wondered if that had been her choice. It was hard to imagine anyone dealing with her. Maria took a deep breath, then wiped her hands down her hips. "But since you're complaining that you feel burned out, perhaps you should take the next two or three weeks off. You've banked enough vacation time. It will give me a chance to better assess some of the talent on our team that you've overshadowed."

Chance swallowed, blinking. "Are you suggesting you're seeing if they could take my place?"

Maria's face softened only a fraction. "I didn't say that. I said, take some time off. You're accusing me of overworking you. So I'm telling you to recuperate. When you come back, I'll expect better from you."

"Maria, I don't need two or three weeks," Chance protested, still worried that Maria was planning to test others to see if they could take on more of the opportunities that came to the firm, which would impede his bonus-earnings. He had just dropped down more than two million dollars on his new house, and it wasn't the time to see a reduction in his salary.

Maria crossed her arms in anger. "First you say I'm driving you too hard. Then you bitch about me giving you time off. Chance, do not come to work for the next three weeks. You always lose vacation at the end of the year. Use some of it instead to get your house in order, or whatever it is you need to do. We'll manage without you."

Maria stormed from the board room, leaving Chance wondering if her last words applied only to the time he'd be away.

* * * *

Chance pulled his BMW up to the three-foot long driveway of his new home. He clicked the automatic garage door opener, then ticked it several more times in frustration, wondering why the door wasn't opening.

"Oh, come on," he muttered. "Now what?"

He exited the car and tried the keypad on the garage door frame. Still, the door wouldn't budge.

He heard a voice call from his left. "Having a problem?"

Chance turned his head to see the latest witness to his humiliating morning. It was a young man watering plants along the sidewalk of the next house over. Since it was San Francisco, Chance mused that the house next door might just as well have been referenced as the house abutting his own. When Chance had bought the place, he had hoped he would like his neighbors as he could open his side windows and clean those belonging to the people living next to him.

Chance shrugged, then pointed at the door. "Doesn't want to open. It's been one of those days."

The young man shot him a smile. He reminded Chance of a guy he had known in college and it made him anxious, as he had been the only man he had ever experimented with sexually. He hoped the guy wouldn't notice his reddened face.

"I'm Arlo," the man announced, walking over to Chance to shake his hand. "I'm your next-door neighbor."

"Oh?" Chance stammered. It had been a dumb assumption that any working-age person landscaping in the middle of the day would be hired help. He recovered, he hoped, quickly enough for Arlo not to notice. "Nice to meet you. I'm Chance."

"So, just moved in a couple of days ago, didn't you?" Arlo asked.

Chance suspected that the neighbors had been watching him and the movers on his first day in the house, wondering what the new occupants would be like. "Yes. The place is still a mess."

Arlo nodded with understanding. "Moving is a lot of work. I was going to come over that day to offer my help, but I saw there were quite a few guys. I didn't want to get in the way or kill a buddy vibe."

Chance grinned. "Ah, that's nice of you. You would have been welcome, but no worries. We had it under control between the professional movers and me." Chance cringed for having just admitted there had been no friends helping. It embarrassed him once more, as it could be read as an indictment of his likeability.

Arlo smiled. His dark eyes looked flirty when he did so. "I was sort of spying. I must admit, I was wondering which one of you or combination of people was moving in. The last couple who lived here weren't the nicest of neighbors. You could walk right past one of them, say hello, and they'd ignore you. They were judgmental residents, which isn't the norm for this city."

Chance wondered what the previous owners had been judging, but decided not to ask a person he'd just met. Arlo's expression turned inquisitive like he was still trying to decide if he'd like Chance any better than the people who preceded him. Despite the scrutiny, Arlo's face was kind. When he smiled, his large white teeth and two pronounced incisors would look menacing were it not for the fact that his whole face lit up when he did. It made Chance think of an overjoyed child, despite Arlo's close-trimmed beard. The man's skin was smooth and his cheekbones and jaw were strong. His dark hair had been cut close on the sides, but was longer on top and heavily streaked platinum. The hair, more than anything, reminded him of his long-ago bed partner, as he had highlighted his hair, too.

It dawned on Chance that he had been staring and hadn't responded to Arlo's last comment. "Um, that sucks they were disapproving. I'd like to think I'm not. Well, unless what they were judging is loud music coming from your house after midnight. I need my sleep." He laughed, hoping his warning came across lighthearted.

Arlo chuckled. "My boyfriend goes to bed early, so you don't have to worry about me cranking up late-night tunes."

Chance's silent question of whether the neighbor was gay was answered. He wondered if it was more than Arlo's hairstyle that reminded Chance of the boy he'd once slept with. "That's cool," he stated, hoping his tone matched his words. He always hesitated to talk about homosexuality with others, feeling he had no right to when he had been too much of a coward to share with anyone his own past encounter. Although he liked women and enjoyed sex with them, he assumed if he told anyone about his past, they'd label him queer. And Chance hated that would bother him, as he supported the gay community and liked to think of himself as an enlightened progressive.

"Want me to check out your garage door?" Arlo offered after they had stood in silence for a moment. "You can't leave your car half-parked on the street all night."

Chance looked back at his BMW. The rear-end was taking up part of a road lane. Fortunately, it was a quiet neighborhood, by San Francisco standards. "Why did they make driveways so short in this city?"

Arlo laughed. "They didn't have automobiles when these houses were built, for one thing. Secondly, every inch of land is worth a gazillion dollars. You want to waste it on pavement?"

Chance nodded knowingly. "Good points. Yeah, if you're handy, I'll take you up on your offer. I'm not very good with my hands." Chance noticed that his comment invited an appreciative look from Arlo at his hands. Out of shyness, Chance stuck them in his pockets.

"Lead the way," Arlo directed, motioning to Chance's front-door steps. When he saw Chance's look of confusion, Arlo added, "I need to check the door from the inside. Unless the batteries are dead in both your remote and your keypad, the malfunction is from within."

"Oh, right," Chance stammered. "Well, they both have new batteries, so..."

He led the neighbor into his home, apologizing for the still unpacked boxes and framed pictures that were scattered across the floor. The two proceeded to a small hall that opened to the garage, and Arlo went inside to inspect the garage door hinges.

Chance was surprised to hear the man let out a laugh. "What?"

Arlo turned, flashing his infectious smile. "I just noticed the door is locked from the inside." He flipped the lock and raised his hands in a 'voila' fashion. "Easy fix. You must have locked it inside and forgotten."

Chance flushed anew, remembering that he had locked the door the night before for added security. He had left his car at his vacated house until he could remove belongings from the new garage, which he had done the night before in preparation of garaging the BMW the next day. What he had forgotten to do was unlock the latch when he arose in the morning. "I'm an idiot."

Arlo placed his hand on Chance's shoulder. Because Arlo was wearing a tank-top, Arlo's bulging bicep and little tuft of underarm hair were on display. Chance noted the armpit fur was the same warm brown tone of the hairs on the man's forearm. He swallowed, wondering why after all these years of ignoring men, Arlo's physical features were drawing his attention.

"You're not an idiot." Arlo smiled. "You probably have a lot on your mind, new house and all."

"Thanks," Chance responded, still self-conscious of his helplessness and his inspection of Arlo's body. "Um, I guess I should move the car in now."

Arlo nodded, reaching over Chance's face to press the automatic garage door opener that was on the interior wall. Chance noticed Arlo's skin smelled like refreshing soap and spicy deodorant. He liked it, and it made him question again why Arlo was having this effect on him.

Arlo looked at Chance with puzzlement when Chance hadn't retreated to the car. "Go ahead. I'll step to the sidewalk so I won't be in your way."

Chance nodded, feeling awkward before following Arlo out to the driveway. He opened his car door and took a seat, then sighed. It would be rude to send away the man who helped him. "Uh, it's mid-afternoon. Do you want to come in for a drink?"

Arlo grinned. "Yes. That would be great."

Chance blinked his eyes in acknowledgment. He started the engine, worried whether he should be encouraging fraternization with a guy who was stirring up old feelings. Even if he had the courage to act on them, it would lead to frustration since Arlo had a boyfriend. Chance saw Arlo follow the car back into the garage—it was too late to undo his invitation.

Chapter Two

Arlo followed Chance back into his house, thinking the man's clumsiness when near him only added to his appeal. When he had seen the group of men moving furniture into the home, he had hoped the guy he now knew as Chance would be the neighbor. Arlo had been attracted to him the moment he had laid eyes on him. He figured Chance was in his early thirties and was likely a successful businessman, based on the way he dressed and his ability to afford an expensive home and German luxury convertible. Arlo was drawn to sexy, accomplished men.

As Arlo ascended the steps behind Chance, he admired the man's well-sculpted butt, hugged tight by his tailored suit pants. Chance's ass was nearly as gorgeous as his face, which resembled an Abercrombie & Fitch model's. Chance ran a hand through his beautiful wavy mane of golden-brown locks, which fell back into place as if untouched.

Chance turned to face him when they reached the kitchen. He had an apologetic expression. "I know the place still looks like it was vandalized. I hope you don't mind."

Arlo shook his head with a smile. "It's not so bad. Don't worry about me. Is it okay to sit at the kitchen counter?" The stools were already in place.

"Sure," Chance responded, pointing at the stool, even though Arlo was already taking a seat. "Um, what do you like to drink? The booze is unpacked, so I might have whatever you like on-hand."

"Hmm. You unpacked with priorities in mind. Red wine?" Arlo requested, assuming a well-stocked cabinet had that. "Any kind is fine. I won't stay long. You must have a lot to do."

Chance sighed. "Yeah, but suddenly I have plenty of time to get it done."

"Oh?" Now, Arlo was curious.

Chance grimaced, wondering why he was sharing his humiliating story. Nevertheless, he plowed ahead, surprised by how comfortable he was with Arlo already. "My boss insisted I take a three-week vacation."

Arlo raised an eyebrow. "You don't sound happy about it. She must think you earned it, no?"

Chance pressed his lips together. "You could say that. She thinks I merited time away like a kid deserves getting expelled from school. I had a marketing presentation earlier that didn't go well. We lost the prospective client. She's pissed." Chance exhaled a laugh hoping it lightened the mood, despite the words he had spoken.

Arlo reached across the counter and patted Chance's arm. "I'm sorry. She sounds like a bitch. I mean, you can't win them all, right? Who treats an adult like that?"

Chance shrugged. "She said she thinks I need time to recuperate."

"Do you?"

"Maybe. She put a lot on me. I think I would have been fine with it if I had won the account and she offered me extra vacation time as a reward. As it stands, it feels like a way of telling me I'm dispensable and that I'd better pick up my game when I get back." He snorted. "If she hasn't already replaced me by then, that is."

"It's one account. That's extreme, isn't it? You must be good at your job to be able to afford this place," Arlo reasoned.

Chance grinned. "I hope you're right. So, now you know I'm in marketing. What do you do that you can be home this early doing landscaping?"

Arlo chuckled. "I work part-time at a nursing home. My grandmother lives there. They had so much turnover that I was worried about the kind of care the residents were receiving. So, when the billionth aide resigned, I decided I would take the job so they could have some continuity."

"Oh." Chance was confused. "That's nice. But you live in a big house in the most expensive city in the country. Do nursing homes pay that well now?"

Arlo laughed out loud. "That would be a hell no. They pay the shit you assume they pay. My boyfriend is the big money-maker."

Chance nodded, remembering the boyfriend. "Right. Where is he? You want to invite him to join us?"

Arlo took a sip of wine, then leaned back on the stool. "He's away on business. Charlie is always on the go."

Chance pursed his lips, understanding that work hours were long for people who lived the way he did—unless they were the person's boyfriend, apparently. "So, what do you do to occupy your time when he's gone?"

Arlo fidgeted with his wine glass, taking a minute to respond. He looked to Chance with apparent apprehension. "Did you mean it when you said you aren't judgmental?"

Chance wondered what he was about to hear, but wanted to prove to himself that he was honest, so he nodded. "I don't think I am. I have the feeling I'm about to find out."

Arlo snickered, then waved a hand through the air. "Okay, what the hell. I guess the worst that will happen is you'll kick me out of your house and I'll have the same kind of relationship with you that I had with the neighbors that lived here before you." He paused when Chance braced his hands on the edge of the counter. "Um, I have a FansOfStuds account."

"A what?" Chance asked, unsure of what that even meant.

Arlo wiped his hands over his thighs. "It's an online adult entertainment thing. You can subscribe to different guys' accounts and, in return, you can watch them…entertain."

Chance blinked a few times before responding. "You do gay porn?"

Arlo wiped his hands on his pants again. "Not gay porn, so much. I suppose it depends on how you define pornography. I mean, there aren't other guys with me. I just do my thing and people watch."

"Your thing?" Chance wondered. "Like, you…jerk off?" Arlo nodded. "And people pay to watch that?"

Arlo laughed. "Okay, guess I know you're straight based on your reaction. Believe it or not, lots of gay guys, and even lots of women, enjoy watching a good-looking guy wank on camera."

Chance swallowed, jerking his head back a bit. "Uh, yeah, sure. I mean, I guess. It's just...don't they get bored after a while just watching you tug your junk?"

Arlo snickered. "Thanks for being curious as opposed to outraged. I was waiting for you to call me some horrible name and ask me to leave."

Chance was offended. "What? No. I'm not like that. I'm just...it's not like every day I meet a sex worker."

Arlo shrugged. "I don't think of it that way, though I guess you're correct, technically. When I hear the term sex-worker, I think of a prostitute."

"Isn't it, kind of?" Chance asked, then held up an apologetic hand. "Sorry. I'm not trying to insult you."

Arlo sighed. "It's okay. It's not like I look down on prostitutes. Hey, everyone needs to find a way to make a living, right? They aren't hurting anyone. There's a much better chance that they're the ones getting hurt. I feel sorry for them. But for me, I work behind a camera so I feel safe. Nobody can do anything to me."

"But why do you do it? You said your boyfriend makes good money, so you must not be doing it for financial reasons. And speaking of your boyfriend—Charlie, was it? He doesn't mind you doing that?" Chance stopped himself—he was beginning to sound judgmental after all.

"Charlie's okay with it, for the most part." Arlo took another sip of wine. "First off, you're right. I don't do it for the money. I do it because it feels good."

Chance squinted. "Uh, yeah. But I don't need to invite the world to watch me making myself feel good."

Arlo laughed. "Hmm, if your boss does replace you, you might change your mind. Trust me, you'd be very successful. *I'd* pay to watch."

Blood rushed to Chance's cheeks before he responded. "Oh."

"When I said it feels good, I wasn't referring to the masturbation. I was talking about entertaining people. It's an art to engage viewers in small talk before removing each article of clothing. Then, you know you've got them panting and stroking while you start playing with yourself, showing more and more until they're begging you to do all sorts of horny shit."

Chance frowned. "Okay…"

Arlo shrugged. "It makes me feel powerful. I like that so many people are getting off because of me. It's an ego-boost every time, reading how much they like my face, my chest, my arms, my legs, my ass, my cock…"

Chance poured himself a glass of wine and took a swig. He looked back to Arlo with amazement. "So, you get off on people watching."

"Yeah, under those controlled circumstances," Arlo responded. "I do. Is that so terrible?"

Chance contemplated, then drank more wine. He rested the glass back on the counter, staring down at it, too embarrassed to look Arlo in the eye. "I guess not. Like you said, you're not hurting anybody. I suppose everyone is getting what they want."

Arlo cleared his throat. "Yeah, and well, I also make a lot of money doing it, so there's that."

"A *lot* of money?" Chance wondered, raising his eyes back to Arlo's as he retrieved the glass for another swig.

Arlo nodded. "I mean, not enough to live here on just that. But I make over half a million a year."

Chance spat out the wine he had been swallowing, coughing. When he collected himself, he stared at Arlo with astonishment. "You make that to shoot your wad?"

Arlo smirked. "Well, not for one wad. I'm not *that* amazing. A year's worth of wads. Anyway, I'm the most-requested model on the site. I have a huge social media presence and, on that site, I have hundreds of subscribers."

"Holy shit," Chance mumbled. "That's unbelievable." He leaned back against the refrigerator. "I don't get it."

Arlo frowned. "Thanks a lot. I know you're straight, but still. You know how to hurt a guy."

Chance blinked, registering how his comment was interpreted. "No, that's not what I meant. You're a handsome man, for sure. What I don't understand is, once they've seen you…do your thing…why would they keep coming back to watch you do it again? It's not like I return to the same porn video."

Arlo shrugged. "What I do isn't stagnant like a video. And the subscribers like me. It's more than them thinking I'm hot. I show them my personality. I talk to them. I answer their questions. I've gotten to know several of them, even if it is by their fake names. I have a knack for remembering what the frequent customers like and I'll mention it when they log a comment. It makes them feel special that I'm singling them out and that I care enough about them that what they've told me is worth retaining and revisiting. They feel a connection to me."

"Hmm," Chance mumbled, surprised and curious.

"Chance, a lot of these people might feel unseen or lonely. I give them something that makes them feel good about themselves, if only for a few moments. And yes, some people are just horny and want to see me do dirty stuff, but that's okay. What's wrong with giving someone sexual gratification? And you know what? I've gotten to like some of the members, too. It makes me smile when certain people log on because I know from experience that we'll have a nice little back-and-forth conversation about all sorts of stuff before we get down to it."

Chance, still absorbing all he was hearing, poured himself another glass. "So, when you're done, isn't it kind of weird? You've been chatting with these people about their dog or some shit, then you all get boned up until you come, then what? You just flick off the camera and everyone scurries away in shame?"

Arlo laughed. "That's a funny image. No, it's nothing like that. Most of the people stay online. Sure, some click off because they got what they paid for, and that's cool. But the viewers who stay on keep chatting, telling me how awesome I was and thanking me. It's sweet. I try to stay engaged for several more minutes, telling them I'm happy that I made them feel good, or stuff like that. Then, I tell them that I'm beat and wish them a good night. You'd be surprised how many of them reply with kind wishes for me."

Chance poked his tongue at his inner cheek, trying to envision the situation. "You make it almost sound wholesome."

"I like giving comfort. Both my jobs allow that."

Chance was unsure. "Don't any of them ever get creepy, asking for sick shit?"

Arlo nodded. "It happens. I warn them when something isn't cool with me. If they don't back off or if they give me crap, I bounce them from the chat room and I don't accept any tips they sent to me during that session. The website bans them and keeps them from subscribing again if they're repeat offenders. You'd be surprised at how supportive the other members are when I'm trying to shut that kind of thing down. They all pile on, calling the obnoxious party names and telling them to shut up. To be honest, even if I wanted to stop doing this, which I don't, I'd feel guilty for leaving my fans. They're good to me and I think they'd miss me."

Chance wasn't convinced. "And what if they stalk you in real life?"

Arlo shot a questioning glance Chance's way. "How would they do that? Chance, I don't use my real name! I'm not an idiot. I have an account-name."

"An account-name?"

Arlo grinned. "*Chatter_butt_box_27.*"

"Huh?"

Arlo shrugged. "I know I'm a chatterbox, but a lot of the fans love that I talk the whole time, and I call them out individually when they log on. Stuff like that makes it feel intimate. As for the butt part, well, I had to pique their interest with something sexual. I figured the butt can be called a box if you think of it as a receptacle." Chance's eyes widened. "And the twenty-seven is my age. So, for now, the name makes sense."

"Okay. I guess," Chance stated with uncertainty.

Arlo crossed his arms. "Come on, Chance. Surely you knew these types of sites exist? You aren't a relic. Are you going to tell me you never logged on to watch a girl finger herself? Maybe fuck herself with a dildo?"

Chance shook his head. "No, I haven't. I've watched porn, of course. You know, a guy fucking a girl, but it wasn't live. They weren't interacting with an audience."

Arlo shrugged. "Well, I think what you watch is boring. I never watch gay porn videos because they're missing that personal element. You should log on to a fan site and you'll see what I mean."

Chance shook his head. "Uh, I don't think so."

Arlo chuckled. "Don't be scared. They won't know who you are."

"They get your credit card information," Chance countered.

"The performer doesn't," Arlo corrected. "In my case, some bookkeeper that works for FansOfStuds processes the payments and, like any good business, that person is audited to ensure they aren't stealing or abusing credit card information. Your name would be one of thousands that person sees as they process transactions—you'd be, for all intents and purposes, anonymous. For example, if you logged onto my account tomorrow night to watch me and created some handle, I'd have no idea it was you watching."

Chance felt anxious again at the notion of logging on to watch Arlo. "That doesn't freak you out?"

"What?"

"That someone you know could stumble upon your account and watch you?" Chance clarified.

Arlo grinned. "If they stumble on my site and still pay to subscribe, then they want what I'm offering. If it was someone I knew, though, I would expect them to ask me first. I think it would be rude of them to watch me without my permission. But if I was convinced that they would be into it and not judge me, then I might say yes. I'd just keep it much tamer than usual. Even I have some modesty." Arlo winked. "If they logged on behind my back, it would make me think less of them. Lying by omission is still lying, and I'm done with dishonest people."

"Does your grandmother know you do this? I can't imagine she'd embrace it," Chance commented with a grin, infusing a bit of a humorous tone to show he wasn't being critical.

"As a matter of fact, she does," Arlo answered. Chance gasped, causing Arlo to snicker. "Grams is cool, unlike my parents. My mother and father are old-school Catholics who are certain I'm going to hell for being gay. I'm sure they'd think there's something even more horrible waiting for me there if they knew I did this for a living, too. Anyway, they don't know because we don't talk much. They're down in El Paso, and I have no desire to ever go back there. Grams moved here decades ago when my grandfather was transferred here for work, and she's been turning more liberal ever since. When Gramps died, she started hanging out with a bunch of Golden-Girl types, and they are a hoot. Unlike my mother and father, Grams has no problem with my sexuality. She's met Charlie, and she loves him. He's good to her."

"That's great," Chance interjected, "but it's one thing to accept you being gay, and another to accept you masturbate for hundreds of people's money."

Arlo narrowed his eyes. "I told you, it's not about the money. Grams understands that. She told me that if I was safe and I was having fun, I should enjoy it while I'm young and can get the attention."

Chance's eyes widened once more. "Yeah, that's so not what either of my grandmothers would say to me."

Arlo laughed. "So, you live your life doing only things that your grandmothers would approve of? You should be doing what makes *you* happy, Chance."

Chance sipped more wine. Yeah, he was pretty sure he hadn't been doing that.

Chapter Three

The sun had begun setting, and Chance and Arlo were into their second bottle of wine. Chance knew he was getting inebriated because alcohol always lowered his inhibitions and had him chattering, which was what he'd been doing the last several minutes. From what he could tell, Arlo didn't mind. Chance hoped Arlo would stay longer, not wanting to be alone to dwell on the day's earlier mortification.

"Maybe I should order a pizza or something," Chance suggested. "I might need something to soak up the liquor."

Arlo laughed. "A lightweight, huh? Sure, *I'll* order a pizza. It's the least I could do since you've been providing the wine."

Chance waved a hand to indicate that it wasn't necessary, pulling his phone from his pocket. While doing so, he checked to see if there was a message from Maria, Aurora or anyone from the office to give him an indication of how much trouble he was in. There was nothing.

Chance was startled when Arlo grabbed the phone from his hand. "Chance, I insist. I'm buying. I know the best place that delivers here. Do you like thin-crust pizza?" Chance nodded. "What do you want on it? Are you a vegetarian?"

Chance grimaced, thinking in such a liberal city that he should say yes—so many he had met since moving to San Francisco were vegan. "Um, I'm not. Sorry?"

Arlo chuckled. "Don't be sorry." He made an obvious glance at Chance's crotch. "I love meat."

"Not subtle," Chance chastised, but found himself laughing anyway, his head more clouded by the minute. "If you're a carnivore, get a combo of sausage and hamburger on it, please."

"That's my man." Arlo nodded, punching in the keys to dial take-out.

While Arlo was talking on his phone, Chance found himself admiring the gym-built muscles of Arlo's arms. He was tipsy enough to admit that he found Arlo very attractive. That he reminded him so much of Chance's one gay encounter played a part, but it didn't change the fact that Chance would have appreciated the man's features anyway.

"Want to sit in the living room while we wait?" Chance asked once Arlo finished the call.

"Sounds good," Arlo agreed. "Sitting so long on your stool is making my butt ache…and not in the way I like."

Chance rolled his eyes. "Is there a good way?"

Arlo shot Chance a naughty grin. "Absolutely. If only I could show you sometime."

The two were walking to the living room, but Chance stopped and jerked his head back. "I don't understand what's happening."

Arlo grabbed Chance's arm and pulled him to sit down on the sofa with him. "*Nothing* is happening. I'm teasing you. I have a bad habit of flirting with cute men." He eyed Chance with appreciation. "Listen, you're really attractive. You must hear that all the time. I didn't think you'd mind me playing around with you about it. If it bothers you, I'll stop."

After the crummy day he'd had, Chance had begun to enjoy the ego-boosting from a good-looking person like Arlo. "Sorry, I'm not an insecure redneck. I promise. Thanks for the compliment, but I don't get it. You said you live with your boyfriend…"

Arlo shrugged. "I still have eyes. Believe me, I've caught him checking out other dudes before."

"Sure, but you're talking about doing stuff with me," Chance pointed out.

Arlo leaned back into the cushions. "This is so much more comfortable. Anyway, yeah, I wouldn't really do anything with another man unless Charlie was on board and participating."

"Wait? What?"

Arlo played with the fringe on one of the sofa pillows. "Okay, since you've been cool about all the other stuff I've told you, I'll tell you everything. Until recently, Charlie and I were in a relationship with another man named Wilson. The three of us lived together. It worked for us. In fact, it was awesome. Since Wilson left, Charlie and I feel like something is missing. Don't get me wrong, I love Charlie. But we don't feel complete anymore." He looked to Chance, but Chance tried not to show a reaction. "So, anyway, Charlie would be all right with me seeking someone to take Wilson's place. I think that's why he's okay with me flirting…testing the waters, if you will. When Wilson was with us, I didn't flirt so much."

Chance tried to make sense of what he was hearing. "I don't understand. Are you saying you've been flirting to test the waters with me?"

Arlo laughed. "Chance, I know you're straight. Of course not. What I meant was, since Wilson left, I've become flirty with good-looking guys because I like the possibility of it happening with *someone*. I just haven't been able to turn it off, even when the opportunity isn't presenting itself. I like flirting."

Chance squinted, rubbing his temples. "Yeah, I guess you'd need to if you do jerk-off shows for people."

Arlo snickered. "Good point. But seriously, when Wilson was with us, I stopped doing the performances. He and Charlie gave me all the attention and admiration I wanted."

"And Charlie alone can't?" Chance wondered.

"It's not just me that feels that way," Arlo replied. "Charlie feels the same. I know he loves me, and he knows I love him. We aren't splitting up or anything. We just want a third person."

"Why?"

Arlo paused before continuing. "Let me give you an example. When I perform my shows, I get off on people making requests and being able to grant them. It excites me to get their compliments when they do. When Wilson was part of our partnership, he and I would do stuff together and Charlie would play that role. He'd tell us what he'd want to see, and he'd talk dirty and encourage us as we did. It added another dimension to the sex that was hot. Of course, it worked the same if Charlie and I were doing things, and I also liked watching them together." Chance's jaw dropped a bit.

Arlo proceeded anyway. "And, Chance, there are things three people together can do that are impossible with just two people."

Chance swallowed hard. "Such as?"

Arlo chuckled. "Come on, Chance. I know you're not as inexperienced as you act. When Wilson was with us, I was able to give oral and get anal at the same time. It was two of my favorite things at once."

Chance ran a hand through his hair. "Christ. I can't believe we're talking about this."

"You asked. Do you want me to stop?"

Chance wondered if he did. He was shocked, a little scared and a little bit turned on. "Uh, it's okay. I'm…yeah, it's fine."

Arlo laughed once more and, after a moment, Chance joined in.

When the two became serious again, Arlo sat up straighter. "Chance, I don't usually tell people all that stuff. I know it's not for most. You're cool and I like you. The truth is, if we're going to be friends, I don't want to keep secrets about myself. If you don't think you could like me because of it, then I will respect that. I mean it. I'll leave, you can have the pizza when it comes and I'll just wave hi when I see you around."

Chance shook his head. "Dude, why do you keep asking me if I want you to leave? I'm fine. Honestly, I'm more intrigued than anything."

"Yeah?" Arlo grinned. "I'm glad you moved next door."

"Hey, if you truly want to be a friend, do you think you can find time this week to help me unpack all this shit?" Chance dared.

Arlo chuckled. "I see how it is. You're putting up a front to get free labor from me."

Chance played along, holding up his hands. "Busted. But if you help me, you'll have unlimited wine or beer and all that time to convince me that your unconventional ways aren't so shocking."

"Okay, I'll help. I have three days that I need to go to the nursing home," Arlo said. "And just to be clear, the living arrangement I had with Charlie and Wilson wasn't just about sex. It was nice to have someone with me when Charlie was doing his job, which was always. And Charlie liked knowing Wilson was there for me. Like I said, it worked for us. But hey, on a different subject, do you want to talk some more about what happened today? I'm a chatty boy, but I can be a good listener, too."

Arlo remained silent, proving he was true to his word. Chance shrugged and shared a more detailed description of the day's events, ending with a shake of his head as he communicated Maria's parting words. He looked to Arlo for his perspective.

Arlo exhaled. "You have a high-pressure job and your boss is a bitch with a capital C."

Chance pursed his lips. "Not really. She has a good side. Maria's very insecure, though, and it doesn't take much to rattle her. Then she becomes a crazy person, making all of us uncomfortable until she has time to calm down. Although she often overreacts, this time she was right. The presentation was a shit-show, so I don't know if she will get over it."

"Sounds like the client was a monster though," Arlo offered.

"Right?" Chance asked, encouraging more support from his new friend. "I mean, the presentation wasn't good, but it wasn't as awful as he made it sound. He was stone-cold from the start and it knocked me off my game. Most of the time, I can charm people into giving me suggestions and delivering something that exceeds their expectations. This guy though was just unforgiving." Chance recalled the incident, shuddering at the encounter. "He was mean, man. Like, who suggests to someone's boss that they consider reassigning their work to other people? Right in front of the person he's singling out? Even if it was the worst pitch he'd ever observed, that was just a crappy thing to do."

Arlo reached over to massage Chance's shoulder. "It was, Chance. The guy must be an asshole. You didn't deserve that."

Chance nodded with appreciation when the doorbell rang. "Must be the pizza guy."

Chance went to fetch the food and tip the deliverer, then returned to the kitchen, surprised that Arlo had already put napkins and plates on the island counter.

Arlo shot Chance a questioning glance. "Where's the pizza delivery guy? Usually that place knows to send over the hot twink who offers his ass as a side-dish. Please tell me you didn't let him leave already."

Chance's jaw dropped. "Huh?"

Arlo laughed at him, shaking his head. "I hope you don't mind—when I saw the plates through the glass-door cupboards, I just went for them. I didn't want to sit here expecting you to wait on me."

"It's fine. More wine?"

"Going to be one of those kinds of nights, huh?" Arlo asked. "Okay, fill it up." Chance retrieved the wine bottle from the counter and Arlo grinned. "Oh, you thought I meant the glass. Okay, you can fill that, too."

Chance paused mid-pour, trying to discern Arlo's meaning, then rolled his eyes when he comprehended. "You're dangerous."

Arlo smirked. "Not for a Boy Scout like you. Maybe you're the smart one. You don't play with fire, so at least you don't have to worry about getting burned."

* * * *

After finishing off a medium pizza, the two men were satisfied and less lightheaded. Although night had fallen, the summer air was still warm and they decided to bring the wine out to Chance's small veranda.

"What a great view you have," Arlo joked since the small deck overlooked the rear of other people's houses. "Maybe you'll get lucky and there'll be a hot chick who leaves her curtains open."

Chance laughed at that. "There isn't much privacy, is there? Dude, did you ever notice that we could open our windows and I could reach over to comb your hair?"

Arlo waggled his eyebrows. "You offering? I like being pampered."

Chance snickered. "Why doesn't that surprise me? Why do you like attention so much? Did someone deprive you as a child?"

Arlo frowned. "Kind of. Were you a psychiatrist before you went into marketing?"

"Huh?" Chance had started tipping the glass to his mouth, but stopped with surprise. "No. I'm sorry. I was just joking around. I didn't know."

Arlo sniggered. "I'm just pulling your leg. No, I wasn't neglected or anything. I was the youngest and the entire family found me adorable. Maybe because I was." Chance shook his head. "I liked the attention then, and I like it now."

"But your parents don't find you so adorable anymore. You said they think you're going to hell," Chance pointed out. When he saw the grimace on Arlo's face, he regretted his words.

"Yeah," Arlo concurred. "They do. They're not cruel to me or anything. My father just kind of shuts me out. Me being gay is a disappointment to them, for sure. My mother told me it was best that we not talk about it, so we don't. The times we chat on the phone, it's pretty much a one-way conversation. I ask a bunch of questions about how the family is doing and my mother answers. My father says hello and good-bye. I get the sense that it's painful for him to do even that. At least he stops short of cutting me out altogether."

"Don't they ask *anything* about your life?" Chance wondered.

"I can't talk about the nursing home because they don't want to hear about Grams since they've grown apart from her. I can't talk about Charlie, of course. And I sure as heck won't talk about my FansOfStuds account." Arlo shrugged. "It doesn't leave much to discuss."

Chance nodded. "Well, I understand why you wouldn't talk about the account. Still, them going silent on you…it's all based on ignorance."

Arlo leaned back in his chair. "Yeah, well, people will always find a way to excuse their own behavior and justify their judgment of others, right? If I got upset every time someone said or believed something uninformed about gay people, I'd be spending my life unhappy." He took another sip of the wine, then smiled. "And I choose not to. I like being happy."

Chance smiled in return. "I'm glad you are, Arlo. You figured out something most of us haven't."

Arlo's smile faded. "Why aren't you, Chance? You have a good job." Chance raised his eyebrows with uncertainty. "Okay, *for now*, you have a good job. You have a nice house, a beautiful car, great looks and a neighbor who is every person's fuck dream."

Chance couldn't help but laugh. "You're too much." He looked down at his glass as if the answer was engraved on the crystal. "I don't know. It should be enough, shouldn't it? I mean, what kind of tool has all that I have and still complains they aren't happy? Forget I said anything."

Arlo sighed. "Don't do that."

"What?"

Arlo reached over and placed a hand on Chance's arm. "Just because there are people who have it worse doesn't mean you need to feel guilty for wanting something different in your life. Screw everyone else if they think you should be content and show gratitude. You only get one life, as the cliché goes. You have a right to make it as happy as possible."

"I guess."

Arlo patted Chance's arm. "Listen, I'm not saying that you should do that without caring about other people's happiness. You can and should still try to bring joy to other people's lives, too. But that doesn't equate to you sacrificing something important to you. So tell me, Chance Findley, what's getting in the way of your happiness?"

Chapter Four

Chance was surprising himself by how much he was revealing to a man who had been a stranger only a day earlier. Maybe it was the booze. The sensible part of his brain was telling him to shut up. His comfort with Arlo was spurring him on.

"I don't know," Chance rambled. "It just all feels like I'm living out someone else's plan for me. Yes, I have a good job, but it mostly makes me miserable. I work too many hours, I have an unpredictable boss and I deal with asshole clients who think they know more about marketing than me. Then they get pissed off when their ideas lead to a poorly received product. They criticize you for doing what they asked, forgetting they insisted on their edits with threats of going elsewhere. I keep thinking, will I be able to stand this for another thirty years?"

"Maybe you shouldn't," Arlo stated.

"And as for my love life, I don't want to get married and have two-point-five kids and a dog. That's the next part of the plan, though. My mother reminds me of that often."

"Where do your parents live?"

"Too close. Missouri," Chance quipped.

Arlo chuckled. "A four-hour plane ride isn't far enough away?"

Chance grimaced. "No. It allows them to visit twice a year, and they expect me to visit them at least twice a year, as well. Hey, guess how I spend the little bit of vacation time I can squeeze into a year? Obligatory family time!" Chance tried to soften his expression. "And now I feel like a shit for talking about them like this. They're not so bad. My mother is intense, but I guess she means well. My dad and I get along fine. He's a good guy. It's just that he's sort of brow-beaten by my mother, so he tends to do his own thing—leaving me and my sister Marybeth to fend for ourselves with Mom. Marybeth is awesome, so I enjoy seeing her."

"Is she married?" Arlo asked.

"Not yet," Chance answered. "So she'd be disappointed if I didn't show up for the holidays. It would be hell for her to be alone with my parents. As it is, a typical get-together involves my dad watching sports on television, leaving me and Marybeth to answer our mother's incessant questions about our work and dating lives. Then we need to listen to her complain about how tough her life is. That's when she starts in about my father not spending enough time with her because of his marketing firm. Marybeth and I are tempted to point out that she doesn't mind the money it provides her for the country club or buying herself things, but it wouldn't go over well. We keep quiet to refrain from being complicit in her criticisms. It all just becomes exhausting."

Arlo nodded. "I get it. You love them, but you don't enjoy most of your time with them."

"Exactly!" Chance agreed. "Then I feel remorseful for that and it makes me even more miserable. And I resent that I feel compelled to find a wife who is the missing puzzle piece to the strategy that my mother laid out for me. God, imagine the agony then. Not only dealing with the job pressures, but also having someone bitching at me the way my mother complains to my father and for all the same reasons—spending too much time at work while assuring her that each year will reap more money. Sometimes I just want to yell at my mother that she just doesn't get it because she's never worked a day in her privileged life. And don't even get me started on the idea of having kids…knowing every time Maria threatens me, I'd need to worry about the security for more than myself. Even if I retained my job and made all the money my family wanted, I'd be spending every free moment with obligatory kids' activities and dealing with their problems. Plus, I'd be squeezing in any vacation I could manage for mandatory Disney trips on top of the miserable visits to Missouri. I almost cry thinking about it."

Arlo started laughing, which lowered Chance's ire a bit. "Chance, take a breath. Okay, you realize you're describing the family from hell, don't you? I know your experience is influencing your perceptions, but I'm sure there are women who wouldn't treat you the way your mother treats your father. You're unfairly judging potential partners before you've even met them. Anyway, why are you pressuring yourself? You don't need to follow your mother's plan. You have a right to stay single if you don't meet the right person. Don't get hitched to a woman like the one you're describing where you'd end up killing yourself."

Chance sighed, then chuckled. "Yeah, but I'd have to because the alternative would be killing her, and I wouldn't do well in prison."

Arlo had taken another sip of wine, then snorted some through his nose. "Fuck! Don't make me laugh when I'm drinking."

Chance took a napkin from the table and handed it to Arlo to clean his mouth and chin. "Sorry. Anyway, I'm kidding about killing. I'm done ranting."

"It's okay," Arlo soothed. "You needed to get it out. So, why can't you just find a girl who thinks like you, who hates the idea of marriage and kids?"

Chance was horrified at Arlo's misconception. "I didn't say I hate kids. I like kids. I hope to be an uncle someday, if Marybeth wants them. I just don't want them for myself. Then I feel more guilt about that."

"Why?"

Chance narrowed his eyes. "Haven't you been listening? The plan, Arlo. They're in my mother's plan. She wants grandchildren from me and she's becoming impatient. And hey, what kind of selfish prick does that make me that I don't want to have kids?"

Arlo shrugged. "I don't want kids. I don't think I'm a selfish prick. I just know myself. I'm way too sex-driven to be distracted by kids."

Chance thought about that. "Yeah, too bad. Unlike me, I have the feeling you'd be a great dad. And it would be nice to see someone raise children without instilling in them the shame and inhibitions that the rest of society places on them. Did you know that in Scandinavian countries, kids see nudity and sex on television at an early age, and they have much lower incidences of sex-related crimes? Maybe there's something to be said for that."

Arlo was smiling. "I like drunk Chance. You're a passionate man. A rambling, passionate man."

Chance bit his lower lip. "God, *I am* rambling, aren't I? I'm sorry, I get that way when I've had too much. Friends always tell me that my mouth goes running and so do my inhibitions. It's a great combination for making a fool of myself."

Arlo's eyebrows raised. "You lose your inhibitions? Hmm. Can I get you more wine?"

Chance grinned. "Shut up."

Arlo leaned back into his chair. "So, forget about your mother's plan. Tell me, what would you do differently to bring more happiness into your life?"

Chance ran his finger around the rim of his glass. "I don't know. Maybe open my own marketing firm so I could at least be my own boss? I wouldn't be penalized for every prospective client that walks. And I would put my foot down with my parents regarding how often I'd visit in-person. And I'd have a more exciting sex life."

Arlo's eyes widened. "Yeah? We should explore that last part more."

Chance chuckled. "Of course you'd say that."

"You brought it up. There must be a part of you that wants to discuss it," Arlo concluded.

Chance sighed. "I'm not as comfortable talking about that stuff as you are, man."

Arlo nodded. "I understand. But look at it this way—because I'm comfortable talking about it, there's nothing you could say that would shock me. You might never find a better person to share with, unless you want to pay for a therapist."

"That's a thought," Chance added.

"Eh," Arlo interjected with a wry smile. "You might want to wait to see if you still have a job in three weeks. Therapy can be pricy." Chance narrowed his eyes, causing Arlo to snicker. "Just fooling with you. Come on, tell me. I promise, I'll try hard not to get a woodie while you discuss sex."

Chance snickered at that. "Jesus. You're crazy." He looked to Arlo, but he sat silent, apparently mastering a class about eliciting information by staring down the person near him. "Fine. I guess…I don't know. I just wish sex wasn't so routinized."

"Routinized? Do you need lessons on different positions or something?" Arlo asked.

Chance shot him a warning look and Arlo pretended to zip his lips. "I don't need your sex education, wise ass. I just mean, I haven't had the guts to ever ask for something beyond traditional vanilla sex. Maybe my mother beat it into me too often that I should be a gentleman with the ladies, so I stick to the missionary position and the same oral moves." Chance looked over to Arlo with an embarrassed frown. "But I want to explore more."

Arlo exhaled. "Chance, I don't mean this to sound flip, but maybe you *should* see a therapist. It sounds like you need to overcome some serious brainwashing. I doubt there are many women who are like your mother, expecting you to be like some guy from a 1950s family sitcom. Did you ever think that maybe some of them have been disappointed that you weren't pushing for more in the bedroom?"

"Yeah, I have thought about it, especially since I'm not even talking about crazy kink stuff. It's just that I'd always chicken out. My desire to be liked overrules any impulse to suggest more adventurous stuff. I guess my non-work ego isn't strong." Chance frowned. "Maybe it's not so strong on the job now, either."

"I can't imagine why. You're a success, and I told you that you're a total stud."

Chance flushed, then fiddled with the wine glass. "I haven't been forthcoming with you, Arlo. Do you want to know what the best sexual experience for me was?"

Arlo nodded. "Does a male dog lick his balls?"

That made Chance chuckle before turning serious once more. He glanced down at his lap, too embarrassed to look at Arlo when he responded. "You keep saying I'm straight, but I'm not sure I'm one-hundred-percent so. I met a pretty girl once, Kathy, and we got on okay. Well, after she and I had been seeing each other for about a week, she introduced me to a good friend of hers, Liam. Turned out he was gay." Chance dared a peep at Arlo, but Arlo acted as though he didn't know where the story was headed.

"Anyway, we were hanging at the bar and, after several drinks, Kathy leaned over and whispered that Liam was into me. I thought she might be telling me because she was annoyed, but when I looked at her, I could tell she was amused and a bit excited. I didn't respond, which she must have assumed was openness on my part. Next thing I knew, Liam was getting closer and closer to my bar stool until he whispered in my other ear that I was cute and he wished I was into guys."

When Chance stopped for a long pause, Arlo nudged him. "Yeah? So, don't leave me hanging. What happened?"

Chance exhaled. "Well, I told you my inhibitions lessen when I've been drinking. That night, I was sloshed. Before I knew it, I agreed to Liam joining me and Kathy at my place." He looked to Arlo, who was transfixed. "Um, we had sex together."

Arlo gasped. "So, what did you do with him?"

"What do you mean? You want the blow-by-blow?"

Arlo chuckled. "No pun intended, I'm sure. Yes, it kind of matters, Chance."

"Why?" Chance wondered.

"Chance, if you just let this guy blow you or jerk you, it doesn't mean much. A lot of straight guys will let another man blow them. It doesn't mean you're gay."

"Would a straight guy let the dude blow him on three different occasions, with the second and third being sober?" Chance challenged.

Arlo's eyes widened. "Oh."

"Yeah. Oh," Chance snapped.

Arlo frowned. "Why are you getting mad at me?"

Chance grimaced. "Sorry. It's just that I've never told anyone that. When I think about it, it scares me that I liked it. He was great at it, though maybe it was because it was…forbidden. And the thing was, he was full of dirty talk about things he'd like to do to me and I fucking loved it. I didn't want to admit it to myself then. The fact that Kathy was watching it all added another level of excitement. I never knew I would like performing for an audience, whether it was for him or for her, but it turned me on as they encouraged me. The filthier their mouths got, the hotter it was."

Arlo grinned a bit. "So, that's why you were understanding when I told you I get off on doing my sex shows, and why I enjoy being with two other people."

Chance nodded. "Yeah, it reminded me how much I liked it. And having someone touching you everywhere while you're having sex with someone else—it was sensory overload."

"Right? You see. So, did you ever kiss him?" Arlo wondered.

Chance cast his eyes down. "Yeah. Liam was assertive. He just pounced and took what he wanted before I even knew what was happening. It shocked me that I enjoyed it. He was a great kisser and it felt decadent. Sex since Liam and Kathy has been…less exciting, I guess."

"So why did it end?" Arlo wondered.

"Well, it was just about sex. A relationship built on nothing else is going to flame out sooner or later. That's what happened," Chance responded.

Arlo shook his head with disbelief. "You've been sitting on that all day while I've been toying with you, making me feel guilty for teasing a straight guy?"

Chance glanced back down at his lap. "Yeah, well, maybe I have hang-ups about homosexuality. I told you that I care what people think about me. As you know, lots of people don't like men who have sex with men."

Arlo moved his chair so that it was abutting Chance's, causing Chance to flinch. "Relax. I'm not going to touch you."

"Jesus, I'm sorry. I didn't mean to do that. You see what I mean? Don't get me wrong, Arlo. I am a hardcore liberal Democrat. I support every marginalized group, including members of the LGBTQ community. I do volunteer work for different organizations when I can. And I swear, I don't do it to try to prove something to others or to myself. I believe in promoting equality."

Arlo sighed. "Chance, it's okay. I believe you. And you don't owe me explanations."

"But I do," Chance pressed. "You're a nice guy, and you're open about who you are, and you have every right to look down on me for being afraid to tell people what I did...or that I liked it."

"I don't look down on you, Chance," Arlo assured him. "Listen, embracing your sexuality when it's anything other than straight is difficult. I get it. There's still a lot of bigotry out there. If it were easy to come out as anything other than heterosexual, you'd see millions more people expressing a degree of fluidity, I promise you. And from the sounds of things, your family has built a little box for you that they'd like you to stay in. I'm sure that plays a part."

"*You* were courageous," Chance pointed out.

"It came with a price, Chance. I don't have a real relationship with my parents anymore. My siblings are better about it, but not a heck of a lot. I'm not a person who pushes others to declare something. You need to decide what you're willing to share with others," Arlo explained. "And I'm grateful you chose to share with me. I'm honored."

Chance nodded, still a bit nervous. "So, are *you* saying that you're fluid?"

Arlo laughed. "I think I'm one of the bands of the rainbow. But, how far to the straight side of the spectrum do you think you are? You liked sex with that guy Liam."

Chance took another swig of wine. "But I didn't do anything to him other than kiss him. Although I'd be lying if I said I didn't like the way he looked naked, or that I didn't like the way he blew me. Liam knew what he was doing. I doubt I'll ever experience a better blow job."

Arlo grinned, waggling his eyebrows. "I love a challenge."

Chance jerked his head back, eyes wide. "Arlo, you're doing more than flirting now. Even if I was interested, you have a boyfriend, remember?"

Arlo laughed. "I wasn't offering. Anyway, if I were ever to give you head, it would need to be with Charlie watching and you wanting it."

"Oh my God," Chance muttered, but he felt a jolt of excitement at the prospect. The damn wine was lowering his inhibitions *too much*.

Arlo quirked his lip. "Oh, come on. Now I'm scandalous for suggesting sex with a third party watching? I have three words for you. Kathy and Liam."

Chance shook his head with confusion. "I...yeah, well, doing it with two guys would be..."

Arlo bit his lower lip. "Yeah, Chance. It would be acknowledging that guys could get you off without a female present." He leaned in closer to Chance's face. "You know what else it would be if it were me and Charlie?" Chance asked 'what' with wide eyes. "It would be hot and dirty—just how you want it."

Chance swallowed, gripping his wine glass hard. "But you said you weren't suggesting... You said you were okay with me staying hidden..."

Arlo squeezed Chance's shoulder. "I never said it was okay to hide from *yourself,* Chance. I just said that you don't owe others an account of what—or who—you do. And if you're ever interested in me...well, I'd say, let's talk. I've put it out there that I think you're super attractive. Of course, you and Charlie don't know each other, so even if you and I wanted to, there's no guarantee something would happen. But you can count on me to be a supportive friend to help you work through your inner turmoil. I wouldn't view anything you say negatively—I heard you when you said it's important for people to like you."

The two sat silent for a few minutes as Chance processed the conversation. He cleared his throat. "Can I ask what happened with the third guy in your relationship? Wilson, was it?"

Arlo's face clouded. He finished the wine that was in his glass. "Wilson broke my heart."

After a long pause, Chance prompted Arlo to continue. "How? What happened?"

Arlo didn't return eye contact. "As much as I like sex and all the stuff we talked about, Chance, I do have the capacity to love, too. I believed Charlie, Wilson and I loved each other. We were a team. There wasn't anything I wouldn't have done for either of them. I assumed it was a given that we were exclusive."

"He cheated on you guys?" Chance asked.

Arlo nodded. "Many times. Charlie found out months before I did. Turns out, he warned Wilson that it wasn't cool and that he'd better stop. Wilson promised it would end, but he kept on going. It was like a trite made-for-television movie how I found out. The nursing home where I work sent employees home earlier than usual one day because there was a case of COVID discovered. We were all told we had to get tested before we could return. Anyway, I went home earlier than usual and caught Wilson in bed with another guy. I was the stereotypical screaming spurned lover, threatening violence and scaring Wilson's boy-toy into running for his life." Arlo paused to take in breath. "I stormed out of the room and waited for Charlie to come home. When he did, and he saw me crying and I told him why, he ordered Wilson out. At first, I tried to intervene. I still loved Wilson—you know? That's when Charlie told me that he knew Wilson had multiple tricks months earlier and likely had continued having them since Charlie first found out."

"That's shitty," Chance offered.

"Yeah. I felt so many emotions. I couldn't understand why two guys weren't enough for Wilson. I mean...*two* guys, Chance! He still needed more? I love sex and even I don't need more. I felt hurt, betrayed and confused. Then, of course, I worried about Charlie's health and mine. We hadn't been practicing safe sex. We didn't think we had a reason to."

"Christ," Chance whispered. "Are you...okay?"

Arlo nodded. "Yes. Wilson assured us he had always used a condom with his hook-ups, as if that fixed everything. Charlie and I got tested anyway and we came back negative. Despite going through that shit, I still waffled on whether I wanted Wilson to leave. It's funny how your heart can remain tied to someone who has been awful to you. To be honest, I still have feelings for him. It doesn't just end. Not for me, anyway. Charlie, on the other hand..."

"He stopped loving Wilson?"

"He did," Arlo confirmed. "Don't get the wrong idea. Charlie is very sweet and caring. And despite being such a serious guy most of the time, he has a surprising side to him where he can be a tease and a prankster. But he's also a lot tougher than me. In many ways, that's good. The downside to that is he's not as forgiving if you wrong him. Sometimes I'm afraid I'll do something that will cross that line. I haven't yet. Maybe I'm the exception to the rule. Charlie loves me so much that I almost fear for him that he's going to take years off his life by how much he worries for me on top of handling a stressful job."

He sighed. "That's what's funny about the Wilson situation. When he first learned of the cheating, Charlie uncharacteristically forgave Wilson. He couldn't quite hide the coolness he was feeling toward him, though. For those few months, I didn't understand what was going on. It turns out, Charlie only let Wilson stay because he knew Wilson leaving us would crush me. Once I was aware of what was happening, and it was clear how upset I was, Charlie decided that was the end for Wilson. The one thing that Charlie will never forgive is someone hurting *me*."

"I'm sorry that happened to you, Arlo," Chance murmured. "I can't imagine why you weren't enough for Wilson. Charlie did the right thing to make him leave. You see that, don't you?"

Arlo nodded. "Yes, I do. It didn't stop me from feeling terrible when I saw Wilson leaving with his bags, looking back at me with a sad face. I know he loved me. Maybe he still does. He told me he has a compulsion. He's a sex addict. He swears he didn't want to hurt me. Perhaps I'm an idiot to believe him, but I do. I'm scared for him."

Chance patted Arlo's arm. "That's because you're a good man. Arlo, are you sure you're ready to move on to a new guy joining you and Charlie? It seems to me you're still a bit stuck on Wilson."

Arlo shook his head. "I'm ready. I'll always have feelings for Wilson, but Charlie is right. Taking Wilson back would just be continuous pain. He's not able to change, and I can't feel good about a partner fooling around with others behind my back. I had suggested to him that he channel his compulsion into doing a sex website like I had done before meeting him, but he told me that wouldn't be enough. He said he needs the physical contact. Well, I'm not a glutton for punishment. I wish him well and who knows? Maybe one day, he and I can be friends."

Chance still had his hand on Arlo's arm, and he reluctantly drew it away. His instinct—even his desire—was to pull the man into an embrace instead. He was still troubled that he found Arlo attractive, despite Arlo's encouraging words to free his mind, but he knew there was no point in doing mental gymnastics to pretend otherwise. "Love sucks, huh?"

Arlo's eyes widened with surprise. "No, Chance. Love is beautiful. You just need to find it with the right person. Or persons." Arlo chuckled a bit at his addendum. "I'm not giving up. And you shouldn't either, Chance."

Chance sighed. "If I can figure out what I want."

Arlo squinted. "I'm guessing deep down, you know. When you remove the other people's opinions from your head, you'll be able to hear your own voice and the message it's delivering." He began to rise. "I'm going back to my place. It's getting late. I'll come over tomorrow to help with the unpacking."

"Are you sure?" Chance asked. "I shouldn't have suggested that. It was super forward of me."

Arlo smiled. "Chance, I like you. You and I are going to be close friends. I can feel it. And close friends help each other with unpacking."

Chance smirked a bit. "Is that right? Is that some bro-code that I haven't read?"

"It is," Arlo replied.

Arlo made his way back into the house and put his glass into the kitchen sink. Chance followed him, noticing how the man's jeans hugged what looked like a nice bubble-butt. He figured he'd get over the ogling once he sobered. For now, he decided to embrace enjoying the view. "Hey, what time do you want to come over?"

"Is ten too late?" Arlo asked, making his way to the front door. "I go to the park at eight o'clock to jog, then I shower. Hey, do you want to join me?"

Chance raised his eyebrows. "For the run or for the shower?"

Arlo snorted a quick laugh. "Either. Both."

Chance hadn't jogged in a long time, and with no job to interfere, he had little excuse not to. "Sure…to the jogging. Should I meet you at your door before your run?"

Arlo beamed at the acceptance. "Sounds good. I wear sexy short-shorts. You do the same if you don't want me hogging all the appreciative stares." He used his comment as an excuse to peruse Chance's body.

"Christ." Chance chuckled. "Go home, Arlo."

"Sweet dreams, Chance." Arlo winked.

Chapter Five

It had been a long time since Chance had been so lightheaded, but he wasn't feeling regret. He was glad he had been unencumbered, allowing himself to be open with Arlo. Chance believed the two had learned a lot about each other, and it made Chance feel closer to Arlo than he did with some long-time friends. Arlo had accepted everything Chance had shared, and he boosted Chance's ego more than anyone had in a long time.

As Chance ascended his stairs to head to his bedroom, he pictured again how similar Arlo and Liam looked physically. That was something Chance hadn't shared with Arlo, as he figured it would make Arlo believe Chance wanted him in bed. Chance *had* been aroused, though, multiple times during their conversation. Still, he wasn't certain that his interest hadn't been piqued simply because of fond Liam memories and booze. He knew he had to consider that before baring his soul to Arlo. And even if he felt the same way the next day when sober, Chance wondered if it made sense to come clean with his new friend. Arlo was in a relationship with another man, and he made it clear he wouldn't cheat on Charlie. The only way an encounter with Arlo was possible would be if both he and Arlo, as well as Charlie, wanted one. Chance couldn't imagine that possibility. He reasoned a threesome had worked for him in the past because Kathy's presence had made it more palatable to a judging, albeit unknowing society. Fooling around with Arlo and Charlie would be embracing and waving the pride flag, and Chance didn't think he'd be able to deal with the blowback if it ever came to light. Still, Chance's dick was in violent disagreement with Chance's brain that sex with Arlo was a bad idea.

Chance went to the bathroom to pee out some of the alcohol, then brushed his teeth and stripped down to his boxer briefs. He entered his darkened bedroom. Light poured from the window on Arlo's house that was directly across from him. Neither Chance nor Arlo had their curtains drawn. Chance moved to his window to close the drapes but stopped in his tracks when a shirtless Arlo came into view.

Chance backed away from the window quickly, afraid Arlo would see him and think he'd been spying on him. But he was guilty because he couldn't tear himself away from watching once he'd started.

Arlo seemed oblivious to the fact that he could be seen by his new neighbor, even making a motion that suggested he was shucking off whatever he was wearing below his waist. The window's sill was low enough that Chance could make out Arlo's trimmed pubes when he turned toward the window and the small of his back and top of his buttocks when he turned away. Chance knew he should stop gazing at the unsuspecting man, but he was transfixed. He'd never seen a man as beautiful as Arlo. Even though the guy's features weren't perfect, the combination of physical traits was mesmerizing. Despite the slight blur from the unwashed windows, Chance noticed Arlo's large pectoral muscles and back were smooth and tanned. His stomach and sides didn't have an ounce of fat.

Arlo had raised his arms to stretch while yawning, showing his nicely shaped triceps and a little bit more of his pubic area. Chance started to become stimulated as he had earlier, and he prayed Arlo couldn't make out his form in the darkened bedroom.

Arlo approached his window, staring at Chance's house. Chance backed up more, worried he had been spotted. Arlo had an odd expression, almost like longing. He had reached down with his right hand, possibly to fondle himself since his eyes closed as if he was feeling pleasure. Just as quickly, Arlo pulled his hand back up and ran it through his hair, looking like he was sighing. Chance watched his neighbor turn away from the window and walk toward the opposite wall, revealing a little more of his smooth, beefy ass. Then, the lights went out in Arlo's house, and Chance couldn't see anything from within.

Chance remained still for a couple of moments, wondering if his eyes would adjust to the darkness, but he only saw the window's panes over a rectangle of black. He was relieved, figuring he must have been just as hidden from Arlo while he had been creeping on the poor guy.

Chance stumbled to his bed, a bit shaky while his shaft uncomfortably stretched against the confines of the boxer brief's fabric. He sat on the edge of the bed, adjusting his alarm clock to ring at seven, then scooched under the covers.

Although he tried to sleep, visuals of Arlo continued to play in his head. He pictured kissing the man, licking his nipples and pushing Arlo's head down until the man's lips were touching his cock.

"Jesus," Chance mumbled, unable to stop himself from grabbing his dick. He shoved down the underwear and started masturbating, pretending it was Arlo sucking him. Chance blew his load within seconds, then wiped himself with a tissue that had been on his nightstand.

After he cleaned up, he turned on his side, figuring he had eased the tension and he'd be able to sleep. His mind couldn't shut down, though. Chance wondered if Arlo had jerked off thinking about him as well. He'd be embarrassed to face Arlo the next day, guilty over summoning imaginary Arlo into his fantasies.

He began mulling over scarier thoughts about his parents discovering he had an attraction to some men, about losing his job and about being out on the street if the latter were to occur. Chance tossed and turned, last glancing at his clock at three in the morning before he finally fell asleep.

* * * *

After Chance showered, he slipped on a sky-colored T-shirt and a pair of light-gray running shorts. He looked in the mirror, pleased that he looked reasonably nice considering he hadn't slept much. He knew the shirt was tight enough to enhance his nicely toned chest and torso, and while the shorts weren't the length Arlo had requested, they were short enough to show off his nice knees and calves. Then, Chance sighed with disappointment. His attraction to Arlo hadn't gone away in the night—not if he was spending time thinking how he could pique Arlo's sexual interest. He wiped a hand over his face as he wondered what was happening to him.

Chance made his way to Arlo's house, reminding himself that he and Arlo would simply be friends. As he approached the man's front door, though, Chance flushed with excitement to see Arlo again. "Christ," he muttered, ringing the doorbell.

When Arlo appeared, Chance's breath hitched—the man had indeed put on a very skimpy pair of nylon running shorts. Most of Arlo's bulked-up thighs were on display, as were the man's arms and sides due to an oversized athletic tank-top.

Arlo turned on his brilliant smile as he emerged from his entrance. "Good morning, Chance. Ready to welcome another gorgeous day?"

"Yeah, sure," Chance mumbled. "I've never liked mornings much. I was afraid I would sleep through the alarm. I was tossing and turning for hours."

Arlo shot him a questioning look, then grinned. "It's a new day. Try to forget your problems and enjoy the run. We can take it slow."

The two began to sprint down the hill toward the city park and its jogging tracks. Chance followed Arlo, enjoying the sight of Arlo's shorts hugging his ass cheeks and cleft as his powerful legs motioned him forward.

"How long do you run for?" Chance panted when they reached the park.

Arlo shot him a wicked smile. "Until you fall to your knees." He looked at Chance's surprised face, then glanced down the man's body. "And what I wouldn't do if you were on your knees." He laughed at Chance's shocked expression. "I told you, tell me any time if you want me to stop teasing."

Chance chuckled. "You just take me by surprise. It's okay."

"Well, in that case..." Arlo smiled, licking his lip. "I need to tell you that your legs are distracting. Very cute. I'll have to loan you a pair of my running shorts so you can show off more of them next time."

Chance huffed a laugh, though his focus was on the words 'next time.' He liked that. "Yeah, well, I thought I was in good shape until I saw your fricking tree-trunk thighs. God. I might not be able to keep up."

Arlo patted Chance's back. "You will. I told you that I'll take it easy on you...today. Tomorrow, all bets are off." He winked and began jogging on the track, looking back to make sure Chance was following.

At first, Chance's limbs were stiff since he hadn't warmed up before leaving the house. He wondered if Arlo had, considering how gracefully and easily he moved. After a few minutes, though, Chance got into a groove—his legs gliding over the beaten path with minimal effort. His breathing became controlled and he felt like he had as a child when he'd run carefree on the playground or in the fields. Chance enjoyed the breeze blowing through his hair and his heart beating at the pace of his steps. He felt good, and he almost had to slow himself from breaking into a full-on run.

"You're doing great!" Arlo shouted from his right as the two men continued to jog past walkers and slow bike riders.

"This is fun!" Chance yelled back. "It's freeing. I haven't done this in a long while. It's so much better than a treadmill."

"Absolutely," Arlo replied, his lungs barely labored.

The friends continued their pace for thirty minutes before Arlo signaled that he was willing to stop if Chance wanted to. Chance nodded. Even though his legs weren't cramping, he was sweating profusely and wanted to cool down.

Arlo pointed to a nearby bench off the track, then jogged to it. Chance followed, watching Arlo bend down to stretch. Chance found himself gaping at the wet fabric clinging to Arlo's ass as the man touched his toes. He could make out the lines of a jock's straps cradling muscular butt cheeks under the nylon.

Chance distracted himself by stretching as well. He figured it was smart anyway, as he'd used leg muscles that his treadmill routine might not have stressed, and he didn't want to be feeling it later.

When the two had limbered, they flopped down on the bench, still breathing heavily. Chance glanced over to Arlo. His face had a sheen, the hair that fell over his forehead was wet and his tank-top was drenched. Arlo reeked of masculine sexiness. Chance turned away, worrying that his attraction was getting out of control.

"Well, I didn't fall to my knees," Chance joked once he could catch his breath.

Arlo bumped his upper arm into Chance's. "Good job. And I wouldn't drive you to your knees unless you wanted me to."

Chance rolled his eyes. "You don't stop, do you? And I'm not sure that would be my thing."

Arlo laughed. "Interesting that you said you aren't sure. Anyway, Charlie never believed it would be his thing, either. He never liked the taste of cum until he met me." He contemplated for a moment. "Then again, maybe it's just because he loves me. I think love changes the way a person views stuff, don't you?"

Chance shook his head, finding it peculiar that they were having such a frank conversation on a park bench. "I guess. I don't know. I've never really been in love."

Arlo's jaw dropped a bit. "What? *Never*?"

Chance shrugged. "No. I mean, I've *liked* plenty of girls I've dated. Maybe I got to a point of feeling some kind of love, but I wasn't *in love* with them. There was never anyone that made me feel like I couldn't live without them. In fact, it was more like I couldn't imagine living my entire life with them."

Arlo continued staring like he'd discovered a new species. "Seriously? Chance, I know we joked about you needing a therapist, but maybe…"

"I know," Chance mumbled, staring down at his lap. "But it's hard to fall in love with someone if you haven't learned to trust them with your darkest secrets. I think I always felt like there was something wrong with me for desiring things that some people would find disgusting, and that whatever affection they felt for me would be gone if they knew."

Arlo studied Chance for a moment, then looked away. "I'm sorry, Chance. I think everyone should experience falling in love. I hope it happens for you."

"Dude, you don't need to get sappy or worry about me. So, what is it about Charlie that made you fall in love with him?"

Arlo grinned shyly. "Oh, he's pretty amazing. First off, he's fucking stunning. I don't mean gorgeous like me." Chance laughed at that. "Charlie could be a movie star. He's got jet-black hair, blue eyes like a misty Irish lake, perfect teeth and a face shaped like a young Cary Grant's."

"Who?" Chance asked.

Arlo's eyes widened. "He was a screen icon from the forties, fifties and sixties."

Chance shrugged. "Well, considering I was born many decades later, I don't think it's odd that I never heard of him."

Arlo narrowed his eyes. "Yes, it is. He's a legend. I guess you don't like old movies."

"Not especially."

"I love them," Arlo defended. "They're all overacted. It's so campy. The men were caricatures of what people in the day believed masculine looked like, and the women behaved like they were either ridiculously stupid or incredibly vampish. When you watch one, you feel like you're viewing something directed by John Wayne and RuPaul."

Chance snickered. "Not sure who they are either. I'm guessing you're suggesting I shouldn't watch old movies if I like gritty reality, huh?"

Arlo shook his head. "I wouldn't recommend it. Anyway, back to my point. Charlie is the epitome of tall, dark and handsome. He's six-foot-four and he has a really muscular body. He isn't body-builder big, where veins are popping all over, thank God. That's too jacked, in my opinion. He's almost as big, though. And he has lots of hair on his chest, arms, stomach and legs. So hot."

Chance laughed. "You like body hair, huh?"

Arlo shrugged. "Not always. But trust me, on him, it is sexy as hell. He's such a daddy."

"A daddy? He has kids?"

Arlo squinted. "How do you live in this city and remain so dense about these things? A daddy is a studly slightly older guy who looks like he'd take care of you...or have his way with you. Either way, there's a happy ending involved."

Chance nodded. "So, you like elderly, abusive guys who have enough body hair to weave a blanket."

Arlo smacked Chance's arm, but he was smiling. "Fuck off. When you meet Charlie, I promise, there won't be anything about your description that will match. He's only thirty-nine, he's jacked and his body hair exists only on places where it's sexy. And he's not abusive. I wouldn't be with someone like that."

Chance shot an apologetic glance. "I was kidding, Arlo. I'm sure he's a nice guy."

Arlo's smile widened. "He is. Charlie takes care of me. I've been told I become more childlike when he's near. I know that probably wasn't a compliment, but I don't care. The feeling of security and love he gives me is everything. Besides Grams, he's all I have. He looks out for me and makes me happy."

"How was he with Wilson before the falling-out?" Chance wondered.

Arlo's expression darkened. "He didn't start off as protective of Wilson. Wilson is older than me, and Wilson sometimes believed Charlie made him feel less-than, if you know what I mean. If poor Charlie tried to soothe Wilson when he was upset, or if he asked him to be careful when he'd need to travel to another city, Wilson resented it. Charlie would feel bad because his intentions were good. He's a caring person, especially when it comes to people he loves. But they mostly got along. They loved each other in their own way, and the sex was on fire."

"Based on what you told me about your three-ways, I imagine Charlie is a top?" Chance asked.

Arlo nodded. "Yeah."

"Wilson was, too?"

Arlo looked to Chance curiously. "Mostly. They liked to take turns fucking me."

Chance swallowed, imagining Arlo's beautiful ass getting pounded by two different men. He could feel his excitement growing, so he placed his hands over his lap. "Uh, so you always bottom?"

Arlo frowned. "I topped Wilson sometimes. But yeah, I always bottom for Charlie. Are you asking me that because you think it's something I should be ashamed of?"

Chance was mortified. "What? No! I was just curious. I promise." Arlo's face relaxed. "So, did you like topping Wilson?"

Arlo shrugged. "Of course, I liked it. But it wasn't Wilson's favorite position. I think he bottomed more out of love than out of desire. It dampened the enjoyment for me a little to know that. Plus, he wasn't my ideal when it came to that position, if I'm being candid. I mean, it was nice, but I prefer a different type when I imagine being a top."

"What kind of guy is the right type?" Chance wondered.

Arlo's eyes got a faraway look. "They'd be sweet and there'd be a bit of vulnerability that would make me want to care for them like Charlie does for me. I'd want to show them a pleasure that they never knew possible. Maybe they'd have such a sweet ass that I can't help but think about my tongue and dick in it."

"Jesus," Chance uttered. "Your *tongue*?"

Arlo laughed. "For someone who hates old movies, you're like a character from one. It's called rimming, and it's not some obscure, primitive ritual. I'll bet right now, in this city, there are several guys getting their holes licked. Women, too, for that matter."

Chance grimaced. "I'll take your word for it."

One of Arlo's eyebrows quirked up. "Chance, you said you want your sex life to be adventurous and dirtier, yet you're pretty closed-minded."

Chance was indignant. "I'm not closed-minded."

"Prove it. Bend over, drop your pants and let me give you a swirlie," Arlo teased.

"Oh my God," Chance panted. "What the fuck?"

Arlo bellowed. "You should see your face right now. It's priceless." He stood from the bench. "Come on, Miss Marple. Let's head back. Those boxes won't unpack themselves."

Chance rose with a pretend huff. "Who the hell is Miss Marple?"

Arlo shrugged. "Wasn't she a character in an Agatha Christie book? I don't remember, but it sounds like a school-marm name that would be appropriate for you."

"I am not a school-marm," Chance grumbled, following Arlo down the path. "Just because I don't want to lick up bacteria."

Arlo chuckled as they walked. "There are ways to be safe, Chance. A good shower, a bidet or douche, some bacteria-killing ointment…"

"I don't get the appeal," Chance mumbled.

Arlo wrapped his arm around Chance's shoulders as they continued their walk back to their street. Chance liked it. He surveyed his surroundings and it was clear that nobody was staring or sending castigating glances their way. They were in the heart of San Francisco, after all, and Chance himself had seen two men do the same multiple times. It was freeing to be affectionate with his friend and still feel safe around others, and he found himself laughing at Arlo's jokes the rest of the way home.

* * * *

Chance's ductless air system was set to a low temperature, but the hours of vigorously ripping and cutting boxes, as well as lifting multiple heavy objects, were making the interior feel like an Arizona summer.

"Chance, did you move from a mansion? I can't believe how many more boxes are still unpacked," Arlo complained mid-afternoon, sweat staining the armpit area of the T-shirt he had changed into after his morning jog and shower.

Chance glanced his way, his own jersey wet in between his pectoral muscles and under his arms. "Shit, sorry, Arlo. We can take a break." They hadn't paused other than for Chance to split a Subway sandwich he had sitting in his refrigerator with Arlo.

Arlo rose from another slain box, putting his closed utility knife in his jeans pocket. He stretched his back, causing the hem of his shirt to rise and reveal his tight abs. Sweat had just pooled on Chance's upper lip and he had the misfortune of licking it in that moment. Chance was glad that Arlo hadn't noticed and read into the gesture, though he wouldn't have been wrong that Chance enjoyed the view.

"Would it be weird for you if I take off my shirt?" Arlo asked. "I don't want to freak you out. It's just so warm in here. And this material is scratchy. It's getting on my nerves."

"Oh," Chance mumbled. "Uh, yeah...sure. I mean, it's cool." He willed himself to shut up. It dawned on him that his bumbling made it sound like it was a big deal, despite his words.

If Arlo noticed, it didn't register. He pulled the shirt over his head, and it was obvious to Chance that there was no seductive intent. The guy really was hot...in two different ways. "Thanks." Arlo smiled, wiping his face with the shirt before dropping it to the floor. "Maybe some water, too?"

"Huh?" Chance asked, jerking himself away from staring at the bronzed man in front of him. Arlo looked even better up-close than he did through the window. "Oh, yeah. Shit, Arlo. I'm sorry, man. Where are my manners? Please, help yourself to anything in the refrigerator, okay? When I get focused on a task, I forget about everything else. Don't wait for me, just treat the place like it's yours."

"You sure?" Arlo asked, but he was already making his way to the refrigerator.

Chance watched his smooth, broad back and narrow waist glide to the kitchen area. "I'm sure."

Arlo opened the appliance, its light radiating on him like a spotlight on a stripper. Chance swallowed hard when Arlo half-turned toward him. "Do you want anything?"

Apparently, Chance wanted Arlo. Instead of voicing that, he shrugged. "I'll have one of the beers. Take one for yourself, too, if you want."

Arlo laughed. "Geez. Don't get me drunk again. I need to do one of my shows tonight."

Chance felt his throat go dry. "One of your shows?" Of course, he knew what Arlo meant. In that moment, he remembered that Arlo had told him the previous day about the timing of his next scheduled web performance.

Before Arlo retrieved the beers, he made a motion with his right hand in a masturbating motion to answer Chance's question. "You want a glass?" he asked, once the cans were in his hands.

"No, but help yourself if you want one," Chance replied, reaching across the island to grab the alcohol. He found that when he was around Arlo, he needed the fortification.

"I'm good," Arlo replied, popping the can top and guzzling a long gulp. Chance watched the man's Adam's apple rise and fall. Arlo could only be more erotic if he poured the beer down his chest. When Arlo stopped for air, he smiled at Chance. "That hit the spot."

Chance was uncomfortable that Arlo's actions continued to hit a spot with him, too. He popped his own can, drinking quickly and hoping to get an early buzz. When he stopped and wiped his mouth with the back of his hand, he noticed Arlo was watching him as well. If Chance wasn't mistaken, Arlo's eyes were lustful. "Well, there's plenty. Just take as many as you want."

Arlo nodded. "Okay. But I think I'll stop at one. Like I said…"

Chance's lips tightened. "The show."

"The show," Arlo repeated. He took another swig of the beer, then put the can on the counter. "Aren't you hot, Chance? I won't jump you if you remove your shirt."

Chance's cheeks heated. He felt warm, for sure. And in that moment, he wasn't certain he would mind Arlo jumping him. "Uh, I'm good." Arlo's expression showed disappointment and perhaps hurt, as if Chance didn't trust him. Chance decided he was behaving like a priss and shook his head. "On second thought, I guess you're right. It is fucking hot in here."

Chance removed his shirt and brought it over to the counter on the kitchen island, trying not to make eye contact with Arlo. When he raised his eyes, Arlo was staring at him in a way that looked like yearning. Arlo blushed when they made eye contact and he looked away quickly before clearing his throat. "Yeah, I guess the air conditioning can't keep up with the heat that seeps into the cracks of these old houses."

Arlo returned to the living room and all became quiet as he resumed his chores. Chance almost regretted stripping off his shirt. The half-naked proximity had made the two awkward with each other. Chance figured it was best to pretend the dynamic hadn't changed, and he went back to putting his belongings in their places.

Chapter Six

Although their camaraderie had diminished when the men first removed their shirts, Chance found that shouting to each other from the two different rooms in which they were working had eased the tension. Before he approached Arlo again, he decided to be fully dressed. He grabbed a different shirt from his bedroom closet and made his way back to the living room. Chance was impressed that dozens of boxes had been broken down and removed, and their belongings had been placed where Chance had instructed.

Arlo frowned when he looked over to Chance. Chance wondered if he was sending a message that he had felt uncomfortable about being shirtless. "It's chilly in the bedrooms," he explained. Arlo nodded, though it wasn't clear he was convinced.

"I left the cabinet doors open so you could see where I put everything," Arlo said, making his way to the kitchen to retrieve his own shirt. He pulled it over his head before looking down at his watch. "I need to get ready for my performance."

"It's only six o'clock," Chance responded, glancing at the clock on his wall. "How long does it take to get ready? I assume your show is much later tonight."

Arlo chuckled. "I need to shower. And it starts at seven. Don't forget, that will be ten o'clock on the east coast. A lot of my fans are there, as well as the Midwest and South America. I'm popular in Brazil, maybe because my profile says my parents are from there."

"Oh." Chance mused that people from Brazil must be very beautiful. "I was planning to offer you dinner. I would have done it sooner if I had known. How about I take you to a restaurant tomorrow night as a thank you?"

"Chance, helping with unpacking is a bro-code requirement, remember? You don't need to do anything to show your thanks." Arlo started toward the door, turning his head back to Chance. "Charlie is back tomorrow anyway. If he isn't too tired from his travels, plan to come over to our house instead. I'll make us something and you and Charlie can become acquainted."

Arlo retreated a few steps and hesitantly pulled Chance into a quick hug, smiled and exited the house with a wave. Chance grimaced watching him go. He was already missing Arlo's brilliant smile and easygoing banter.

* * * *

Chance returned to his bedroom to finish putting away the items that were still scattered on his floor. When he looked toward his window, he saw the light go on in Arlo's own bedroom. It reminded Chance of his intrusive behavior the previous evening.

"I can't spy on him again," Chance mumbled to himself. Still, he turned off his bedroom light so Arlo wouldn't see him.

Chance's breath hitched when he saw Arlo strip off his shirt once more. He was beyond denying that he enjoyed looking at Arlo, and he was hoping he'd see even more skin.

Arlo moved away from the window and out of sight for the next twenty minutes, leaving Chance to imagine Arlo taking a shower. When Arlo re-emerged, it appeared that he was wearing a white Henley shirt. Arlo moved about the room, and at one point, disappeared again. Chance wondered if Arlo might have gone to his bed, which was out of view of the window.

Chance warred with himself about logging onto Arlo's site. He remembered the web page name, and he recalled the handle Arlo used. Arlo had told him that the performers didn't know who was logging in, and they weren't privy to the subscriber information. Apparently, Chance could watch the whole thing and Arlo would be none the wiser.

He pulled his laptop off the desk and brought it to the bed. Once he was lying down, he positioned the computer on his lap. Chance typed in the web address and was hit with a barrage of pictures of half-naked men. Apparently, they were some of the featured talents. Arlo had said he was the site's most popular performer, and it explained why a shirtless Arlo was front-and-center of the picture collage.

There was a warning that viewers needed to be at least eighteen years of age to enter, and it was another reminder that Chance was doing something questionable. In this case, it wasn't because he was viewing porn—it was that he was observing Arlo without the man's knowledge.

Chance rationalized that he wasn't betraying Arlo. After all, Arlo had provided the web information, almost as if he had been coaxing Chance to check it out. Arlo had even said he wasn't opposed to people he knew watching him perform. He was also the one who had been encouraging Chance to be less uptight and focus on his happiness.

Chance tried blocking the part of his brain that was shooting down his excuses and reminding him that Arlo had also said he'd want a friend to ask permission before logging on. Chance played a mental game of semantics, thinking to himself that knowing someone for two days might be too early to consider them a friend, so Arlo's comment didn't apply. Before he could debate it more in his head, Chance advanced through the screens and punched in his credit card information. He figured he could stop viewing at any time if it started to feel weird or invasive.

Once he was granted entry, Chance searched for Arlo's show using the *Chatter-butt-box* performer name, then a different picture of a shirtless Arlo appeared. Chance deliberated for several more minutes, even closing the laptop at one point. When the thought of Arlo already engaging his fans while Chance was missing it entered his mind, he flipped the screen back open.

Before he could talk himself out of it, Chance punched in a user-name at the prompt. He chose *MBW_1217* to stand for Marketing Boy Wonder, followed by the house number of his building. Chance figured he could remember the name if he ever wanted to log in again, and it was cryptic enough that Arlo wouldn't know who he was.

Once the user-name was accepted, a message displayed that Chance was being taken to the live performance. Within seconds, the interior of Arlo's bedroom displayed where Arlo was sitting on his bed, smiling as he welcomed the members who were joining.

"Hi *MBW_1217*," Arlo chuckled. "Wow, that will be a hard one to call out. Do you want to give me a first name in case I want to interact with you? It doesn't have to be your real one."

Chance panicked. What the hell was he doing? He sat frozen, thinking he should just log off. When he didn't type a response, Arlo shrugged and continued greeting other members who were joining.

Chance hadn't planned on interacting anyway, so to avoid being rude, he provided a fake name to Arlo. Chance ended up typing 'Charles,' because Arlo's boyfriend's name of Charlie was the first one that came to mind.

Arlo must have seen Chance's response scroll up the screen because he grinned. "Thank you, MBW. I'll call you Charles, if that's okay. That name is rather special to me, in fact."

Chance could feel a bead of sweat on his temple. He didn't do well with being underhanded and devious. He debated turning off the computer once more, but he feared that Arlo would be hurt and insulted that the new member decided he didn't want to see what Arlo had to offer.

What Chance had believed to be a white Henley shirt on Arlo was, in fact, a white union suit—only this one had short sleeves and legs. Arlo had the first several buttons undone, and the cotton fabric was stretched tight over Arlo's muscled body. Since there was no computer on Arlo's lap, Chance assumed Arlo was watching his television screen. Arlo must have hidden the microphone that allowed him to speak to his viewers. Chance mused that the camera and lighting were great, as there was no blur and it was easy to see every detail of Arlo's body. Chance could even make out the outline of Arlo's cock and balls through the crotch of the cotton sleepwear. Although Chance had hoped that seeing the man's privates would be what would ultimately disinterest him, it excited him more.

Arlo continued greeting members with effusive charm and friendliness, which Chance knew to be genuine.

"Hi, Chad. Hi, Steve. Hi, Jeremy. Good to connect again, Jessica. Hey, Timmy." Arlo smiled, recognizing every person that was logging in. "Let's just give folks a couple of more minutes, okay?" he asked the group.

Many of the members were responding with their own hellos, usually with flirtatious comments like 'hi sexy' or 'looking good, buddy.'

"Okay, guys, thanks for being patient," Arlo stated, still with a warm grin on his face. As if pretending he had a slight chest itch, Arlo casually reached a hand into the opened front of his suit and rubbed his pectoral muscle, making sure the viewers caught a glimpse of a pretty nipple.

"Love the outfit, CB," *Tommy from Springfield* typed.

"So sexy, CB," *Hunter27* concurred.

Chance noted that members called Arlo 'CB' as an abbreviation for the Chatter Box handle.

Arlo was soaking up the compliments, thanking each person as he did so. Chance remembered that Arlo mentioned he tried to build a rapport with his viewers and make each person feel respected. Chance was tempted to type something, too, but refrained.

"Let's see your chest," *Huge_cock476* typed.

Within seconds, several other members were making demands to see not only Arlo's chest, but also his more intimate places. Chance wanted that, too, but he didn't like that people were pushing Arlo.

Chance couldn't stop himself from typing. "Let CB do what he wants, when he wants…if he wants."

Josh_in_Boston24 typed a statement that he concurred, and put a 'like' emoji on Chance's statement. Chance immediately decided Josh in Boston was a decent man.

Arlo smiled broadly. "Thanks, Charles. Thanks, Josh. It's okay. I don't mind that everyone's eager. It's flattering." Arlo paused, rubbing his hand over the fabric that clung to his chest. "Charles and Josh, I'm ready to show off my chest. Hope you won't think I'm going too fast." He winked.

Josh responded immediately. "Of course not, CB. Can't wait. Just agreeing with Charles that you shouldn't be forced to do something you don't want."

Chance swallowed. Shit. This was getting weird. He wasn't expecting to engage with Arlo and other members online. He simply typed 'same' in agreement with Josh's statement.

Arlo popped a few more buttons, then pushed the fabric away from his chest. He slid the top part of the suit from his shoulders and arms until the material sat bunched at his sides. Arlo had opened enough that his stomach and pubes were also on display. "Better, guys?"

There were many comments of approval, along with scrolling heart emojis. Someone had found dirtier emojis and sent one of a penis getting hard. It made Arlo chuckle.

Chance was surprised at how long Arlo dragged out the suspense. He rubbed his fingers over his nipples several times during the ongoing chat, making them erect. Chance found himself wanting to lick and suck them. He glanced at the comments and saw several other members voicing the same. "He's mine," he muttered before admonishing himself with a reminder that he had no claim to Arlo.

Comments continued to flood in so fast, Chance wondered how Arlo could read all of them. Arlo continued to smile, though, muttering 'thank you' frequently, acknowledging the many compliments.

Arlo upped the ante after a few minutes, rubbing his cock through the fabric. It had become fully erect—thicker than average. The fact that Chance wanted Arlo to pull it out ended any denial that he had regarding gay tendencies.

Chance swallowed. His throat was uncomfortably dry as he watched Arlo reach into the suit to grab his dick. Arlo was massaging it while maintaining eye contact with the camera.

One of the members typed a message to Arlo, asking him what he was thinking about while he was playing with himself. Another viewer, *Mark_is_horny555*, latched onto the comment, suggesting Arlo envision him.

Arlo chuckled. "Oh, Mark, I can't see you guys, remember? I'm sure watching you jerking your dick would turn me on, though. You are jerking, aren't you?"

Mark_is_horny555 responded that he was. He felt the need to add that he was playing with all ten inches. Chance rolled his eyes. He figured Mark was likely half that size.

Arlo played along, though. "Mm. Lucky you, Mark."

Paolo_99 shot a follow-up question. "Do you have a boyfriend, CB? Is he who you're picturing?"

Arlo's smile slipped a bit. "Now, Paolo, you know I won't talk about my personal life. But if I do have a boyfriend, I'll just get the real thing from him. I did meet a super handsome guy yesterday, though. I think we're becoming good friends already. Maybe I'll picture him since I'll never have him for real."

Chance gasped. Arlo had to be talking about him. He would have had no time to make friends with someone else when he'd spent all his time with Chance.

"Why can't you have him for real?" one of the nosy members asked.

Arlo laughed. "Because he told me that he's mostly straight. He's only let a gay boy blow him. You know how that goes, guys. Even if he was interested, he'd run for the hills when we're done. I like him too much to let that happen."

Chad_from_Denver77 typed that was too bad, and that it was a loss for the 'closet-case.' Others started typing that they agreed. Chance felt embarrassed. Even though he had never met these people, they were disparaging him. Then again, they weren't wrong about his cowardice—especially since he was hiding in his dark room, watching Arlo pleasuring himself instead of having been honest with Arlo and admitting he found him attractive.

"Stop it, everyone." Arlo chuckled. "He's a super nice guy. I don't criticize people who struggle with their sexuality. It's not easy. Besides, like I said, I believe him when he says he's mostly straight. I'll just enjoy having a friend who's a stud."

"Describe him to us," Josh from Boston suggested.

Arlo's eyes clouded and he grabbed his dick harder, creating some wetness on the fabric that covered the head. Arlo's excitement was for him. Chance opened his jeans and shoved them and his boxers down his thighs. He couldn't stand the constraint any longer. His cock bounced toward his stomach and Chance started stroking.

"He's sexy as fuck," Arlo finally responded. "He's thinner than me, but really toned. He has a body like a runway model. I saw him without a shirt today. Oh my God. His chest is so beautiful. Gorgeous nipples and just enough hair to rub your face over." As Arlo spoke of Chance, he started more aggressively tugging on his cock. "His face is so cute. Well, handsome and cute, if you know what I mean. And his hair is so pretty. When the sun shines on it, it's like glass. And his smile…it melts me."

"LOL. You have it bad," *Sara7435* typed.

Arlo smiled. "You would too, if you saw him, Sara."

"I have it bad for *you*," she replied in writing.

"Yeah, CB. Let us see that hot dick," *Sean-the-meat-lover* demanded.

That spurred on many other members to request the same, encouraging Arlo to turn up the heat. He retrieved his hand from the suit and held it toward the camera.

"I'm so wet. Can you see the pre-cum on my fingers?" Arlo asked. He then put the digits to his mouth and licked them.

Chance had never tasted himself, but he liked watching Arlo do it. Especially when Arlo told the group that he was pretending he was licking his new friend. Chance stopped masturbating. He knew if he kept stimulating himself, he'd erupt before Arlo made it further. The idea of logging off was now far from his mind. He was as eager as everyone else to see Arlo finish himself.

Arlo sat up on the bed, then he repositioned himself to a kneeling position facing the camera. The suit fell farther down his hips, revealing half of the man's hard cock. Chance groaned, finding the slow tease to be exquisite torture.

"Should I take off everything, guys?" Arlo asked.

Of course, that was just baiting the group to send numerous replies of yes, accompanied by more emojis of hearts and spraying dicks.

"Charles? Want to see my cock?" Arlo asked.

Chance felt heat rise to his neck and spread to his face. He wondered why he was being singled out. His hands were shaking as he typed a response. "Yes. Please."

Arlo laughed lightly. "I like you, Charles. So polite."

Chance watched as Arlo slowly slipped the suit down farther until his very hard prick sprang from its confines. Arlo continued pushing down, revealing his balls as well, before resuming his stroking.

Chance thought he should comment, since Arlo's action directly followed a call-out to him. "It's beautiful, CB. *You're* beautiful." Chance had double-checked before hitting send, making sure he hadn't typed Arlo's real name. He had almost done so more than once.

Arlo had a curious look on his face, but then the broad smile returned. "You're so sweet, Charles. I'm glad you joined us tonight."

"Tug on your balls," one of the members demanded. Arlo complied and his prick rose higher. More clear liquid started to escape his piss-slit.

"So hot," another member typed.

Chance was starting to ignore what people were typing. He was transfixed, staring at naked Arlo. He had never seen an uncircumcised cock other than in a picture, and he liked it. Arlo's foreskin was the same tannish color as the rest of him, but his bulbous cockhead was the color of light raspberry. Chance was surprised that his first instinct was to lick it. So much for giving oral to a man not being 'his scene.'

"You picturing your new friend sucking your cock?" *Hunter27* asked. Chance flushed. It was as if Hunter could see into his bedroom and his thoughts.

"Mm." Arlo nodded, tilting his head back, rubbing one of his nipples with his left-hand and continuing long, slow strokes over his erection with his right-hand.

Chance resumed stroking himself in rhythm with Arlo, mesmerized by how hot his friend looked masturbating.

Soon, multiple requests were streaming in to see Arlo's butt. Chance found himself agreeing with them. He even typed it himself. "Yes. Please, CB. Want to see your ass."

Arlo grinned. "That's it, Charles. You don't have to be bashful. I want to know what you'd like."

Arlo pulled the suit off his legs, then turned around, wiggling his muscular ass at the camera. He looked back over his shoulder with a sexy expression.

Chance had to remove his hand once again from his lap. He was on the precipice. It was a good thing he had, because Arlo then bent forward and spread his legs, revealing his hole. Chance had never found an asshole pretty, but everything about Arlo was proving an exception. Arlo's butt was incredible—full, smooth and shapely. His crack had very little hair that might have been manscaped, and his pinkish hole looked clean and tight. Chance wanted to fuck the man right then.

More compliments flooded the screen about Arlo's privates, focusing on his anus and the sexy way his scrotum hung between his legs. "So hot, CB. You are perfect," he typed.

Arlo turned back around to face the camera, then leaned back on the pillows, raising one of his knees toward his chest. The guy was purposely displaying his chest, his genitals and his hole. Chance could see why members kept coming back for more. He was wondering how he'd resist.

"Thanks, Charles," Arlo mentioned, along with thanks to several other visitors who were complimenting him.

"Use your dildo," *Jay_Minneapolis1983* typed. That opened the door to several other viewers requesting the same. Chance wasn't sure he could handle the added stimulation of watching Arlo fucking himself.

Arlo chuckled. "You all like that, huh?"

"Yes," was the reply from dozens.

Arlo reached over to the nightstand and pulled out a thin, lavender-colored dildo and a bottle of lubricant.

Before slicking it up, he poured some of the lube on his finger and began massaging his entrance. Chance swallowed again, wishing he had brought up a bottle of water. But there was no way in hell he was leaving the scene to retrieve one.

Arlo started to press his slippery finger in his hole, earning many thanks and cheers from his fans. Arlo began to moan as he pushed more of his finger in and out of his opening.

"You picturing your friend fucking you?" *Hunter27* asked.

Chance hoped he was, because Chance was envisioning burying himself in Arlo.

"Yeah," Arlo admitted softly.

Chance inhaled. He spit on his hand and resumed palming his aching shaft.

Arlo removed his finger, reaching for more lubricant and slathering the dildo. With one slow push, Arlo fully inserted the toy as he moaned.

More comments filled the screen, but Chance ignored them. He was intent on watching the dildo slide in and out of the man. As Arlo sped up his motions, Chance accelerated the pace of fisting his cock.

"I'm not going to last long tonight," Arlo apologized to the group. "Just so horny."

"It's okay," Josh from Boston typed. "We're ready, too. Give us a nice load, CB. Shoot it for the new buddy you made a couple of days ago."

That put Arlo over the top and he gasped, blowing four or five extended jets of cum over his stomach and chest. Chance whined as he quickly followed, blasting his own jism across his abs before the final spurts cascaded down his shaft. "Fuck," he shouted to nobody.

As Chance panted, he watched Arlo's breathing slow before the man reached for a tissue to wipe himself.

"Eat it," someone ordered.

Arlo shook his head with a little laugh. "Not tonight. I don't want to ruin the vision I had in my head with reality."

Chance sighed. Was Arlo still thinking about him? He found himself hoping so. Chance reached for his own tissues to clean himself, feeling embarrassed at what he'd done. He considered logging off.

"Charles? You still there?" Arlo asked. "I think it was your first time with us. I hope you liked it."

Chance's eyes widened. Now that he was feeling shame, he was less comfortable chatting. "Yes." He couldn't bring himself to type more.

Arlo chuckled. "Okay. I never want to disappoint a newcomer. Please tell me you came, Charles."

Chance swallowed hard. God, why couldn't Arlo speak to someone else? "Yes."

Arlo grinned. "Okay. You're shy now. That's sweet. I hope you'll come back."

Chance didn't know what to type, but making Arlo feel good was important to him. "You were wonderful. Thank you so much." *Thank you so much*? Now he knew he should log off since he was sounding like the schoolmarm Arlo had accused him of being earlier in the day.

Arlo laughed. "Thank *you* so much, Charles."

With that, more viewers began chatting it up with Arlo, and he politely engaged with them. Mostly, the members shared their appreciation with Arlo, making Chance feel less stupid about his remark. There were several members wishing Arlo a good night and he was offering the same in return.

When there was hardly anyone left on the site, Arlo smiled and waved at those who remained online.

"Goodnight, CB," Chance typed. "It was one of the hottest nights of my life."

Arlo literally jerked his head back with surprise. His voice choked a bit when he responded. "Gosh, Charles. Thank you. I'm glad. Goodnight to you, too." He then composed himself and smiled at the group one last time. "Have a good night, everyone."

The screen went black, and Chance dropped his head down on his pillow with a groan.

Chapter Seven

When Chance awoke, he remembered coming all over himself when watching Arlo's performance. He placed his hands over his face, wishing he could fall back to sleep to block the shame.

It wasn't that he felt bad for wanting Arlo. He was past that. He could learn to live with right-wing disparagers. But he hated himself for having betrayed someone who trusted him. He couldn't enjoy recalling how hot Arlo had been—it just reminded him of how he had creepily watched and pretended to be someone else. Chance hadn't had the guts to ask permission to log on to Arlo's site, and he worried that if Arlo knew what he'd done, it would end their budding friendship.

Chance remembered that he was supposed to meet Arlo for an eight o'clock run, then join Arlo and Charlie for dinner that evening. He didn't feel he could under the circumstances. He imagined the introductions with embarrassment. *Oh, hello…I'm the neighbor who spied on your lover as he undressed, then pretended to be someone else on his website so I could watch him whack off. So, what's for dinner?*

He wanted to excuse himself from the run and the get-together. It would be awkward enough whenever he met Charlie, but he didn't want it to be when he was in the man's home, eating the man's food and drinking his wine. It would make Chance feel even slimier.

Chance rolled off the bed and grabbed his iPhone. There were still no messages from Maria or others from the firm. He would have expected one of his co-workers, at least, would have contacted him. He wondered if they sensed his job was in jeopardy and decided it was best to cut ties with him. It made him question whether he had any real friends at work.

There were two messages, though. One was from his mother complaining that he hadn't called for two days. She'd have to wait because he was in no mood to engage with her. The second was from Arlo. They had exchanged phone numbers the day they had met, but seeing his new friend's name pop up twisted the knife of guilt in deeper. It didn't help that the message was a sweetly worded text about looking forward to their run and that Charlie was eager to meet him for dinner.

Before he could overthink it, Chance typed a declination to both the jog and the dinner. He lied that he was feeling under the weather and he didn't want to get Arlo and Charlie sick. He felt it best to stay indoors and isolated until he felt better.

Chance sat on the floor by the bed, staring at the phone as if summoning a response from Arlo. He hoped Arlo would text that he understood, wish him well, and that would be the end. The last thing Chance needed was for Arlo to start asking specifics of what was wrong with him or suggesting that he determine how he was feeling later in the day before deciding about dinner.

More than an hour went by with no response. Chance was still sitting on the floor at the foot of his bed. His butt and his neck were beginning to ache. It served him right.

When the phone pinged at seven-forty-five a.m., it nearly made Chance jump. He looked to his messages. Arlo had replied. The message began with a sad-face emoji, followed by the words 'oh no.' Arlo went on to say that he was sorry that Chance wasn't feeling well and that he should rest in bed. He told Chance not to worry about dinner and that they'd reschedule. Arlo finished the message with a wish that Chance would feel better quickly and to call Arlo if he needed anything.

Chance wiped a hand over his face. "Don't be nice to me, Arlo," he whispered to the phone. "If you knew what I did…"

Feeling depressed and without energy, Chance took Arlo's advice and went back to bed. He pulled up the covers and worried more about his job and whether he'd ruined the possibility of a real friendship before falling back to sleep.

When Chance awoke, it was to a buzzing sound. Sleepily, he looked at the alarm clock, noticing it was one in the afternoon. He lifted the clock to turn off the alarm, then understood that wasn't what had made the noise. He heard another buzz and Chance remembered it was the sound that his new home's doorbell made.

Chance groaned, wondering who would be calling on him and, more importantly, why they weren't going away. He looked toward the window. It was pouring rain. He hoped the fool would tire of getting sopping wet while standing on his front doorstep.

When the doorbell rang once again, Chance exhaled and swore, then forced himself out of bed. He feared the person who'd be this persistent might be Arlo, probably worried about him. Why wouldn't he just accept Chance wasn't feeling well and leave him in peace?

Chance bumbled down the stairs, getting a quick glance of himself in the mirror. He looked like shit. His hair was askew, he had a five-o'clock shadow and he was still in a rumpled T-shirt and boxers.

He opened the front door with some annoyance, finding a drenched Arlo on the other side. The man looked like a wet puppy, big eyes all worried but adorable. Arlo was holding a plastic container that was enclosed in a clear storage bag.

"Chance, I'm sorry to bother you. I know you're sick. I considered leaving when you weren't answering, but then I worried you might be unconscious or something. Anyway, I didn't think you'd have the energy to make yourself a meal. I brought homemade chicken soup. And, well, I was just concerned."

Arlo pushed the container toward Chance, and Chance tentatively took it. He was feeling more guilt-ridden by the minute. "Arlo, you didn't have to…"

"It's no problem." Arlo smiled. "I like cooking, especially for people I care about."

Chance knew he should invite Arlo in, but he remembered that the sweet guy had no idea what a bum he was befriending. "Um, that's really nice of you, Arlo. Actually, I was sleeping. I think I'll just put this in the refrigerator for later."

Arlo took the hint, nodding apologetically. "Yes, of course. I'm sorry I woke you, Chance. You look terrible. Well, not terrible because you're so handsome and the boxers are sexy, but you know what I mean. Go back to bed, but call me if you need anything. Do you have enough medicine?"

"Yes," Chance replied with less patience than he would have liked. He imagined there was some universal force that was putting kind words in Arlo's mouth to make him feel even more reprehensible.

Arlo grimaced ever-so-slightly at the terse response. "Oh, okay. Well, I'll leave you alone, then. Take care, Chance. Call me if you need anything."

Arlo turned and scurried down the steep front steps, leaving Chance holding the bowl of guilt. He closed the door and brought it to the kitchen, debating whether to dump it down the sink. He didn't feel he deserved the soup, and his shame wouldn't let him enjoy it anyway. But Arlo had labored to make it just for him, and he couldn't bear to do so. He put the bag in the refrigerator, shutting the door so he wouldn't have to see it.

Chance made his way back up the stairs and eyed his laptop as if it was a portal to hell. He grabbed it and logged onto the FansOfStuds site and found his account information. Once Chance saw where he could unsubscribe, he plowed through the prompts that intended to stop him with warnings that he would lose access to the 'best men' on the net. One last question asked whether the reader was certain, and Chance typed 'yes.' A message returned that his account would stay active for the remainder of the month for which Chance had paid, but then would be terminated. Chance wished it would cancel right away. He didn't want the temptation of ever watching Arlo again. Maybe he could excuse one-time bad judgment. A second time would certify him as a despicable friend.

He fell back on the bed, still exhausted. Chance wondered if that was a manifestation of depression. He wasn't sure, as he had never been tempted to do anything but work hard each day after graduating from college. In that moment, though, he was glad sleepiness was coming easily.

* * * *

When Chance awoke, it was a little past midnight. He felt a severe ache in his side and stomach, and he figured it was because he hadn't eaten all day. Still, he wasn't hungry, and he didn't want to be tempted to eat the food Arlo had brought to him. Chance wondered if he'd ever eat it, or let it sit in the refrigerator for eternity, its eventual foul smell a reminder that he messed up. It made him think of an Edgar Allan Poe story where the main character had buried the heart of his murder victim under the floorboards of his home, and the killer continued to hear the heartbeat that nobody else could, leading him to confess as he was slowly driven to madness. Would the constant sight and smell of Arlo's soup do the same to Chance, forcing him to confess his sin to his friend before it drove him insane?

He rose to drink some water, feeling a bit dizzy. Chance was surprised at how quickly a body reacted to a lack of food. He figured that come morning, whether he was hungry or not, he would force himself to eat something—even if it was just a bowl of cereal. He wasn't inclined to starve himself to death for committing one selfish act.

Chance was able to fall back to sleep for a couple of additional hours, despite the pain in his stomach. When he woke again, though, the discomfort was more severe and Chance was shivering. He knew the air-conditioning was set to seventy-three degrees, which shouldn't have caused him to be so cold. He pulled up more blankets, but it was as if they were made of cotton gauze for all the warmth they were providing.

Chance stumbled out of bed, feeling like a wave of acid or mucus was making its way up his esophagus. He started to gag. He wrapped the covers tighter around himself and stumbled to the ensuite. When he looked at himself in the mirror, he was deathly white. He had never seen himself so pale and it scared him. He started to dry-heave, hoping something would escape his throat that would give him relief from the violent distress. Nothing was happening, though, other than Chance shivering over the sink, gagging and struggling to keep himself upright. The pain in his stomach and side had intensified, and he wondered if it was his appendix.

Chance returned to the bedroom and crawled back onto the mattress. He knew he should call an ambulance. This was worse than the flu, and it wasn't flu season. Also, he hadn't eaten anything for several hours, so it couldn't be food-poisoning. The idea of an ambulance showing up to his house, though, was embarrassing. He didn't have the energy to get dressed, and he didn't want to be hauled away—unwashed and wearing nothing but his underclothes. In the morning, surely, he'd feel a little better. He told himself that he just had to make it through the night.

Several hours lapsed where Chance tossed and turned, trying desperately to find a position that stopped the pain in his abdomen. The chills had subsided somewhat, which was a relief. He wondered if maybe it was a bug of some sort after all and he would feel better in a few hours.

When the sun started to rise, he forced himself to shave, take a hot shower and brush his teeth. When he emerged from the steamy bathroom, though, he started to quake, feeling frigid again. He put on his warmest sweater and a pair of briefs before he started collapsing to the floor. His body was shaking uncontrollably, and the pain in his stomach had become unbearable once he had started moving around.

When the nausea hit him again with no ability to vomit, he knew something was seriously wrong and he couldn't continue to ignore it. He grabbed his iPhone and pressed the icon that would connect him to Arlo. Chance hoped he'd answer, because the fallback was making a nine-one-one emergency call.

"Chance? How are you feeling?" Arlo asked within seconds.

Chance's teeth were clattering so much, and there was so much clogging in his esophagus, he wasn't sure if Arlo would even hear his response. "I need help."

He heard the words "I'm coming," and Chance clicked off the phone with relief. He still had the wits to remember Arlo saying those words erotically during his online performance and he wondered if, ironically, they'd be the last words he ever heard.

Chapter Eight

Charlie had been about to head out the door to the office when Arlo grabbed him and begged him to accompany him to Chance's house.

"Charlie, please. He sounded awful. He said he needs help." Arlo was panicked.

Charlie had heard a lot from Arlo about their new neighbor, and he had been curious to meet him. The last time he had seen Arlo take a liking to someone so fast, it had resulted in the couple welcoming Wilson into their relationship. Truth be told, Arlo had always loved Wilson more than Charlie did, and he knew Wilson's greater affection had been for Arlo. Charlie could never refuse Arlo, though, and when he had hinted about trying a threesome, Charlie had been eager to please. In time, he had begun to enjoy it, as well. Though Wilson never became as important to him as Arlo, Charlie had grown to care for the man. The sex was incredible, for sure, and the unusual living arrangement had started to feel like any *other* would have been abnormal. That was, until Wilson started sleeping with other men.

Charlie had been the first to discover Wilson's cheating, and he had wanted Wilson to pack and leave the day of the discovery. Because he knew Arlo would be devastated by the news and the departure, he kept the secret and elicited a promise from Wilson to remain monogamous with him and Arlo. When Arlo had discovered Wilson cheating several months later—again—Charlie was infuriated. He had seen the pain in Arlo's eyes that day, and he swore he'd protect his boyfriend from ever experiencing that kind of hurt again.

So, when Arlo began telling Charlie about Chance, Charlie was wary. Arlo had been bursting with happiness and excitement, and he had admitted to Charlie that he found the man to be one of the most handsome he'd ever met. Arlo had been quick to add that Charlie would always be at the top of the list for him, but he wondered if Chance could be that guy who'd make for a great threesome once more. Charlie had to laugh when Arlo tried to dismiss the fact that Chance, apparently, was mostly straight. Charlie wasn't opposed to trying to reintroduce a third party, as there had been many benefits to the arrangement. With his frequent business travels, it had been comforting to know that Arlo wasn't lonely. Also, Arlo had stopped performing online because, sexually, his desire to be watched and guided had been fulfilled. That had given Charlie peace of mind, as he had no idea what types of people were subscribers to Arlo's site.

Charlie also knew that since he himself tended to be mostly take-charge, paternalistic and nurturing, Arlo felt complete when he had a 'buddy' type of relationship in the mix. Certainly, the three incomes and added help taking care of the house and errands didn't hurt. Finally, Charlie missed the sex possibilities, too. He loved Arlo, and if he went through the rest of his life with only him, Charlie would still consider himself the luckiest man in the world. But there was a part of him that was highly aroused watching Arlo with another man, and he enjoyed satisfying two partners in one encounter. The combination had allowed him to indulge in some erotic role-play sessions, too, which had resulted in some of his favorite sex memories. Finding a guy who would be the perfect fit, however—that would be like finding a lost rare coin in the city's largest dump. Charlie assumed it would never happen, considering even Wilson hadn't been the perfect fit. Arlo, on the other hand, was determined to find the unicorn, and his hope was that Chance was that mythical creature. Charlie had reminded Arlo that he and Chance had never met. The odds of both being attracted to each other was unlikely, and that was if Chance was even attracted to Arlo since no such declaration had been made. Arlo was hopeful, though.

Now, Charlie would be meeting the guy under the strangest of circumstances. He and Arlo would be bounding into the man's home to tend to whatever emergency was underway.

As the two raced up the steps to Chance's house, Arlo was fidgeting with worry. Charlie placed a soothing hand on Arlo's shoulder while Arlo incessantly rang the doorbell. Arlo turned more than once, terror on his face, when minutes were passing without an answer. Finally, Charlie and Arlo heard the click of a lock and Arlo nearly shoved the door open.

Charlie saw that the man he assumed was Chance, slid partly down to the floor on his knees. He must have struggled to make his way down the stairs. Charlie noticed the guy hadn't even had a chance to put on trousers.

"Chance!" Arlo shouted, dropping to his knees and putting his arms around his friend. Arlo turned back to Charlie with wide eyes after putting his hand on Chance's forehead. "Charlie, he's burning up."

Charlie dropped to a haunch position, lifting Chance's chin. He recognized the man, but couldn't remember where from. He placed the back of his hand on Chance's cheek and nodded, concurring with Arlo's assessment. "Chance? Chance, I'm Charlie. I'm a doctor. Tell me where you have pain."

Chance looked at the man and gasped, his eyes squinting as if he couldn't believe what he was seeing. "It's you. The monster."

Arlo glanced between the two, confused and distraught. "Charlie, what's he saying? Is he delirious?"

"Dr. Kendall," Chance whispered. "Have you come to finish me off?"

"What's he talking about, Charlie?" Arlo asked, looking stricken. "How does he know your last name?"

In that second, Charlie remembered Chance. He had forgotten the man's first name from their previous unfortunate encounter. He had been thinking the guy's name was Chase. Truthfully, he hadn't been paying much attention during the introduction, as he had other things on his mind at the time. But there was no question when Charlie gazed into the man's eyes—the same eyes that had looked pleadingly at him, hoping for a lifeline when his marketing presentation had bombed. Charlie winced when he remembered how he'd been unempathetic, suggesting to Chance's boss that she should consider other talent. It hadn't been Charlie's finest moment.

How could Chance have known it was the same day that Charlie had run into Wilson, and Wilson had wanted to re-enter his life? It was something he had kept from Arlo, praying Wilson wouldn't contact him directly. Or how could Chance have known that the previous evening, the charity board on which Charlie was a member found out that their major donor decided giving their money to climate change was more important than contributing to the community's immediate welfare? And, of course, Chance wouldn't have been aware that Charlie had recalled Chance's sad expression many times since their encounter, wishing for a do-over.

"Charlie? Do you know Chance?" Arlo asked again when he hadn't heard a response.

"We've met," Charlie replied tersely. "Arlo, we need to get Chance to the hospital. He's very ill. Run upstairs to his bedroom to try to find him a pair of trousers."

Arlo followed the order and headed for the stairs.

"Chance? Listen to me. Where do you have pain?" Charlie asked the foggy-eyed man. Charlie wasn't liking the pallor of Chance's skin.

"Stomach," Chance mumbled.

"Show me," Charlie commanded.

Chance felt his lower abdomen, toward the side. He began to wretch a bit, shaking with chills as he did so. "Am I dying?"

Charlie stroked the man's hair. He knew it was awkward, considering their last encounter. "I won't let you die, Chance. You have appendicitis. Your appendix might have burst. We need to get you to the hospital."

Chance leaned into Charlie. "You're warm," he muttered with a small smile.

"I've got the pants," Arlo shouted as he bounded down the stairs.

"Okay. Go get the car. I don't want to wait for an ambulance," Charlie ordered. "Just take the slacks with you. I'm not going to try to put them on him at this point. He'll probably be angry later, though, if he has none to wear home."

"What's wrong with him?" Arlo dared to ask with obvious fear.

"It's his appendix," Charlie replied. "Now, Arlo. Get the car!"

As Arlo raced down the front steps that led from Chance's front door, Charlie considered how he would get his patient to navigate the same route. It wasn't the first time he'd noticed how poorly designed the city homes were when it came to safety.

"Chance, listen to me," Charlie instructed. "I'm going to lift you and carry you down the steps. You're too weak to risk descending them."

Chance acquiesced to the humiliation with a weak nod. Charlie was able to lift the man easily into his massive arms and he transported him to the curb below.

Arlo pulled the car up to where Charlie stood holding Chance before exiting to open the rear door for Charlie to place Chance within. "Charlie, don't let him die. Please!"

Charlie quickly kissed Arlo's temple. "Arlo, get in the back seat with Chance. You're in no state to drive to the hospital. Just hold him and try to keep him warm."

Arlo jumped in the car, cradling Chance while Charlie took to the driver's seat and sped away from the curb. Charlie glanced in the rearview mirror and was surprised to see that Chance was grinning at Arlo.

"Bet you wish you had the old neighbors back," Chance whispered.

Arlo brushed his hand along Chance's heated face. "Never. You're coming right back here, Chance. Good neighbors are hard to find, and we're not letting you leave."

* * * *

Chance didn't remember much of the ride to the hospital. He knew Charlie and Arlo had exchanged conversation, but it was a blur to him. His entire goal during the drive had been to stop shivering uncontrollably. He was glad Arlo had brought a blanket with his trousers, which Arlo had wrapped around Chance. Arlo rubbed his hands over Chance's still uncovered bare legs to warm them as well. Chance mused how just two days earlier, that would have given him an erection. That, however, was a physical impossibility since the previous evening.

When they arrived at the emergency room, Charlie had instructed a reluctant Arlo to part with Chance and take the car to park it in the visitor lot. Charlie told him he'd handle getting Chance admitted, as his hospital affiliation would ensure an immediate examination.

Chance was humiliated to enter the building with no pants, but considering everyone's ailments, nobody noticed. Even the receptionist who greeted Charlie focused only on what the doctor told her, and within seconds, he was being helped down a corridor to an examining room.

A nurse greeted them, and Chance did his best to shiver out responses as Charlie helped him climb onto the examining table. Charlie was considerate enough to cover Chance's lower extremities with the blanket to which Chance had been clinging.

"So cold," Chance muttered through chattering teeth. "Can't they turn down the air conditioning?"

Chance was surprised that Charlie gently stroked his hair. "I'm sorry, Chance. Germs thrive in warmth. They keep it cool for health reasons. When Arlo gets in here, I'll get some additional blankets from the nursing station. A doctor will give you some medication to reduce the fever, then you'll stop shivering."

"When?" Chance asked, wondering why there wasn't a doctor already there.

Charlie squeezed Chance's arm. "I'm sure they're busy. I'll get someone in here. You'll stay put, yes?"

Chance nodded. He found it an odd question, considering he wasn't about to walk off in his condition—without trousers—to take a tour of the hospital.

A few minutes went by before the door reopened. Chance was almost disappointed that it was Arlo and not Charlie or another doctor with medicine. He groaned, hugging himself to make the sweater he was wearing compress around his chest.

"Where's Charlie?" Arlo asked, sounding irritated that his boyfriend had left Chance alone.

"He went to get help for me," Chance responded.

Arlo resumed the stroking of Chance's hair that Charlie had started. Chance was beginning to wonder if the two men were more concerned with shaping his locks than trying to assist him.

"It's going to be okay, Chance," Arlo soothed. "They'll take care of you. Charlie will make sure you get the best treatment."

Chance wanted to disagree, considering the man had apparently left him alone to die of frostbite—or at least suffer by delaying aid.

As the morbid thoughts played out in his head, Arlo began vigorously rubbing Chance's arms. The look of concern on Arlo's face made Chance worry. He wondered if he was as deathly pale as he had been the previous evening. When he had awoken, he was relieved the color had returned to his face, but he also hadn't been shivering like he was now.

The door opened and a new nurse appeared along with Charlie. He was pleasant enough, making small talk as if they were enjoying a mai tai at the beach while Charlie placed more blankets on the patient. Chance was relieved when the nurse gave him instructions to prepare for an intravenous tube which had the alleged potion for regulating his body temperature. As the nurse warned him of a pinch, he almost laughed. He didn't care if he slammed the needle into his vein as long as it brought relief.

Once the tube was in place, Charlie and the nurse started conversing in the corner of the room. Chance wanted to hear what they were saying, but Arlo was in his ear trying to cheer him up with stories of when he was a child in the hospital.

After a few minutes, Chance's teeth were no longer banging against each other and the frigidness was lessening. Conversation ceased as the nurse returned to the table to check more vitals, starting with his blood pressure.

"Chance, in a few minutes, they'll bring you to the lab for some tests to take a look in your abdomen," Charlie explained. "It won't hurt. You'll just need to lie still."

"What do they need to see? You said it was my appendix."

"Yes," Charlie acknowledged. "It's my educated guess. But they can't operate without confirmation, and the pictures will tell them just what they're dealing with. Hopefully, your appendix is just inflamed and infected. If that's the case, there's a good chance they can remove it laparoscopically and you'll heal fast."

"And if it's worse than that?"

Chance felt Arlo squeeze his hand as he watched Charlie's face tighten. "Chance, there's no reason to be thinking the worst. If your appendix ruptured, though, it will be more complicated. It will mean toxins are in your bloodstream and getting you back to normal will take longer. You'd be looking at a few days here, at least."

"But it's not fatal, right?" Arlo whispered to Charlie.

Charlie pursed his lips. "Chance is going to be fine, Arlo. He's already responding to the medicine, which makes me think we're simply looking at acute appendicitis." Charlie turned to Chance. "They'll take good care of you."

"Aren't you going to operate?" Arlo asked. "Please, Charlie?"

Chance wanted to tell Arlo to zip it, as he still wasn't so sure Charlie wouldn't love to lose the patient on the operating table. "Arlo, it's fine," Chance murmured.

Charlie walked over to Arlo and massaged his shoulder followed by a kiss on the head, apparently unconcerned that the nurse was watching their interaction. "Baby, I'm not a specialist in this. I know you think I'm some kind of superhero, but trust me, the surgeon who will be performing the operation is the one you want doing this. She's done this hundreds of times. Chance will be in the best hands."

Chance was beginning to feel calmer as well as warmer, and he pondered what was being pumped into his body. He wasn't going to complain. "I feel like I can put my pants on now. Is that okay?"

Charlie gave a weak smile. "Sure, Chance. If your appendix hasn't burst, it will be a few hours before they operate."

Arlo retrieved the slacks he had laid on a nearby chair and brought them over to Chance. Then he removed the blanket and stared appreciatively at Chance's body. "Are you sure? Your legs would be nice to look at while we're waiting here. Not to mention…everything else."

Charlie lightly slapped Arlo's butt, causing him to yelp. "The poor guy is sick as a dog. He doesn't need you acting like one right now."

Chance was surprised at how unperturbed Charlie was by Arlo's blatant flirtation, and just as surprised the nurse was observing and chuckling like there was nothing odd happening. "Arlo, just hand them over," he snipped.

Arlo sighed with a smile, giving the trousers to Chance who tried to sit up to put them on.

The nurse touched Chance's arm. "Technicians will be in shortly to take you to the lab." He gave Chance an encouraging nod before leaving the room. Chance was irritated that the guy hadn't offered to assist him with his slacks, as Chance was struggling to put them on.

Charlie took possession of the garment, positioning the opening at Chance's feet and pulling the pants up Chance's calves. Once the waist of the trousers was over Chance's knees, Charlie let Chance finish dressing himself by tugging the fabric the rest of the way up his legs.

Arlo shook his head, making a tsk-tsk sound. "Such a shame. It's like throwing a tarp over the statue of David."

Chance blushed and mouthed 'oh my God.' "Arlo, what is wrong with you? Your boyfriend is standing right there."

Charlie let out a loud exhale, pretending to have the weight of the world on his shoulders. "I'm used to it, Chance. Arlo has talked about the cute guy next door since he met you. I'm well aware that I'm second banana now."

Arlo's eyes widened and he punched the big slab of beef that was Charlie's upper arm. "Stop being so dramatic. You know I'm crazy about you, Charlie. You'll always be my guy and you'll always turn me on."

Charlie smiled, as if forgetting that his boyfriend's declaration was on the heels of eyeing another guy. Charlie leaned into a kiss from Arlo, and Chance hadn't turned his head away from watching. Instead of feeling uncomfortable, he found the two of them together endearing. Their relationship was unconventional, for sure, but there was an obvious understanding between them.

"Sorry," Charlie uttered to Chance when he pulled his lips from Arlo's. "This isn't professional of me."

Chance half-shrugged. "It's okay. You aren't *my* doctor, right?"

Arlo nodded. "That's true. Right now, he's just a friend of yours who knows doctor stuff."

Chance tried not to snort a sarcastic laugh at Arlo calling Charlie a friend. He was still struggling to shake the icy demeanor and unkind words from Charlie at the marketing meeting.

Charlie kissed Arlo's cheek and told him he had to get to his own job. "Chance, you'll be fine. There's nothing more I can do for you at this point. Arlo will keep me informed of how things are going."

"Yeah, that's fine," Chance responded. "Thanks for helping me."

"Arlo, I need my car keys," Charlie stated. Arlo blinked with realization, then went to the other side of the room to pull them from his jacket pocket. As he was doing so, Charlie looked to Chance with a sad expression. He leaned toward Chance's ear. "Arlo will want to know how we met. You can tell him. He'll be very angry with me for how I behaved, but I deserve it. I'm sorry, Chance. I've had regrets since the day I met you."

Charlie pulled away from the examining table as Arlo approached, holding out the keys. Charlie took them, but paused to squeeze Arlo's hand. Arlo looked perplexed as to what Charlie might have said to Chance and equally confused by Charlie's apprehensive expression.

"How will I get home?" Arlo asked.

Charlie smirked. "As if you're leaving Chance's side before the surgery is done. I'll come back later to sit with you while Chance is undergoing the operation. I know you'll need me to hold your hand." Charlie turned to Chance once more. "Try not to worry. I'll see you later."

Once Charlie left the room, Arlo sat back down on the chair that was at the side of the examining table. "Okay, so what did he whisper to you?"

Chance wasn't sure how to answer. In that moment, he didn't want to deal with drama, hurt Arlo or appear spiteful to a doctor who had just helped him. He decided to hide the truth. "He just wished me good luck."

Arlo eyed him with skepticism. "He didn't have to whisper to wish you good luck."

Chance had always been quick on his feet. He gave Arlo a side-eye grin. "He might have said something about you having the hots for me."

That worked. Arlo laughed. "Yeah, well, I think I established that already. Don't be concerned about that, Chance. Charlie is okay with it. He knows I wouldn't cheat on him."

Chance nodded. "I can see you love him."

"I really do," Arlo replied. "He's my proverbial knight in shining armor. I'd never hurt him." Arlo waggled his eyebrows. "That said, if you two were to ignite a little spark, and you could ever see me as more than a friend, I'd be happy to share my knight with you."

Chance exhaled a laugh. "Jesus, Arlo. I'm in no state to be thinking about that right now."

Arlo's face sobered. "God, you're right. I'm sorry, Chance. I'm being insensitive and stupid. Let's talk about something else. How did you meet Charlie, anyway? Why did you call him 'the monster' when you first saw him?"

Chance didn't even remember having done so. However, he did remember the conversation he had had with Arlo the day they'd met, where he had told

Arlo about the marketing meeting and Arlo referred to the client as a monster. The label must have stuck in his head.

"I did? Arlo, I was kind of out of it. Maybe I was seeing things. Anyway, we met at a business meeting. He investigated what our firm could do for him. I think he was shopping around. We never ended up doing business together."

"Huh," Arlo muttered. "Small world. Well, it was his loss."

Chance was spared from telling additional lies by the entry of two technicians who informed Chance the lab was ready for him.

Chapter Nine

Chance had been in surgery for over thirty minutes when Charlie arrived at the waiting room. Arlo stood from his chair and rushed to him. "Aren't they supposed to be coming out to inform people how things are going? I haven't heard anything yet."

Charlie gave Arlo a small grin and a quick peck. "Hello to you, too."

"Charlie!"

"Baby, it's not a football game. There isn't an announcer who's going to give you the play-by-play. The doctor will come out when she's done. Since you aren't even family, they don't owe you an update at all. The only reason they're doing so is because I asked them to," Charlie explained.

"Well, that's asinine," Arlo whined. "His family is halfway across the country, and Chance didn't even want to notify them. Who else is the doctor supposed to inform if not me? If Chance died and they didn't tell me, would he just mysteriously disappear into the basement of this building never to be spoken of again?"

"Calm down," Charlie soothed. "You're becoming anxious and dramatic like you always do when you're stressed. Come sit down with me. This isn't going to be over in twenty minutes."

Arlo sat, but narrowed his eyes at Charlie as he took the seat next to him. "That would have been helpful to know if you had arrived twenty minutes ago. How am I supposed to know how long a surgery takes? That's why I asked you to be with me."

"I'm sorry I couldn't get here sooner. It was a crazy day. As it is, I had to ask my staff to take on extra so I could be here."

Arlo leaned into Charlie's side and sighed. "I know. I'm sorry. I'm just scared. You've always said people can die under anesthesia."

Charlie chuckled. "And I've told you that it's rare. Arlo, the odds are like one in one-hundred and eighty-five thousand. You're far more likely to die in a car accident. Yet you don't stop me from getting in one, and it doesn't panic you when you see me drive away."

"Sometimes it does," Arlo countered. "There have been times when it's raining hard or when you've been working late that I do think about it, and the relief I feel when I know you've made it safely is something I just hide."

Charlie wrapped his arm around Arlo and kissed the side of his head. "Don't make yourself sick over things you can't control."

"But I don't know what I'd do without you, Charlie. I know we talk about how we liked having a third person to love and be affectionate with, but *you're* my rock. You're the one I could never be without. You know that, don't you?"

Charlie brushed his fingers along Arlo's hand. "And you're my beautiful guy, Arlo. I could never be without you either."

Arlo nodded. "Maybe we shouldn't think about adding a third person ever again. I mean, it was nice to have someone there and the sex was fun—but maybe it's asking for too much."

Charlie ran his tongue over his upper teeth, contemplating. "I think you were more content when Wilson was with us. I liked that you didn't feel the need to do your shows. The admiration you got from me and Wilson was enough for you."

"Are you mad at me that I started doing them again?" Arlo asked.

"No, baby. I'm not mad. I just liked it better when you saved all your orgasms for me and Wilson." Charlie smiled.

Arlo frowned. "You're away a lot. I don't know why I crave the attention so much..."

Charlie gently held Arlo's chin. "I understand. It's intoxicating. I know what you and I have is wonderful, but I can tell you always got off more on having me or Wilson giving you extra attention while you were getting plowed by the other." Charlie grinned to show the crudeness was meant to make Arlo chuckle.

Arlo pouted instead. "I'm pathetic."

Charlie stroked Arlo's cheek. "Says who? You like what you like. I enjoyed it, too, Arlo. It doesn't mean I love you less just because I liked seeing you with another man."

"Why *do* you like it? You've never explained why."

Charlie shrugged. "I guess, when you and I make love, I can only see so much of you. I feel like I don't get to see my whole beautiful Arlo in the throes of ecstasy. You turn me on. What can I say?"

Arlo contemplated. "Yet you refuse to watch my shows. Wouldn't that do it for you?"

Charlie frowned. "It's not the same, Arlo. Watching you with a man we both care for isn't the same as reading a bunch of lewd comments coming from strangers. I've told you that I'd rather not log onto that."

Arlo nodded. "I understand. I liked watching you with Wilson, too, for the same reasons you said you liked watching me with him."

"Until I stopped loving him," Charlie added. "I know it was hard for you when I sent him away, but I can't forgive someone who's hurt you."

"I like how you protect me," Arlo murmured. "I know I shouldn't. I should be a big boy by now, but I like it all the same."

Charlie squeezed Arlo's hand. "Good, because I like looking out for you, Arlo. I want to take care of you. And I want to make you as happy as you can be." He paused, turning Arlo's head to face his. "You really like Chance, don't you?" Before Arlo could answer, Charlie rolled his eyes. "Forget that. It was a dumb question. Look at you. You haven't left his side since you met him, including all day here at the hospital."

"It's not just that he's cute, you know," Arlo explained. "He's really nice, Charlie. Spending time with him was…easy and comfortable. He was open, and kind and vulnerable. And he's really smart, like you. I think you'll feel the same about him if you get to know him."

Charlie kissed Arlo's cheek. "Maybe. Arlo, I'm glad he was nice to you while I was away. And I understand the attraction. Chance is a very handsome guy. But don't rush it. If Chance has limited experience with men, sex with one man is probably daunting. Imagine how intimidated he must have been when you suggested the three of us together."

Arlo sighed. "I guess. It's just that the bond I feel is quicker than I've ever felt with anyone, other than you. I knew right away you were the one for me."

Charlie laughed. "You were just horny for me."

Arlo shrugged. "That, too. I still knew you'd be something more to me, though. And my gut was telling me Chance could be special. If he wanted something with us..." He paused. "You said he's good-looking, but do you think you could be attracted to him?"

Charlie looked down at his lap. "I suppose. Look, Arlo, I don't even know him. I trust your judgment, though. If you say he's a great guy, then I imagine he is." He hesitated before speaking again. "Arlo, did Chance tell you how he and I met?"

Arlo nodded. "Chance told me that he met you in a business meeting. He mentioned something about how you were investigating marketing possibilities for your firm, but then nothing materialized."

"That's it?" Charlie asked.

Arlo frowned. "Yes. Is there something you two are hiding? Did you sleep with him?"

Charlie gasped. "What? No, of course not! I told you that I don't even know him. How did you jump to that? Arlo, I have never cheated on you."

Arlo's expression relaxed. "Okay. It's just odd that you're so interested in what he had to say about a casual meeting where nothing unusual happened."

Charlie shrugged, wondering if he should come clean. If Chance didn't share, then maybe he was too embarrassed about how he'd failed the presentation. Charlie decided it might be best to withhold specifics. "I'm not *so* interested. I just wondered if he had a bad impression of me for not going with his firm. After all, he did call me a monster when he saw me this morning."

Arlo grimaced. "I asked him what he meant. He didn't even remember saying that. Don't be offended, Charlie. He was delirious this morning. I want you to like him."

Charlie sighed. "I know you do, baby. But for you to see this fantasy come true, he and I would have to bond like the two of you have, and he'd have to be open to doing stuff that's likely outside his comfort zone. You're hoping for a lot."

"No, I'm not," Arlo stated. "There's no reason why two attractive guys who are super nice and smart wouldn't like each other. I know he has inclinations regarding sex with men. He's said as much. Just don't fall for each other and leave me in the lurch."

Charlie snuggled Arlo closer to his body. "That will never happen, Arlo."

* * * *

Once the surgery was over, Arlo stood close to Charlie as Chance's surgeon explained the outcome. Arlo was frustrated that the surgeon spoke very softly with a heavy foreign accent and used many medical terms since she was speaking to another doctor. When the conversation was over, Arlo still wasn't certain everything was okay with Chance.

After Charlie assured Arlo that Chance was fine, Arlo exhaled with relief. Though they knew from the lab results that Chance's appendix hadn't burst, they had been concerned about a mass on the organ. It turned out the image had depicted a terrible infection—one of the worst the surgeon had ever seen. Though his recuperation would keep Chance in the hospital for a couple of days, there was no reason to believe he wouldn't make a full recovery. The surgeon had also commented that they had been able to perform laparoscopic surgery to remove the appendix. Arlo chastised himself for his selfish gratitude that Chance wouldn't have a scar marring his sexy abdomen.

Charlie tried to convince Arlo that they should go home for the evening, as Chance would be brought to his room to sleep away the night and not allowed visitors. Arlo protested, though, pointing out that the hospital would allow Charlie, as a physician, entry to Chance's room. Arlo wanted Charlie to inform Chance that they had been there during his surgery thinking about him, and that they would see him the next day. Arlo wouldn't budge until he agreed. Charlie sighed and told Arlo to wait for him in the hospital lobby.

After some inquiries, Charlie discovered where Chance had been taken and he made his way there. Chance had been fortunate enough to be assigned a single-occupancy room. He appeared comfortable, despite the harsh overhead lights shining on him.

"Chance?" Charlie whispered. "Are you awake?"

Chance opened his eyes, looking surprised to see Charlie standing outside his room. "Yes?"

Charlie entered the doorway quietly. The poor guy was probably still coming out of the anesthesia. "I just wanted to check on you."

Chance gaped a bit. "Why?"

Charlie frowned and approached the bed. "Chance, I'm not the demon you think I am. I know I was awful to you the day you did your pitch for me. I meant it when I apologized. I had many horrible things happening at that time and I took it out on you. It doesn't excuse my behavior. I just want you to know that you can expect better of me going forward. You've made quite an impression with Arlo, and I don't want awkwardness between us to hurt what's started between you two."

Chance blinked a few times and Charlie wondered again if he might still be too groggy to follow the conversation. "You came here to tell me that?"

"I came here to tell you that Arlo has been worried and he's been here since we admitted you. He'd be here now with you, if he could. They won't allow visitors at this hour. I told him I'd check on you since doctors are permitted access."

"Oh...he's nice. I like him a lot."

Charlie sighed. "He likes you a lot, too, Chance. I hope you and I can be friends. Please forgive me for how I treated you."

Chance nodded. "I didn't do a good job that day. I had a lot of things happening then, too. It also isn't an excuse. None of those things were your problem. You had a right to expect more. I apologize for letting you down."

Charlie walked to the bed and squeezed Chance's hand. "I can see why Arlo likes you, Chance. You're an upstanding guy. I wish I could do over that day."

Chance pursed his lips. "Yeah, me too. I think I'm going to lose my job."

Charlie gasped. "Because of me? No! Please tell me that's not true." Chance shrugged. "Chance, I…I don't know how I can make this up to you. Why would she fire you over one disappointing outcome? You're the boy wonder of marketing, for Christ's sake."

Chance shrugged. "You know what they say—you're only as good as your last presentation. The firm is hurting. Big expenses, dropping revenue. There are some talented newcomers on the team. If she can replace me with one of them, it's a big cut to the budget."

Charlie squeezed Chance's hand tighter. "Chance, I'm going to call that boss of yours. What was her name? Irina?"

"Maria." Chance smirked.

"Maria. Sorry. I'm not good at remembering names. I'm going to tell her that I was out of line and that I've heard many good things about you since our meeting. I'll add that if she wants the board's business in the future, she should disregard my earlier, misguided complaint and ensure you're part of her team."

Chance shook his head. "You don't have to do that, Charlie. It's not even the truth. You haven't heard good things about me."

"Not true," Charlie countered. "Someone from the charity board had recommended you. Don't you remember that I said that to her? She had said the firm was good and there was an award-winning marketing guy there. I'm sure she meant you. And since meeting you, Arlo learned a lot about your work. He showed me some of the print ads attributed to you, as well as one of the commercials on television. You are very good, Chance. I don't know how I didn't connect the dots that Arlo's new friend was the guy I had met. I was thinking your name was Chase. As I said, I'm not good with names. And I was in such a shitty mood that day—my mind was elsewhere. Arlo told me that he shared with you the story of our past relationship with Wilson and why it ended. The night before your presentation, Wilson came to see me to ask if I would let him come back. He had hurt Arlo so badly. I was afraid he'd go around me to plead his case to Arlo. I know that's a lot of drama to drop on you, but I want you to understand that I wasn't myself that day. I'll make this right."

"Charlie…"

"It's settled, Chance," Charlie interrupted. "And, by the way, thank you for not telling Arlo about how I treated you. You had every right to."

Chance cast his eyes down. "He loves you. Why would I do that? To hurt him? To hurt you? That's not who I am, Charlie."

In that moment, Charlie felt as though he could see everything in this man that Arlo had been gushing about. With a few words, Chance had shown his character.

Charlie cleared his throat. "Well, thank you, all the same. I meant what I said, Chance. I hope we can put the past behind us and be friends. I know Arlo would like that."

Chance chuckled. "Arlo would like even more." He blushed. "Oh shit, did Arlo even tell you that? He was joking…"

Charlie smiled. "He did…and he wasn't. It's okay, Chance. One thing you'll get used to is the words from Arlo's mouth are not triggered by his brain—they're straight from the heart…and his dick."

Chance laughed. “Well, he doesn’t shut up about you. He loves you a lot. And he thinks very highly of you.”

Charlie flushed. “Thanks.” He shoved his hands in his pockets. “Well, you’ll be fine, Chance. Arlo and I will come back in the morning. I’m glad the operation was a success. Get some rest.” He turned to leave, but paused at the door. Charlie glanced back at Chance who was still watching him. “And, Chance…I can see why Arlo has taken to you.”

Chapter Ten

A week had passed since Chance's operation, and once the hospital discharged him, he had been staying at Charlie and Arlo's house under their care. His recuperation was almost complete, aside from the fading abdominal bruising and lingering swelling from the surgical gas and resulting fluids passing through his stomach and genitals. At one point, he had asked Charlie if that was normal and Charlie had assured him it was. However, Chance had refused to let Charlie examine him to verify his healing was progressing as it should. Charlie had been amused by Chance's shyness but Chance figured if he ever leaned into Arlo's fantasy of the three men together, he didn't want Charlie picturing how awful he had looked—especially his disfigured-looking penis and swollen scrotum.

And the more time Chance spent in the men's home, the more he warmed to the idea of sex with them. Seeing Arlo's smile every day and basking in the care and sweetness he showered upon him was making Chance feel sentiments he had only had for women in the past. It was becoming hard for Chance to imagine Arlo not in his life. And when Chance saw Arlo walking around in boxers, his gaze was appreciative even if a physical rise from him was still a struggle.

More surprising, though, was Chance's growing attraction to Charlie. When Chance had first met him, his reaction was that the man's body was too big and brutish. The few men he'd found attractive in the past had been built more like himself with slender, toned bodies and angular faces. Maybe that was because Chance never pictured himself in anything other than a dominant role with another male. There was something about Charlie, though. It was hard to deny the man's handsomeness. He was much taller than most. His chest, arms and legs were thick and bulging with muscle. When Charlie rolled up his shirt sleeves and unfastened a couple of buttons, dark hair was abundant. From Arlo's comment about Charlie's hirsute disposition, Chance had figured that the body hair would be tufty, wiry or wooly like a carpet. Instead, it was almost pretty the way it laid flat and looked soft. And it wasn't so dense that he couldn't see nice tanned skin beneath. Because Charlie wore fitted shirts, Chance had found himself more than once gazing at the massive pectoral muscles that swelled against the silky-textured cotton. He began wondering if he could enjoy sex with a man who was bigger and stronger, and if that sex would have to be anal with Chance as a bottom. That notion still caused him anxiety.

It helped that Charlie didn't act like he had to be top-dog or have others submit outside the bedroom. On the contrary. Chance could see that Charlie was what Arlo had described as a caretaking alpha—a man who wanted to guide, protect and care for the person or people he loved. Every action Charlie had taken since the second encounter with Chance cemented that impression. Not only had he helped Arlo rescue Chance, but he was the one who had insisted Chance stay with them rather than try to recuperate alone in his house. On several evenings, it was Charlie who had cooked dinner, and he consistently ran the menu by Chance in advance to ensure every food item would be to his liking. Charlie had also checked on Chance's comfort often, bringing him blankets, pillows and re-chilled ice-packs.

Above all else, Chance was appreciative of Charlie's reach-out to Maria. Charlie had made the call when Chance was within earshot, no doubt to prove to Chance he was a man of his word. From what Chance could discern from the conversation, Maria had been her typical kiss-ass self when talking to a prospective client, telling Charlie that she, too, had nothing but admiration for Chance. After the call, Charlie shared that Maria had assured him that Chance was an important part of the firm's future.

When Chance later called Maria to let her know that he was recovering from surgery, she gushed sympathies and well wishes, telling him to rest for as long as he needed. Unlike the previous time she had encouraged him to take a leave, she added that his job would be waiting for him when he returned and she'd be happy to see him.

"Chance, Charlie just called from work. He's picking up a chef salad for each of us at Rose's Restaurant, if that's okay for you," Arlo informed as he bustled into the living room where Chance was reading.

"Let me order them on my credit card," Chance pleaded. "I'm feeling guilty about how much you guys are doing for me."

Arlo waved a hand through the air. "Don't be silly. If you want, when you're well, you can invite us over for dinner."

"Arlo…"

"Chance," Arlo teased, using the same castigating tone Chance was using. "Does it look like we're struggling to make ends meet? I promise, Charlie isn't worried about the money, and it would hurt him to think you are. I told you that he relishes pampering. Let him have his fun." Arlo dropped on the sofa, pushing aside Chance's feet to make room for himself. "He said again last night that he's enjoyed having you here."

"Really?" Chance wondered. "How is that possible? I've been nothing but a burden the whole time."

Arlo narrowed his eyes. "You have not. Being a caregiver makes him happy. Horny, too. He and I have had wild sex… Well, anyway, he liked the conversations you two have had about history, politics and God-knows-why—sports."

Chance chuckled. Arlo had zero interest in anything involving athletics, other than the attractive men in tight uniforms. Charlie, on the other hand, shared Chance's interest in baseball, football, hockey and tennis. While both men were transplants to San Francisco, they agreed on supporting the local teams and were looking forward to attending games together. Arlo, not wanting to be left out, had asked to join them, though he had admitted he'd be spending most of his time at each event playing on his phone.

"I've enjoyed his company, too," Chance admitted. "He's a great guy. And he's crazy about you, Arlo. Every time I see him looking at you, his eyes shine."

Arlo blushed. "If I tell you something, will you promise not to freak out?"

Chance wondered what it could be, but he shrugged. "Sure."

"Charlie told me that he thinks you look at me that way, too," Arlo admitted, biting his lower lip. Chance could see that Arlo was waiting for him to be upset or hurl a vehement denial.

"Was he angry?"

Arlo shook his head. "No, not at all. He thought it was cute. He thinks we have a mutual crush happening." Arlo paused, then took a deep breath. "Do we, Chance?"

Chance gulped. "Do *you* have a crush on *me*?"

Arlo blushed, but chuckled. "Come on, Chance. I haven't been subtle about it from the day I met you."

Chance frowned. "Oh. And that really doesn't bother Charlie?"

Arlo shook his head. "You still don't get us? No, it doesn't bother him. I mean, I'm sure it would trouble him if we acted on it without him. That is, if he's right about what he's perceiving from you. Is he?"

Chance looked down at the book, unsure what he should admit. He couldn't deny what he was feeling any longer—he just wasn't sure if he should confess. If he admitted it, then it opened the door to the question of a three-way with Charlie. But when Chance glanced back to Arlo's hopeful eyes and nervous lip-biting, he couldn't bring himself to hurt him with another lie. He knew he would need to deal with the fallout, whatever it might be.

"I think you're very attractive, Arlo," Charlie confessed. Almost realizing it sounded like a cop-out and the start of a rejection, he swallowed and continued. "More than attractive. I think you're hot and pictured sex with you." He looked at Arlo's widening eyes. "And I liked it."

Arlo's face relaxed and he broke into a huge smile. "Yeah? Chance, I was really hoping you felt that way. It's getting harder and harder to be around you and not be able to touch you."

Chance placed a tentative hand on Arlo's forearm. "I'm still not sure how any of this would work. I mean, aside from my own hang-ups, there's Charlie. And…"

"And?"

"And what does that mean? If Charlie is into it, are we just going to have sex to see what it's like? Then what? We go back to being friends?" Chance cast his eyes back to his lap. "I don't know if that's what I want."

"What do you want, Chance?" Arlo pressed.

Chance shrugged. "I'm not sure. I wish I could tell you."

Arlo sighed. "Do you care about us?"

Chance jerked back his head with surprise. "Yes, of course."

Arlo nodded. "We care about you, too, Chance. Maybe we could see where it goes? I know the idea of two men scares you, but are you opposed to thinking about a possible relationship? If the caring part is already there, and you acknowledge that you find me sexually attractive, would it be so foreign an idea?"

Chance sucked in a breath, feeling like his words were pushing him closer to the open door of a plane, and he had to decide whether to trust a parachute and jump. "Well, there's still the big question of whether Charlie finds me attractive, right? Caring for me isn't going to make him want to share you with me...that way."

Arlo smiled. "Charlie told me last night that he understands why I think you're hot. He shared that the more time he spends with you, the more he's attracted to you, too. Honestly, he just assumes you don't feel the same. He told me not to get my hopes up because if you aren't into him, he doesn't want to feel like you tolerate his presence—or worse, are repulsed by it—but endure it to be with me." Arlo resumed biting his lower lip. "Chance, this really comes down to you...not me or Charlie. We want you. But was he right? Should I not get my hopes up? I don't want him to feel like a third wheel in his own house."

Chance felt like his Adam's apple was doing pull-ups. "I wouldn't do that to him. He's been kind to me. I don't know if that's why, but I'm finding him more attractive every day, too. But, Arlo, I'm nervous. I wish I could just man up and push the voices from my head like you had suggested, but it's taken a lot for me to get to this place where I can admit how I'm feeling about the two of you. The next step is even scarier."

Arlo rubbed his hand soothingly over Chance's knee. "I know, Chance. Feelings for someone else are scary regardless of orientation. You make yourself vulnerable. And the idea of sex with someone for the first time is exciting, but it's intimidating, too. I can only imagine what it would be like for you, knowing how limited your experience with men is. And this would be with two men. I get it. So, you're frightened. But, Chance, if you push away those fears and think about the nice time the three of us have together, and you picture it being that way always, isn't it worth a try? We could go as slow as you need."

Chance pushed away the book he had been holding so his anxiety wouldn't cause him to leave sweat marks on the pages. Then he looked into Arlo's expectant eyes and he knew he was lost. Maybe too scared to say the words, Chance simply nodded.

Arlo broke into another smile. "Chance, thank you. I'm falling for you hard." He blinked back the mist that had formed in his eyes. "I'll talk to Charlie. Chance, we both want to make you happy. We'll try so hard. I promise."

Chance pulled Arlo into a side-hug. "If Charlie even agrees. But if he does agree to this, yes, we need to go slow. Please. This is all so…"

"I know," Arlo whispered. "Chance? Can I kiss you on the cheek now?"

Chance huffed a short laugh. "If I couldn't let you do that, there wouldn't be much chance for us to progress further, would there?"

Arlo chuckled, then slowly leaned in to press his lips against the side of his friend's face. Instead of pulling away, he put his arms around Chance and hugged him. Chance sighed, the tension leaving his body simply by nestling in Arlo's arms. It was nice, and despite his nerves, he was starting to hope Charlie would want to give the three a try, too.

* * * *

More days had passed and though Chance had healed and resumed working at the office, he returned each night to the house next to his. Charlie and Arlo had asked him why he'd choose to spend time alone at home when they could enjoy each other's company. Chance was finding it hard to argue that point. He knew being away from Charlie and Arlo would just leave Chance wondering what they were doing without him.

Arlo had told Chance that Charlie had been pleasantly surprised by Chance's revelation. Chance found himself excited when Arlo added that Charlie was growing fond of him and wanted him in their lives. He was also relieved that Charlie cautioned Arlo about moving slowly when it came to initiating sex.

And while Arlo had heeded the advice, it was Charlie who had started testing the waters. He had found ways to orchestrate the three of them sitting together on the sofa to watch a movie or television show, increasing the amount of touching and snuggling each time. When he'd put a dinner plate in front of Chance, he'd caress the man's shoulder. When they'd clean up together, he'd find an excuse to joke with him and bump Chance's hip with his own.

After a couple of days of that, Arlo had picked up on Charlie's cues and began to interact with Chance by showing more affection, as well. Arlo had dared even more than his partner by kissing Chance's cheek goodbye and hello each day, and hugging Chance when opportunities arose for celebratory or consoling gestures.

Chance was aware of the tactics the men were applying, and he was grateful that they were taking their time with him. Every night, he fantasized about sex with Arlo or with both Arlo and Charlie, and it was arousing him more on each occasion. Within time, his excitement at the idea overshadowed his apprehension. The two men were so gentle and kind with him, he knew they'd never push him to do something that made him panic. Plus, he was growing fonder of the two as time passed, recognizing they had become the most important people in his life. Chance's buoyed spirits even translated to greater creativity at work, and he was nailing each presentation he gave. That triggered Maria to praise him each day, and Chance was thrilled at how much positive attention he was receiving at work and in his personal life.

When he spoke to his parents, he shared the news of his operation, but appeased their worries by sharing with them the good care he was receiving from new friends. During initial conversations on the topic, his parents focused on Chance's health, grateful he wasn't alone. As days passed and it became clearer that Charlie and Arlo were still involved in Chance's life, his mother's tone started darkening. In the most recent conversation, she had asked Chance if he thought the two men were just hoping to 'get in his pants.' Chance had to hold back his anger. Even though he knew it was true his friends were attracted to him, he also knew that they would have cared for him regardless of whether Chance had an interest in return.

While Chance's parents weren't outwardly bigoted, on occasion, Chance had caught glimpses of it with his mother. In the case of her remark about Arlo and Charlie, Chance had felt compelled to chastise her, reminding her that if his friends were a man and a woman, his mother wouldn't have asked if the wife had been trying to seduce him. Chance's mother had been unfazed by the call-out, still warning Chance to be careful.

When Chance shared the conversation with Charlie and Arlo during dinner, the two men frowned and

Charlie abruptly began clearing the table. Arlo shot a worried look to Chance, and Chance put a reassuring hand on Arlo's shoulder before following Charlie into the kitchen.

"I'm sorry, Charlie," Chance said when he pulled up behind the man who had begun scrubbing pots in the kitchen sink.

"For what?" Charlie asked, though he didn't turn to face Chance.

Chance moved closer, pulling the big man into a hug from behind. "That I shared what she said and that her words hurt you. You don't have to worry that she's getting into my head."

Charlie sighed, then twisted around to look Chance in the eye. He placed his hands on Chance's hips. "Her remarks make me feel ashamed because she isn't wrong. Arlo and I would love to sleep with you. But Chance, we like you very much as a friend, first and foremost. If you never want sex to happen, it wouldn't change how we feel about you. We will always be here for you. I don't want you to have doubts about that."

Chance mirrored Charlie's pose, placing his hands on Charlie's wider hips. "She pissed me off and I was venting. There was no hidden agenda, need for affirmation or subtle message that I'm disinterested in you. And I'm not questioning your motives."

Charlie smiled. "You can vent any time, Chance. I'm thrilled you're interested in me and Arlo. I'll be as patient as you need. If you ever change your mind, I'm still lucky to know you. You aren't just breathtaking. You're impressive in so many ways."

Chance swallowed, looking down at where the two men connected. "Charlie, I *am* ready."

Charlie's eyes widened. He paused a moment before speaking. "Chance, do you mean sex…with both me and Arlo? I swear, none of what I said was to manipulate you."

Chance chuckled. "I'm not a child, Charlie. You're not leading some innocent into a den of sin. I like sex. I like it a lot. I've been thinking about sex with you and Arlo for a while now, and it just keeps getting more exciting. I know I'll like it. You don't need to worry."

Charlie laughed. "Wow, that was bolder than I was expecting. But all the same, it's different from what you've experienced…"

"And so was sex with a girl the first time I tried it," Chance pointed out. "I still liked it, though."

Charlie nodded, scrutinizing Chance's face as if to make sure the expression matched the words. "Okay, Chance. Uh, when exactly, do you want to try this?"

"How long will it take to finish cleaning up?" Chance asked with a mischievous grin.

Chapter Eleven

When the kitchen chores were completed, Charlie walked Chance back to the living room to meet with an anxious Arlo. Charlie took a seat next to his boyfriend.

"You look worried," Charlie whispered.

Arlo looked back and forth between the two men. "Are you both okay? You were in there a while. You're not mad at Chance, are you? He can't help what his parents said."

Charlie lifted Arlo's chin and kissed him.

"I'm not mad," Charlie soothed. "I felt shitty that his mom wasn't wrong about what I wanted. And it bothered me to think that Chance's parents might be making him feel guilty that he was having feelings, too."

Arlo turned to Chance who was standing behind the sofa, hands in pockets appearing unsure of what to do. "Were they, Chance? Were they making you feel bad about what's happening between us?"

Chance shook his head. "No. It made me angry, if anything. I'm tired of trying to live my life for my mother. They haven't changed my mind about anything."

Charlie kissed Arlo's cheek. "Chance said he'd like to take things to the next step."

Arlo inhaled sharply. "The next step?"

Charlie nodded, smiling at how excited Arlo was becoming. "Yes, Arlo."

Arlo gasped. "Chance, are you sure?"

Chance grinned, clearly still nervous. "Yeah. I mean, I'm still a little unsure what to do or what I'll want, but I know this. I don't want to sleep in the other room another night just wishing I could be with you two."

"Come here," Charlie commanded, motioning Chance to take a seat on the sofa with them. Charlie moved toward the end of the couch, pulling Arlo with him, leaving a space on the other side of Arlo for Chance.

Chance bounded round the sofa and took a seat, awaiting instruction on what they should do next.

"I really like you, Chance," Arlo whispered. "I mean, I like you a *lot*."

"I really like you, too, Chance," Charlie stated. Then, with a bit of a teasing tone to Arlo, he added, "I mean, like a *lot*."

Arlo playfully punched Charlie's arm. "If you want me to keep liking *you* a lot, you'd better stop making fun of me."

Charlie caressed Arlo's cheek. "I'm not making fun, baby. I just think you're so adorable when you're excited. And I can't wait to see you and Chance together."

Chance's swallow was loud. "How do we do this? Starting is probably the hardest part…it's kind of awkward with three people, isn't it?"

"It won't be," Arlo promised. "Charlie will take care of us."

Charlie chuckled when their expectant faces turned toward him. He stood from the sofa and motioned for the two men to follow. They rose with curiosity, traipsing behind Charlie as he led them to Charlie and Arlo's bedroom. Charlie then asked Chance and Arlo to sit on the carpeted floor at the foot of the bed. The two men exchanged questioning glances, but assumed the positions Charlie had requested.

Charlie walked over to a desk and pulled out a pack of playing cards, then took a seat on the floor as well, forming a human circle.

"We're going to play cards?" Chance asked, baffled.

Charlie grinned. "Yup. You're eager, Chance, but you're still a little skittish. So, we're going to play cards first."

Arlo pouted. "I don't want to play cards, Charlie! You got me all excited, and now we're going to waste time..."

Charlie shushed Arlo with a finger to his lips. "Arlo, Chance's comfort is important right now. You want him to have a nice experience, don't you?"

Arlo frowned. "Yes, of course."

Charlie retrieved the cards from the carton and shuffled them a few times, watching Chance and Arlo glance at each other with curiosity. "Chance, do you know how to play twenty-one?"

"Sure." Chance shrugged.

"The rules are simple, boys," Charlie explained. "We each get dealt two cards. When you see your hand, you can request another card or you can hold. The person with the lowest total score without exceeding twenty-one needs to remove an article of clothing. If someone exceeds twenty-one, then they are the one who needs to take off something."

Arlo brightened at the turn of events. "I've never played with those stakes. Hey, what happens if more than one of us exceeds twenty-one?"

"Then whichever person has the higher score takes off an article of clothing." Charlie looked to Chance. "Any objections to the rules of this game?"

Chance swallowed hard again. "Maybe we could have alcohol, too?"

Charlie reached over to Chance and kissed him on the mouth. He pulled back to a shocked Chance and frowned. "Do you need to be drunk to want this, Chance?"

Chance shook his head no, eyes wide.

Arlo half-laughed. "He's a very convincing kisser, Chance." Chance nodded with surprised agreement.

"Oh, one other rule," Charlie added.

"Is it going to be that socks come off before we start playing? I don't care about feet," Arlo griped.

Charlie laughed. "Chance will be sad if he has a foot fetish."

Chance shook his head. "I don't. I never understood that."

Charlie continued to chuckle. "Well, I never did either. I guess we all have something in common. Socks off, boys."

The three men removed their socks and tossed them to the side of the room.

"What's the other rule?" Arlo asked.

"Oh, you're going to let me finish now?" Charlie mused. Arlo rolled his eyes in response. "The other rule is that whoever removes an article of clothing is exempt from the following round. That's because whoever next removes an article of clothing has to do something sexy with what's been exposed on the guy before him."

Chance gulped. "Something sexy?"

Charlie pursed his lips, studying Chance's adorable expression. "Yes, Chance—involving touching and tongue. In your case, because of your inexperience, I'll guide you through what to do."

"Oh," Chance murmured.

Arlo stroked Chance's arm. "Do you still want to do this? You don't have to."

Chance took a breath, then nodded. "I'm okay."

Charlie clapped Chance's shoulder. "I'll make things comfortable for you, Chance. Trust me."

Arlo looked to Chance with longing. "Please go with this, Chance. Charlie makes everything good and I don't think I could bear it if you backed out now."

Chance put on a courageous face. "Yeah, I said I'm okay. Let's do this."

Arlo smiled. "Good. Charlie, deal the cards already, before my dick stretches over there to do it for you."

Chance laughed at that, relieving some of the tension for the three as Charlie dealt two cards to each of them. The men looked at their cards and only Chance requested a third card.

Charlie knew what the result would be when Chance huffed with disappointment at seeing his third card. Charlie asked everyone to reveal the hands they were dealt, and Chance's total was the only one that exceeded twenty-one.

Charlie leaned toward Chance. "As much as I want to see you, Chance, I wish it hadn't been you losing the first round. I know you're nervous. But hey, it's just a shirt, right? You'd think nothing of removing it if you were at the beach."

Chance undid the garment button by button while Charlie and Arlo watched. The two men eyed Chance appreciatively once the shirt was removed.

"You are so beautiful, Chance," Arlo whispered. "I love your chest."

"Mm. Me, too," Charlie agreed. "I don't know why, but I pictured you smooth there like Arlo. Nature finds a way to do the right thing for each guy. I love Arlo's chest, but I like the light hairs on your pecs. And your nipples are…"

"Fucking sexy," Arlo finished. "So pretty."

Chance blushed. "Okay, move on. There's only so much I can listen to talk about my tits without getting embarrassed. I get to sit out this round, right?"

Arlo smiled. "Yes, but depending on the outcome of the next round, me or Charlie get to stop talking about those tits and start licking and sucking them."

Chance's eyes popped. "Oh. Yeah, I guess…"

Charlie and Arlo played another round and Arlo looked disappointed that he lost.

"Stupid cards," Arlo mumbled. "Winning feels like losing. I should have cheated so I could have fun with Chance."

Charlie narrowed his eyes. "Now Arlo, you'd better play fair or I'll make you sit on the bed and watch Chance and me play the rest of the game."

Arlo looked horrified, eliciting a laugh from Chance.

Charlie removed his top. It was the first time that Chance was seeing him without a shirt. He was glad that Chance didn't look disappointed.

"Chance, look at how powerful and sexy Charlie is," Arlo gushed. "Doesn't it just make you want him to come pull you into that mass of muscle and hold you close?"

Chance nodded and though his expression was shy, it was clear to Charlie that the man was turned on by what he was seeing.

Charlie shuffled over to him and placed a hand on his knee to calm him. "I'll stop anything you don't like as soon as you ask, okay?" When Chance nodded once more, Charlie pushed Chance's legs apart to give him greater access. Then he ran the back of his hand down Chance's chest. "So hard, but your chest hair is so soft."

"Kiss him again," Arlo suggested.

"Can I, Chance? I'd like to very much," Charlie whispered.

Charlie saw Chance's throat move when he took a deep gulp. He was surprised when Chance reached his hand to Charlie's cheek to beckon him. Charlie leaned forward and kissed him more passionately than their first time. After a few seconds of caressing Chance's jaw, Charlie licked Chance's lips, which made Chance respond by parting them. Charlie slipped his tongue into Chance's mouth, tasting the man as they continued to embrace. Charlie brushed his fingers over Chance's nipples before gently playing with one of them as they stayed lip-locked.

Arlo was watching intently. "So hot. Charlie, suck them."

Charlie worked his way down to Chance's chest, planting soft kisses before circling one of the nipples with his tongue. Chance's face tightened as he suppressed a moan, thrusting his chest forward to get more of Charlie's mouth on his sensitive nub. Charlie groaned as he alternated between licking and sucking the nipple while pinching and caressing the other. When he stopped and pulled away, Chance's eyes were closed and Arlo's were glazed. He reached a hand over to Arlo's crotch and squeezed lightly. "Don't worry, Arlo. You'll be free soon enough."

Per the rules of the game, Charlie dealt two more cards to Arlo and Chance, trying to ignore his own aching erection. He looked to Chance who appeared to be both aroused and hesitant. Charlie wanted to give him another reassuring kiss, but he knew whatever happened next would just ratchet up both emotions.

When Chance and Arlo flipped their cards, it was Arlo who ended up with the lower number. He smiled broadly at losing, lifting his shirt over his head. Charlie remembered that Arlo had shared that he and Chance had already seen each other shirtless when they were unpacking Chance's house, but Chance still eyed Arlo with awe. It was understandable. Arlo's body was perfect and his skin was flawless.

"Get over here," Charlie commanded.

Arlo practically leaped into Charlie's arms, pulling Charlie into an open-mouthed kiss. Arlo ran his hands up and down Charlie's massive torso while they made out. From the corner of his eye, Charlie saw that Chance was observing with a sense of wonder. He almost wanted to end the game and pull the man into the huddle.

Charlie gave Arlo a gentle nudge to return to where he had been sitting, then dealt another round of cards to himself and Chance. Charlie could tell that Chance was debating whether to ask for a third card, which signaled his total was going to be low if he refrained. When Chance declined a third card, Charlie kept the hand he had. He had a total of seventeen and assumed it would outscore Chance's. When the cards were flipped, Charlie's intuition was proven correct.

Chance emitted a small groan. "I don't have anything to remove except my jeans."

Arlo laughed. "We've already seen you without your pants the day your appendix was blowing up, remember? Come on, take them off. I want you to get over here and kiss me like you kissed Charlie."

Chance grinned and shrugged. He unzipped the denim and pushed his jeans down his legs until they were lying on the floor in front of him.

"You have legs like a dancer," Charlie noted with admiration. "Nice thighs, defined calf muscles—and your body hair is perfect, Chance. You are so fucking sexy."

Arlo licked his lower lip. "And I can't wait to see your cock. Somehow, I don't remember it being so prominent when we last saw you without pants."

Charlie swatted Arlo's head. "He was in pain, Arlo. I'm pretty sure he wasn't sporting a hard-on that day."

Chance blushed, but moved over to Arlo. Charlie was surprised by the man's assertiveness as he pulled Arlo's face to his before his boyfriend could say anything more. Arlo wasted no time using his tongue and the two began exploring each other's mouths with vigor. The men continued their passion while Chance ran his open palms over Arlo's chest, arms and back.

"You are so beautiful together," Charlie commented. Chance pulled away from Arlo, his lips puffy and his eyes lusty.

"I'm sorry," Chance apologized to Charlie. "I got a little carried away."

Charlie pulled Chance into a hug. "Chance, don't apologize. I'm glad you're enjoying this. We want you so much. Believe me, watching you with Arlo has me hard as steel. Lick Arlo's gorgeous pecs."

Arlo nodded. "Yeah, Chance. Don't be gentle."

Charlie chuckled. "Arlo's always eager for a little tit play."

Chance licked his lower lip before sucking on one of Arlo's nipples and rubbing his thumb over the other. Charlie could see Chance's cloth-covered prick expand more when Arlo started making throaty moans.

"I can't wait for you to get inside me," Arlo whispered.

Chance gasped.

Charlie chuckled. "In good time, Arlo. The point of the card game is to break Chance in. I'd say it's working." He looked at Chance and winked, causing Chance's cheeks to redden.

"Quick, another round," Arlo pressured Charlie.

Charlie snorted a laugh as he dealt cards for himself and Arlo. When they finished the round, Arlo was once again the reluctant 'winner.' "Sorry, Arlo," Charlie lied, shrugging at Arlo's disappointed face.

Arlo snarled. "Why is it when you want to lose, you can't?"

Chance was laughing until his attention was drawn to Charlie unbuckling his belt. Charlie proceeded to unzip his trousers and slowly slide them down his enormous, hairy thighs. Chance's gaze went to the crotch of Charlie's boxer briefs.

"Jesus," Chance muttered. "You're huge everywhere."

Charlie removed the pants entirely, motioning Chance to approach him. Chance walked on his knees until he was in front of the bigger man. Charlie resumed kissing Chance as he had earlier, but this time he greedily palmed Chance's underwear-covered ass. When Charlie pulled away for air, he grabbed Chance's butt cheeks more firmly. "Chance, your ass is exquisite. You might be in a tie with Arlo for men with the nicest butts."

Chance blinked, maybe never having had his butt admired like that. He leaned back in for more kissing. Charlie moved one of his hands to the front of Chance's shorts, grabbing Chance's erection through the fabric and rubbing his thumb over the shaft. Chance's mouth opened, his head falling back a bit. "Fuck."

Charlie kissed Chance's throat. "Arlo is right. You have such a nice, long dick. You're circumcised, aren't you?"

Chance appeared panicked for a second. "Yes. Is that okay?"

Charlie smiled. "Of course. I can feel the big head of your prick. I like men who are circumcised and I like men who aren't. It will be nice to have variety."

Arlo groaned. "As much as I like watching, I can't much longer. Please, let's play another round."

Charlie returned to his sitting place, almost wondering if the game was becoming too torturous. Nevertheless, he dealt a pair of cards to both Chance and Arlo, and with an odds-defying consistent pattern, it was Arlo who lost. Arlo was glad to shuck his jeans, doing so in firefighter time.

"So hot, baby," Charlie gushed when he saw his lover kneeling only in his white briefs, the man's erection stretching the fabric to its limits.

"Yeah, yeah," Arlo grumbled, pouncing on Charlie. Within seconds, Arlo moved his face down Charlie's body, nuzzling his mouth over the boxer-brief covered hard-on. Charlie's composure cracked. He leaned back and gasped as Arlo rubbed and mouthed his prick through the fabric, causing Charlie to secrete a tell-tale sign of excitement into the dark-colored shorts.

Arlo kneeled back and appraised his boyfriend appreciatively. "I love it when your cock starts leaking. Even better when you're naked. Take them off."

"But the game..."

"Fuck the game, Charlie," Arlo protested, grabbing the waistband of Charlie's underwear and yanking them down to his knees. Charlie's oversized member sprang up against his stomach, oozing a stream of precum that hung several inches from its slit. Arlo licked it up, then retracted Charlie's foreskin to suck on the mushroom-shaped crown.

Charlie looked to Chance, who was enthralled with Arlo's oral skills, particularly when Arlo took Charlie to the root. Charlie began gasping with pleasure as Arlo repeated the deep-throating action while drool from his lips coated Charlie's rigid prick.

"Okay, Arlo. Slow down. You're going to make me come," Charlie warned.

"Mm," Arlo hummed with a mouthful of cock, apparently liking that idea very much.

Charlie gently pushed Arlo's head away. "Arlo, don't move too fast for Chance."

Arlo smacked his lips, then wiped them with the back of his hand. "Am I moving too fast, Chance?"

Chance was quiet for a moment, then swallowed. "Take your briefs off, Arlo."

Arlo smiled broadly and grinned at Charlie. "See, not too fast for Chance." He pinched the sides of his underwear and glided them down his hips. When his dick and balls were freed, Arlo sighed with relief.

Arlo held the base of his dick and showed it off to Chance. "Do you like it?" Arlo asked with his first sign of apprehension.

It appeared Chance decided to let his actions speak for themselves. He moved cautiously to Arlo, reaching down and gently touching his friend's cock. "It's velvet-like...but hard at the same time," he said before running his thumb over the head. Arlo gasped.

Chance leaned in to suck the man's tongue while he lightly tugged Arlo's retracted foreskin. "Is that okay? It doesn't hurt to slide the foreskin?"

"Hell no," Arlo answered, pulling Chance back in for more kissing.

Charlie moved behind Chance and began to remove Chance's underwear. When the fabric was down to Chance's knees, Charlie lifted each of Chance's legs so he could remove the garment altogether. Arlo took the opportunity to align his dick with Chance's and begin stroking them.

Charlie huddled in closer, pressing his strong chest against Chance's back, putting a hand on each of Chance's ass cheeks, massaging them lightly. Charlie dared to run his hard, wet cock in Chance's crease while kissing him behind his ear. "Chance, don't be scared. There'll be no fucking tonight. We all need to be tested before introducing you into the mix that way. Just relax and let yourself feel good."

Charlie could hear Chance exhale with relief before he reached behind himself to pull Charlie's hips closer to his butt. Charlie took that as an invitation to use Chance's ass-crack for friction.

Arlo pulled away long enough to look down at Chance's dick. He backed up a bit to eye it better. "Chance…just wow. Everything about you is gorgeous. Your cock is perfect. And those beautiful nuts…I want to suck them."

Charlie leaned his head over Chance's shoulder to peek himself. "I knew it was going to be hot, Chance. I could shoot just from looking at your incredible body."

Charlie stroked Chance's hair, still nuzzling Chance's throat. "I want to see everything, Chance. Can I?" Charlie whispered.

Chance nodded, in a daze, and Charlie wondered if the man had understood his question. He decided to go for it, spreading Chance's buttocks. Chance jerked forward, so Charlie kissed him on his shoulders. "It's okay. Don't be shy. You can look at us there, too, if you want. I want to know your whole body, Chance." Charlie kneed Chance's thighs apart, then opened Chance with his long, thick fingers. "Chance, you are incredibly beautiful. Such a sweet, tight little hole."

"Can I look?" Arlo asked like a five-year-old wanting to see what his friends were hiding.

Charlie was relieved when Chance chuckled. "Oh my God. This is fucking weird." Then he half-shrugged. "Sure."

Charlie laughed, too, before switching places with Arlo. Charlie pulled Chance into more wet kissing while Arlo spread and admired Chance's ass.

Charlie moved his lips to Chance's cheek, jaw and throat, making Chance moan with pleasure. "You are so fucking hot, Chance. Look how hard you make me." Chance reached down and ran his fingers over Charlie's prick, causing him to hiss.

Arlo had started circling Chance's anus with his thumb and Chance gasped at the sensation. "Can I lick it, Chance? Please," Arlo panted.

"Oh God," Chance whispered, his chest falling against Charlie. Charlie pulled Chance forward a bit, making Chance's butt stick out more in offering to Arlo. Arlo appeared to think it was an invitation and he pressed his tongue against Chance's opening.

"Just feel good," Charlie reminded Chance. "Don't overthink. Let Arlo take care of you, baby."

"So good," Arlo said when he'd pulled away for air. "Chance, I can't get enough of you."

"Oh God," Chance repeated when Arlo resumed the action, dropping his head in abandon on Charlie's chest.

Charlie held both his and Chance's cocks together, then he began stroking them. Charlie marveled at the sensation of jerking their conjoined flesh, reveling in the sound it made because of the precum on each.

"Does it feel good, Chance?" Charlie panted, increasing the friction of his hand over their pricks.

"Yes," Chance whimpered.

Arlo came up for air. "I could keep doing this all night, but I don't want to deprive Charlie of his favorite thing."

Chance blinked a few times at Charlie. "Rimming is your favorite thing?"

Charlie grinned. "Fucking someone as hot as you or Arlo is my favorite thing. But eating a beautiful ass is a close second."

"Oh," Chance sighed.

Arlo maneuvered around Chance, caressing the man's side, arm and chest before bumping Charlie from his position. Charlie pulled Arlo into an open kiss before repositioning himself behind Chance.

Charlie caressed Chance's back, gliding his hand down the man's spine to the end of his tailbone. "Bend forward, Chance. Arlo will milk you while I eat your sweet hole."

Arlo helped position Chance on all fours before kneeling before him, kissing him, and reaching under him to grab his hanging tool. Arlo stroked while Charlie used his tongue to give pleasure to Chance from behind.

Charlie applied a strong grip on each of Chance's cheeks and pulled hard so the man was spread as open as possible. "You like that, baby? You like me exposing you for my pleasure?" He didn't wait for a response, instead lapping his tongue over Chance's crease and taint before flattening it and rubbing it against Chance's entrance. Chance began to utter nonsensical words when Charlie used his tongue to breach him.

"Oh my God," Chance cried out when Arlo gave him some air.

"You taste so good," Charlie murmured when he took a breath, then dove back in, plunging his tongue into Chance's channel. Charlie tugged lightly on Chance's dangling scrotum. It firmed in preparation for release.

"I can't last much longer," Chance panted.

"It's okay," Arlo told him through kisses. "Want to see you come so bad, Chance. Tell me when you're ready."

Chance's eyes rolled to the back of his head. "I'm fucking ready now!"

Arlo leaned forward, watching as he stroked Chance to completion.

"That's it, baby," Charlie encouraged from behind, pulling away to watch Chance's cum spewing from his red, swollen cock and landing on the jeans that were splayed on the floor below him. Charlie had inserted his fingertip into Chance and had been swirling it as Chance erupted.

"Oh my God, fuck!" Chance screamed at the pleasurable assault on his most private places. "Oh, fuck!"

"Yeah, Chance, that's it." Arlo smiled. "You're so fucking hot. I love watching you blow your wad."

Charlie murmured an agreement before resuming gentle kisses to Chance's clenching ass cheeks. Arlo used his clean hand to massage one of Chance's shoulders as the man's breathing continued to run rapid, and leaned in for more kissing when he believed Chance's lungs could withstand it.

Chance lifted a hand to hold Arlo's head and used his tongue to probe the man's mouth. Charlie had hunched back to his knees and had started pressing strong, soothing rubs along Chance's back.

When Charlie saw Chance part for breath, he stroked the man's hair. "Are you doing okay, Chance?"

Chance huffed a quick laugh. "Yeah, I'm doing okay. It was…amazing."

Arlo beamed. "Thank God. I would have been miserable if you said this wasn't for you. So, you think you would do this again?"

Chance rolled his eyes. "Arlo, I'm not freaking out. I promise. I've been thinking about this for a few days. I didn't expect to like it *this* much, though. It was…intense."

"And it was dirty enough for you?" Arlo asked.

Chance bellowed a laugh. "Are you kidding me? I don't expect your grandmother's nursing home will be asking us to repeat our performance there."

"What the hell are you two talking about?" Charlie gasped.

Arlo shrugged. "Chance said he never gets to do dirty stuff." He turned back to Chance. "But it wasn't scary dirty for you, right? Charlie made it good for you?"

Chance pushed back up to his knees and stroked Arlo's cheek. "You both did, Arlo. I was a little afraid, if I'm being honest. Of what, I'm not sure. Maybe it's knowing there's no plausible denial after—I don't know. I don't care at this point. I don't want to deny you guys. I'm falling for you, too." He turned his head back to Charlie. "Both of you."

Arlo leaned in for more kisses. Charlie pressed his big body into the two and held them tight.

"So, important question for you…did you like my tongue and fingertip penetrating you?" Charlie asked.

Chance snickered. "That's an important question?"

Arlo nodded seriously. "Of course, Chance. If you liked it, it means you could like getting fucked."

Chance's eyes widened. "Oh."

From behind Chance, Charlie rubbed Chance's chest and stomach. "So, did you?"

He nodded with hesitance. "I did, but it wasn't big and hard…"

Charlie pressed kisses along Chance's neck. "I would never hurt you, Chance. Neither would Arlo. Trust us."

"Do you want to watch Charlie fuck me?" Arlo asked as easily as if he'd asked Chance if he wanted a tissue to wipe up his semen. "You'll see that he's really careful, and you'll see how much pleasure it gives me."

"You mean, right now?" Chance asked, swallowing hard.

Arlo chuckled. "Yes, right now. You're the only one who got to come. I'm still aching over here."

Chance glanced down at Arlo's still erect cock. "Oh, shit. Sorry. I didn't mean to be selfish."

Charlie kissed Chance's ear. "You weren't, baby. We wanted to take care of you. If you're feeling like you need a break from this, we won't be upset. But you're welcome to stay, if you want to."

Arlo shot Chance a hopeful glance that Chance would remain with them, and Chance almost laughed at how much Arlo enjoyed being an exhibitionist. Chance did want to see Arlo get fucked, but he wondered if it would have the same excitement for him now that he was sated. He decided maybe that was better, as he'd pay more attention to what it would be like for him if he were ever to submit, and not acquiesce simply in a moment of passion.

"Um, if you're sure you guys are okay with it," Chance whispered.

"We want you to stay with us," Charlie assured him. "We want you to feel your place is with us."

Charlie instructed the men to get onto the mattress. Charlie walked over to the nightstand to retrieve lubricant, then asked Arlo to turn over and get on all fours. Arlo happily agreed, spreading his legs and jutting his butt with anticipation.

Chance kept his distance, too shy to watch the intimacies of the preparation. Charlie grinned and crooked his finger for Chance to join him behind Arlo's ass.

Chance flushed, but was happy that Charlie was letting him watch close up. He moved down the bed and kneeled next to Charlie, admiring Arlo's incredible ass. Chance liked the way the man's genitals looked, as well. Arlo's pink balls were perfect—symmetrical and proportioned to the rest of the man.

Charlie handed Chance the bottle. The invitation to prep Arlo was clear. Chance swallowed hard. "Oh."

"I'll get him started," Charlie stated, placing his hands on Arlo's cheeks and spreading them so that Chance saw Arlo's hole appear between the slightly puckered skin. Charlie bent forward and began licking Arlo's crease, then slathered his spit over the man's entrance.

Chance was becoming erect again, turned on by the wet sounds Charlie was making accompanied by the whimpers Arlo was emitting. He wanted to try it.

As if reading his mind, Charlie pulled back and gave Chance a questioning look, followed by a side-eye at Arlo's waiting ass. "It's okay if you're not ready for this."

Chance parted his lips for a second, debating. He shot another longing glance at Arlo then maneuvered behind him to begin tentatively licking the man's taint and the sides of his ass cheeks.

"Oh, Chance," Arlo murmured. "Yes."

"You're doing great, baby," Charlie coaxed. "Eat his hot ass, Chance."

That spurred on Chance as he dared to flick his tongue over Arlo's hole, finding that Arlo had been right—his showering, use of a bidet and body deodorant had left only the smell of Arlo's soapy, sweaty skin. Chance began to rim Arlo like when he had performed cunnilingus in the past and Arlo was soon squirming with pleasure, moaning more with each motion Chance made.

Charlie eventually pulled Chance back with a mischievous grin. "You're going to make him lose it if you keep going. Pick the bottle back up and lube your forefinger."

Chance did as he was instructed, eager to feel Arlo's tightness and warmth. When he was slicked up, Charlie gave Chance a little nod and Chance gently inserted the tip of his finger. He was pleased that Arlo groaned in appreciation, even pushing his butt back a bit to accelerate the intrusion. Chance found there was no resistance to sliding his whole finger in, and he was transfixed by watching himself finger-fuck Arlo.

"Chance, so good," Arlo moaned. "Need more."

Chance looked to Charlie and Charlie nodded. "Pull out. Then put more lube on your forefinger, but lube your middle finger, too. Slowly push them both in."

Chance followed the instructions, marveling at watching himself stretching Arlo. He felt a bit more resistance than before, but eventually had both fingers inserted.

"That's it, Chance. Nice and easy. Slide your fingers back and forth. When he's bucking for more friction, start to scissor your fingers to stretch him."

Chance worried about hurting Arlo, but Arlo glanced back with a wide grin. It was clear he was blissed out and eager to get pummeled. Chance accelerated the sliding of his fingers and Arlo was rearing and grunting with pleasure. Chance remembered to start stretching. Arlo leaned forward on his elbows, willing himself open.

Chance saw from the corner of his eye that Charlie had taken the bottle of lubricant and had slathered a good amount on his prick. He bent forward to kiss Chance. "You did a good job, baby—and it was so hot watching you get Arlo ready for me." Chance took that as his cue to slowly withdraw his fingers from Arlo's ass.

"God, fuck me, Charlie. Please. I need it now," Arlo begged.

Chance watched Charlie line up the head of his enormous cock to Arlo's hole and slowly push partway in. Arlo's breath hitched and Charlie ran a soothing hand along Arlo's back. "That's it, Arlo," Charlie cooed. "I can't wait to be all the way inside you."

Chance found it odd that he was so closely watching a man breaching another, but he couldn't pull away. His own dick got harder as Charlie's sank deeper into Arlo's ass. When Charlie hit bottom, Arlo moaned.

"Is he okay?" Chance asked, even though he loved the sight of Charlie fully embedded in Arlo.

Charlie half-smiled. "Are you okay, Arlo?"

"Hell yes," Arlo gasped. "Please, Charlie. Start fucking me."

Charlie let out a small laugh, clearly knowing how Arlo would respond. He began to pull back, then push in with a bit more force. When Arlo began whimpering, Charlie accelerated the pace, his crotch slapping against Arlo's sweaty ass.

Chance wondered if he should ask Arlo once again if he was okay, but when he saw the ecstasy on Arlo's face, he knew it was unnecessary. He glanced at Charlie, and his face appeared full of affection. Chance stared at Charlie's hard cock drilling Arlo's pretty butt. His own dick needed another release.

"Have you ever watched from behind? Go ahead, Chance. It's hot as fuck," Charlie managed to say to Chance while furiously nailing his lover. "It's one of the great things about threesomes. You see angles you don't get to see otherwise. Bend down and you'll see me sliding in and out of our beautiful boy."

Chance didn't even feel awkward at this point. He moved behind Charlie and watched the man push Arlo forward more, giving Chance an unobstructed view of Charlie's super-sized tool pumping in and out of Arlo's rectum. Chance was fascinated, watching the back of Charlie's massive, hairy thighs flex and his hanging sack slap against Arlo's pale cheeks. The thwacking noise with each thrust was titillatingly filthy. Chance even found that he was turned on by seeing Charlie's hairy crease open and close, revealing his own dark hole clenching with his movements.

"I'm going to come," Arlo shouted.

"Yeah, baby. Come for me," Charlie encouraged. "I'm so close."

Chance was mesmerized as Arlo's hot, white stream erupted from his swinging cock, spraying pools of cream along the bed sheets. Within seconds, Charlie slammed down hard and growled with pleasure, dumping his own load into Arlo's channel. Maybe for Chance's pleasure, Charlie pulled out quickly, shooting the last of his load onto Arlo's entrance before sliding his cum-covered dick back inside his boyfriend.

The two men collapsed on the sheets, panting heavily, leaving Chance a little embarrassed but incredibly horny. "Fuck," he whispered.

Charlie laughed through his panting. "You like that, Chance?"

Chance could only nod.

When Charlie and Arlo started breathing normally again, Charlie motioned for Chance to join them lying on the mattress. Chance moved to their sides and Charlie used his strong arms to flip Chance on his back.

"What...what are you doing?" Chance asked.

Charlie eyed Chance's erection appreciatively. "I think we need to make you comfortable again."

Arlo peeked over Charlie's shoulder. "Mm, Chance, I'm going to like how fast you recover."

Charlie maneuvered so that he took one side of Chance and he let Arlo sidle up to Chance's other. The two men kissed Chance and, together, moved their hands and tongues down Chance's erect nipples, stomach and hips before kissing and licking Chance's member.

"Jesus," Chance muttered when Arlo sucked in Chance's dickhead while Charlie simultaneously laved his shaft and balls.

This time, it was Arlo who breached Chance's anus with his whole finger as he and his boyfriend alternated between sucking Chance's dick. Within seconds, Chance warned them he was about to ejaculate once more. The two men let Chance shoot at both their waiting mouths, then they licked his still-twitching cock and his release until Chance was clean.

Arlo wiped his mouth and smiled up at Chance. "You taste as good as you look, Chance."

Charlie laughed. "You really do. You're amazing, Chance."

The two men used tissues to clean their faces, then navigated their way back to Chance so that their three heads aligned. Arlo was still smiling as he ran the tips of his fingers through Chance's chest hair. "Are you okay still?"

Chance grinned with a small amount of embarrassment. "Yeah. It was…holy shit. This is so outside my realm of experience."

Charlie shot Chance a concerned look, stroking the man's cheek. "But in a good way?"

Chance nodded. "Yes. In a good way. It's a lot to take in, though."

Charlie touched Chance's jaw and gently turned his face toward him. "After your first time admitting to yourself you enjoyed gay sex, guilt or shame can start to seep into your brain. Try not to think about everything right away. Just relax, Chance. Sleep with us. Let us be here for you."

Arlo nodded. "Yes, Chance. Stay here. Cuddle with us. That's the best part when you're in a relationship."

"Is that what we are?" Chance dared to ask.

"I hope so," Charlie answered. "Who else cares about you as much as we do, Chance?"

Chance looked at the two men, each hoping for him to want them back. He saw kindness and maybe the start of love—and that outweighed whatever complications the lifestyle might bring. "I feel the same about you guys, though it's such an adjustment from what I always pictured I'd want. But right now, what I want is to be with you guys. I can't even picture going home alone and feeling good about that."

Charlie smiled softly. "Good. That's enough for now. Sleep, baby."

Chance glanced between the two men. "Um, shouldn't Arlo or you be in the middle?"

"Tonight, it's about you," Charlie replied.

Arlo nodded. "It's okay, Chance. Charlie has long arms. He can reach over you and still rest his hand on me. I want to feel both of you. I'm happy you're with us, Chance."

Chance saw a little tear in Arlo's eye and it warmed his heart. The man was so sweet. "Thanks, Arlo. I'm happy I'm here, too."

Chapter Twelve

As Chance awoke, it looked like it would be a bright Saturday morning. The rays of sun were making their way through the bedroom window and illuminating his face along with Charlie and Arlo's. As if to block the brightness from his eyes, Charlie pushed his body closer to Chance's, burying his face in the man's neck. Chance mused how different it felt to have a large, hairy arm lying over his torso. It was strange, but comforting—evoking childlike yearnings for security and support. He remembered how Arlo had shared that it was one of the things he appreciated about being with Charlie. Chance hadn't known he had craved that until it became available.

Chance looked to his right. Arlo was lying on his side, facing him. He had an angelic look on his sleeping face, a hint of a smile on his lips. Chance wondered if the guy was capable of being anything other than happy for an extended period. Chance snuggled closer to him, lightly stroking the magnificent curves of the man's upper arm.

Arlo's eyes opened and he immediately smiled broadly at seeing Chance. "Good morning."

"Hey," Chance whispered.

Charlie must have heard the talking as he grunted in annoyance, grabbing Chance's belly and pulling him into a tight embrace. Chance felt Charlie's morning wood firmly pressed against his butt, and he almost laughed at how casual he was about it.

"Are you okay still?" Arlo asked.

Chance nodded. He didn't want the two men to continue worrying about his mental state, but he also appreciated that they were considerate of his feelings. "It was nice to wake up to your face. You were smiling in your sleep, you know."

Arlo beamed even brighter. "My subconscious was aware you were here with us. I like it, Chance. I want it all the time. Is that wrong? Should I be encouraging you to move slowly?"

Charlie must have awakened some, as he started pressing light kisses along Chance's shoulder.

Chance half-shrugged. "I don't feel like I'm moving too fast. I like it here. I like being with you...and Charlie. You were right about him. He knew just what to say and how much to push or hold back. He knows me better than I know myself."

Charlie began to stroke Chance's hip under the bedsheet. "I hope I can be what you need, Chance. But Arlo was right to ask. You need to tell us if I read you wrong about anything."

Arlo's eyebrow quirked up. "But just in case you do want to move fast, maybe we can all get tested today."

Chance tensed and Charlie laughed before speaking. "Arlo, what am I going to do with you?"

Arlo smiled mischievously. "I can think of dozens of things. Feel like watching, Chance?"

Chance snickered. "God, you're insatiable. Sorry, but I need to pee." He scrutinized the path to the bathroom from the center of the mattress. "I'm not used to having to crawl over someone to exit a bed."

Arlo sighed. "Okay, fine. Go pee."

Charlie looked over at the alarm clock. "If you were serious about being tested, we should rise and get ready. The clinic closes at noon on Saturdays, and we've already slept away half the morning. Chance, don't eat anything or drink anything but water."

Chance glanced back at Charlie with a questioning glance. "So, we really are getting tested?"

Charlie lightly smacked Chance's bottom. "It doesn't *commit* you to anything, Chance. But it would *allow* us to do anything without worrying if you decide you're ready. Hmm? Now, go pee and brush your teeth. You don't need to get your toothbrush from the spare bathroom. There are extra unopened ones in the medicine cabinet." Charlie narrowed his eyes at Arlo. "Get that horny look off your face. You use the bathroom when he's done."

* * * *

Chance wondered if passersby found it odd to see the three men walking side-by-side, each with Band-Aids at the bends of their arms. The day was too warm for them to have worn long-sleeved shirts. Chance pictured people concocting all sorts of stories about them.

Chance was noticing Charlie was highly intuitive as the man glanced down at Chance's hand fidgeting with the dressing on his arm. "You're subconsciously or consciously trying to cover that when people near us."

"Huh?" Chance asked.

"Stop worrying what people are thinking. We could be three friends who just donated blood," Charlie noted. When Chance relaxed, Charlie squeezed his shoulder. "One of the things I've learned in life, Chance, is that we think people are far more interested in us than they really are. I'm pretty certain most people haven't even noticed that we all have bandages. And for those who have, I'm quite sure that they couldn't care less as to why. I also think it's safe to say that probably none of them are suspecting that we're three lovers who just got tested for HIV, hoping for a green light to raw-dog each other."

Chance halted, choking out a cough which elicited a snort from Arlo. "Charlie! Don't give Chance a heart attack on the streets of San Francisco."

Charlie chuckled. "I'm sorry, Chance." His smile signaled otherwise. "It's fun to tease a newbie."

Arlo rolled his eyes. "I warned you, Chance. Charlie might be all doctor-serious, but he's a chronic prankster and likes to knock you off-kilter."

People continued to pass by the men, barely noticing them. That bolstered Chance's confidence and made him realize how true Charlie's words were. He resumed walking, and Charlie and Arlo followed suit. "Where are we going anyway?"

"For lunch," Charlie replied. "I'm starving. I don't like skipping breakfast. I need a lot of calories to keep this machine going."

"Is there a reason you got so bulked up?" Chance asked, slowing as they neared a street corner and faced a 'don't walk' sign.

Charlie shrugged. "Do you think I'm too bulked up?"

Chance raised his eyebrows while his mouth opened. "No! I mean, I didn't ask because I dislike your body. I didn't realize I was giving that vibe. I like your body. No, I love your body. I was just wondering." Charlie grinned at Chance's discomfort. "Ugh, you're playing with me again, aren't you? I only asked because it must be a conscious effort to get as big as you are, and I wondered if it was just a vanity thing or if you do it for some other reason."

Charlie squeezed Chance's shoulder once again, partly to reassure him that he hadn't been insulted, and partly to signal to Chance that he should begin walking now that they had a 'walk' sign. "You're right," he said as the three made their way across the street. "In college, my roommate, Tyler, suspected there was something going on between me and a guy I met named Stu. When Tyler told me he was going to be spending most of the night at our school's basketball game, I invited Stu to our dorm room. We didn't do anything but kiss and hug, but it was enough. Unbeknownst to me, Tyler had set up a hidden camera facing my bed. The next day, my make-out session with Stu was posted on the internet. There were screenshots printed and taped up around campus."

"Shit! What a jerk thing for Tyler to have done," Chance muttered. "What did you do?"

"I confronted Tyler," Charlie replied. "He admitted he had planted the device, wanting to see if his suspicions were true. I took a swing at him and missed, and he returned one and didn't. He knocked me to the floor. Then he called me a bunch of hateful things, told me he was asking for a room transfer then kicked me in the ribs for good measure."

"You should have gone to the police," Arlo spat. "I told Charlie this a hundred times."

Charlie shot Arlo a sad glance. "And I answered you a hundred times that I wasn't mentally in a frame of mind to do so. It didn't feel like anyone was on my side, and I doubted the campus police would be either." Charlie reset his eyes on Chance while occasionally glancing forward to see where he was walking. "I decided that day, I wouldn't be anyone's punching bag again. I joined a gym and worked for years to build up my body. I don't know that I'm any better a fighter now, but I think my size makes bullies wonder."

"I'm sorry that happened to you," Chance offered. The story reinforced in Chance's mind that the relationships he was forging could have ugly consequences. He felt anger more than fear, wondering what motivated such levels of hatred toward people who were minding their own business.

Charlie pointed to a burger joint that was a block from them. "I don't allow myself this kind of lunch often. But hey, I think today, we should treat ourselves. What do you say?"

Arlo groaned before laughing. "You're killing me. I'm going to have to work out twice as long later to keep this cam-ready body."

Charlie's smile faltered a bit and Chance wondered why it wasn't obvious to Arlo that Charlie wasn't a fan of his boyfriend's side hustle.

"Um, I could go for a cheeseburger," Chance interjected, hoping to distract Charlie. "I haven't had one in ages. Are they good here?"

As they reached the restaurant door, Charlie opened it for his mates with a wink. "The best. And their fries are to die for. If we're going to be bad, we might as well go all the way."

Arlo chortled by Chance's side. "That's the line he used on me to introduce me to kink."

Chance started to laugh before stopping himself with a gulp. "Say what now?"

* * * *

Chance was still questioning what Arlo's kink comment meant as he was ushered into the establishment, seated by the hostess and informed of daily specials by the waiter. The fact that Charlie and Arlo were making small talk about the menu options after dropping a bombshell increased his frustration. Even though Chance had been wanting more sexual adventure for years, he knew the word kink could cover many things—some of which were not to his liking.

His two companions stopped their chatter when Chance hadn't been engaging in the conversation. They peered at him with concern.

"Something wrong, Chance?" Charlie asked.

Chance was seated across from Charlie and he jumped slightly when he felt Charlie's hand gently squeeze his knee under the table. Chance glanced at other patrons—nobody had been watching.

"Maybe we shouldn't do PDA here," Chance suggested. "This looks like the kind of place tourists come to and they're probably not used to…it."

Charlie frowned, removing his hand. "I don't give a fuck about what tourists think, but I'm sorry if I made you uncomfortable."

Arlo sighed. "Chance, relax. If people come to San Francisco expecting they'll see only heterosexuals, they're pretty dim. I'm guessing they're hoping to witness openly gay behavior so they can tell their friends back home about the decadent big city."

That didn't make Chance less self-conscious, but he did feel ashamed of his cowardice. More importantly, he regretted spurning Charlie's affection.

"I'm sorry, Charlie," Chance offered, hoping his eyes showed Charlie that he meant it. "I'm not embarrassed by you or Arlo. I guess maybe your story about the bully is in my head. I haven't had to deal with people treating me like shit because of who I am, and it's a little scary to think about it happening now. I've always cared too much what others think of me."

Charlie's face softened as he leaned toward Chance. "I understand. This is all new to you and I need to remember that. And you're right to be cautious about the hate that's around us. There are times and places where you need to be careful. But you'll also get a sixth sense for when you can be yourself. I know this area and I know this restaurant. I can see from my surroundings that my touching your knee isn't likely to start a brawl." He winked at Chance. "But if it did, I also know I can stare down any asshole who harasses us."

Chance laughed. "Well, I'm not totally helpless." He surveyed the restaurant before returning his attention to Charlie. "And I'm pretty sure I can take down any of these guys myself. They look like they frequent this place a bit too often."

Charlie smiled. "See? That's the spirit. And we have Arlo, too. He's very strong."

Arlo shuddered. "God, let's stop talking about fist fights. I hope it never comes to that. I like my face the way it is, thank you. But, Chance, if I ever needed to come to your defense, I would. I doubt you'd need my help, though."

Chance nodded, feeling a sudden rush of warmth through his body at the notion the two men would fight for him. It was different but pleasant to have someone look out for him while still allowing him to be a protector in a relationship. He decided Charlie was right about the surroundings and he reached across the table, using his hands to take one of Charlie's and one of Arlo's in his. "Thanks, guys."

"Are you ready to order?" the waiter asked, causing Chance to quickly pull his hands back to himself. When he looked at the waiter, however, the man was standing there without judgment. Charlie and Arlo were trying to suppress laughter.

Chance felt flushed throughout his request for a cheeseburger and fries, then his companions calmly ordered their own meals. The waiter smiled before leaving the table to head to the kitchen.

Chance wiped a hand over his face and groaned. "I'll try to get better at this."

Charlie chuckled. "It's okay, Chance. We're here for you."

Arlo changed the subject to comments about the song that was playing, which led to Charlie talking about a concert they had attended. The discussion continued with the two debating which musician they'd next want to see.

"Who would you want to see?" Arlo asked Chance.

"What kind of kink are you two into?" Chance blurted. He hadn't been paying attention to their talk of singers and bands. He was still agonizing over what the two might have planned for him.

"Excuse me?" Charlie asked, surprised but somewhat amused.

"Arlo said you introduced him to kink. What was that about? Are you guys into some freaky shit that I should know about?"

Arlo snickered. "Chance, you've already seen most of the kink. Come on. Three guys together, voyeurism and exhibitionism."

Chance sighed with relief. "Oh. Yeah, I guess. Maybe I hadn't thought about what we did as kink, but I guess it would be considered that by most people."

"Pretty sure it would," Charlie concurred. "And you can tell that I like to please and take care of my partners. That's considered a kink by many."

Chance raised his eyebrows in surprise. "Really? I don't think that qualifies."

Charlie shrugged. "So, there you have it. That's mostly everything about us that's kinky."

Arlo sipped at his unsweetened iced tea while Charlie popped some of the free peanuts that had been left as a meal-starter into his mouth.

Chance narrowed his eyes at the two. "Wait. What's that supposed to mean? *Mostly* everything?"

Arlo and Charlie exchanged glances, followed by a slight nod and blink of the eyes from Charlie to Arlo.

"It's nothing that I think would bother you, Chance. But if it did, you don't have to participate," Arlo replied.

"Jesus, you guys have been worrying me about this since we entered the restaurant. Just tell me what it is, already," Chance pressed.

Arlo scratched his ear, and his expression made it clear he wasn't as certain Chance would approve as his earlier statement suggested. "Um, we sometimes…not often…like to role-play."

"Role-play?" Chance wondered. "Like dress up in costumes? You don't pretend that you're animals or anything weird like that, do you?"

Charlie bellowed a laugh. "Animals? That's the first place your mind went? Please tell me that isn't a secret fantasy of *yours*, Chance."

Chance flushed again. "No! Didn't I just say that would be weird shit?"

Arlo began to chuckle, as well. "Chance, I can assure you, we have never been inclined to dress up like animals."

"Then what? Cowboys?" Chance asked, not sure what made him think of that either.

Charlie continued laughing. "It appears you've had a lot of thoughts about role-playing. I might have a ten-gallon hat souvenir from somewhere I visited in Texas if you have an itch to play a cowboy, Chance. You'd be a cute ranch-hand."

Chance's face heated even more. "I wasn't saying it was my fantasy. Jesus, just tell me…"

Arlo put a soothing hand on Chance's arm. "As fun as the cowboy scenario sounds, Chance, it isn't something Charlie and I have done. We don't even wear costumes, per se. We just create little scenarios and act them out."

"Such as?" Chance pressed.

Arlo shrugged. "Like Charlie being a cop who pulled me over for driving recklessly. Or Charlie being a TSA agent who needs to pull me into a back room when my *package* looks suspicious."

Charlie chuckled. "Let's just say, both situations required a thorough body search and some pretend non-consensual sex."

Chance pictured the scene and felt his dick twitch. Maybe the role-play thing wasn't so strange.

Arlo bounced his straw up and down into the iced tea. "And of course, there's the obvious role-play. Charlie as my doctor, giving me a full physical."

Now Chance's cock was reacting by stiffening—he would very much like to witness that scenario. "Oh," was all he could muster in response.

Charlie's expression became serious. "Like Arlo said, we don't do it often. You wouldn't need to play…"

"I would," Chance blurted, then felt the burn in his cheeks return.

Arlo and Charlie each jerked their heads back with surprise before snickering. Charlie reached under the table and steadied Chance's bouncing knee. "Chance…you are so right for us." He leaned his head across the table so he could whisper to Chance. "I think Dr. Stone, the college soccer physician, and his assistant Arlo will need to examine the new student athlete soon. I've been told the young buck is worried he isn't ejaculating enough."

Chance swallowed hard, watching Charlie lean back with a mischievous grin.

"Here's your food," the waiter announced, startling Chance from the images that had formed in his head.

Chance glanced over at his companions. They were both trying to keep from laughing.

Chapter Thirteen

It had been a fun yet stressful week for Chance. He was still getting his bearings living in Charlie and Arlo's house and trying to feel like he belonged there. His companions had done everything they could to make Chance comfortable and encourage him to treat the place as his own, but little things like helping himself to food or lounging on a sofa still felt like overstepping. He almost wished Charlie and Arlo would move into his house instead.

The living arrangements also raised the question of what Chance would do if, in fact, the relationship continued. It made no sense to pay a large mortgage on a home that was doing nothing more than garaging his car. And if he did retain his house, he had to think about how he could financially contribute to their shared home while still paying his other bills.

Adding to his stress had been that his boss, Maria, had run into him and Charlie on a Sunday excursion they had made to pick up ice cream for an ailing Arlo.

Arlo had an allergy-related sore throat, and Charlie had wanted to provide relief as well as baby his boyfriend. Chance had been happy to accompany him to help carry home the desserts. He regretted that decision when Maria had tapped his shoulder while he was waiting in the customer line. Chance had been holding Charlie's hand. The public display of affection was something Chance had forced himself to do to make up for his squeamishness the day before. When Maria had seen the conjoined hands, her negative expression was noticeable. She had mumbled a hello, and Chance had felt compelled to admit that he was seeing Charlie. He refrained from mentioning Arlo, as it was likely shocking enough for Maria to find out that Chance liked men—and the man he was dating was the guy who had recommended Maria replace him.

Each day that Chance had gone to work since, Maria had made no mention of the encounter. She had remained cool to him, though. He was relatively certain that Maria was not homophobic, as her politics were liberal and she often spoke of a gay friend. Chance could only deduce that Maria's aloofness resulted from her feeling Chance had lied to her about his past relationships, hiding that he was gay. Although that wasn't true since he also liked women, Maria was the type of person who would take it personally if she felt untrusted by a colleague—even about personal matters.

The fun part of the week had been the ongoing banter, movie nights and sexual explorations with Arlo and Charlie. Contrary to what Chance feared would happen—which was once he'd tried a few same-sex acts, the desire would leave his system—the added experiences confirmed he liked relationships with men.

Or, at least, he liked them when it came to Arlo and Charlie.

Charlie had been protective, slowing down what Arlo wanted to try—even slowing down Chance. He felt it was important to ease Chance into the physical aspects of the relationship, not wanting to push Chance past his comfort-level and readiness. On the previous evening, Chance had wanted to protest that Charlie was sexually frustrating him by the glacial speed he was navigating. Chance knew in his heart that he was ready for more than mutual touching, masturbation and receiving rim and blow-jobs. It was true that Chance had been rimming Arlo, too, but that only made Chance eager to try oral sex on the man. Chance loved the sounds and squirming he could elicit from Arlo when he'd rim him, and he could only imagine the pleasure it would provide both him and Arlo if he could finish off his new boyfriend by giving head. Charlie warned Chance that the first time could be less pleasant than he hoped, as he wouldn't have the experience taking a cock to the throat or swallowing semen. Chance understood that, but he wanted to try because that dick and cum would belong to Arlo. He was curious to attempt it with Charlie, too, though the man's overly blessed endowment did give him pause.

The day earlier, the three had received their HIV test results and all proved negative. With that news, Chance was even more obsessed with fucking Arlo than he was with performing oral sex. Every time Chance saw Arlo's nicely curved butt-cheeks part for him, all he could think about was burying his dick deep inside.

Despite the physical fun he was having, it led to more stress as Chance had to acknowledge he was bisexual and prepare himself for the ramifications. Not only did he like sex with *two* men—he was falling in love with them. Neither was something he could imagine telling his parents or his friends from college. Charlie's 'fuck them' attitude was inspiring until Chance applied it to the people in his life. Try as he might, Chance couldn't bring himself to dismiss their opinions of him.

It was after dinner and Chance was nursing a glass of wine at the kitchen island in Charlie and Arlo's house. He thought the boys were still preoccupied in the family room playing a game of chess, so he was startled when Charlie approached from behind and clasped his shoulders.

"Something troubling you?" Charlie whispered before nuzzling the back of Chance's ear.

Chance exhaled a contented sigh. "No, not really. Just thinking. Charlie, I can't keep sponging off you guys..."

Charlie began kissing Chance's neck while massaging his shoulders. "You aren't. The expenses would be the same regardless of whether you're here or not. You know the old saying...three can live as cheaply as two."

Chance smirked. "I don't think that's the saying."

Charlie began massaging Chance's back while resting his chin on Chance's right shoulder. "What's really bothering you, Chance?"

Chance shrugged. "Nothing. Everything. I don't know. It's a lot of change, I guess. Sooner or later, this temporary situation—me staying here and living on the down-low—isn't sustainable."

Charlie reached his arms around Chance's chest and hugged him to his front. "Then make it permanent. Arlo and I want you here, Chance."

Chance leaned his head back so the side of his face could rest against Charlie's. "It's fast. And what about my house? What would I tell my parents? And the people at work...who knows if Maria has told people about us? If she has and people start asking questions, do I tell them about Arlo, too? It's...a lot."

Charlie was silent for a moment, then began to rub soft, gentle circles over Chance's pectoral muscles. "I know, Chance. I'm not trying to rush you."

Chance pulled away so he could swivel the counter-stool and face Charlie. "None of this is on you," Chance whispered, placing a hand over Charlie's heart. "You've been amazing. I'm just saying, I can't live two realities forever. I need to decide if I'm in or out and accept the consequences of that decision."

Charlie bristled. "I see. I was rather hoping the in-or-out decision was already made."

Chance leaned forward, resting his forehead on Charlie's chest. "I know. I think it is, Charlie. I'm just...scared."

Charlie ran his hand through Chance's locks, then bent his head to kiss the top of his head. "I know, baby. I just ask you to do what makes *you* happy, then we'll figure out the rest. Okay?" Chance nodded his head against Charlie's chest. "Okay. Anyway, we have something more pressing to consider right now."

Chance pulled his face away and raised his eyes to meet Charlie's. "We do?"

"Mm." Charlie grinned. "We need to decide whether you want chocolate or vanilla cake for your birthday tomorrow. Arlo has been pushing me to figure out your preference without blowing the surprise that he's baking for you."

Chance jerked back his head with shock. "How did you know it was my birthday tomorrow? I purposely didn't say anything."

Charlie chuckled. "Everything is available on the internet, Chance. What, didn't you think I would do a search on the man we were letting into our home?"

Chance groaned and dropped his head back against Charlie's chest. "I don't like birthdays."

"I guessed from your silence about it," Charlie mused, tousling Chance's hair some more. "But Arlo does, so indulge him. And don't tell him I said anything, okay? I'm giving you the heads-up because I figured you wouldn't like being ambushed tomorrow. There would be nothing worse than Arlo all excited about surprising you, followed by you reacting in annoyance."

Chance pulled away from the embrace, placing his hands on Charlie's hips. "I wouldn't, Charlie. I could never crush Arlo's happiness like that."

Charlie bent to drop a soft kiss to Chance's lips. "Thank you, Chance. You're a good guy. And for what it's worth, as you make your in-or-out decision, the man in the other room is crazy about you."

Chance sighed, thinking about his affection for Arlo. Then he gazed up to Charlie with need. "And you, Charlie?"

Charlie stroked Chance's cheek, and Chance knew the answer just from the look he was receiving. "Chance...baby...the only other person to ever make me feel this way in just a few short weeks was Arlo. Not even Wilson did. You have my heart...if you want it."

Chance leaned back into Charlie's chest, feeling warm and secure. "I want it. And I prefer vanilla—unlike my sex, apparently."

Charlie chuckled before landing more kisses to the top of Chance's head. "Speaking of…I was thinking. Maybe tomorrow night, it would make for a nice birthday memory to…take our lovemaking to the next step?"

Chance's lips involuntarily parted. "Yeah?"

"I think you're ready now," Charlie mused. "Come on. Arlo was searching for a movie that we can watch. He's going to wonder what's taking us so long to join him."

Chance nodded, unable to keep a broad smile from forming on his face. The prospect of new sexual experiences was exciting, but the confirmation that the two men were falling in love with him was overwhelming his heart. As frightening as it was, he knew his decision was all-in. He'd have to start thinking about how to deal with the fallout.

* * * *

Chance awoke the next morning with a new spring in his step. The night's lovemaking had been slow and sensual, with Charlie abstaining from topping Arlo so the three could orgasm together through mutual masturbation. Chance could tell that Charlie had subtly coaxed Arlo to join him in giving Chance extra attention and affection. He had fallen asleep between the two of them. Chance had never awakened on a birthday feeling so loved.

Chance needed to head into work earlier than Charlie, so he rose and began his walk to the guest room ensuite to prepare for his day. He smiled fondly as he peeked back into the master bedroom, seeing the two men had maneuvered their way to the center of the bed, locking arms around each other.

Once Chance cleaned up after his breakfast, he grabbed his keys and made his way out the front door to head to his house to retrieve his car. When he started descending the front steps, he stopped abruptly, horrified by what he saw. His parents and sister were sitting on his front stoop looking quite perturbed that there was nobody there to greet them.

"Fuck," Chance mumbled to himself before bounding down the remaining steps of his neighbors' house.

Chapter Fourteen

"Mom? Dad?" Chance called out to his parents as he approached them from his next-door neighbors' house. "Marybeth? What are you all doing here?"

Chance's mother Ann was the first to respond, rising from the stoop. "We flew out to surprise you for your birthday." She walked slowly to Chance to pull him into a hug.

"Oh," Chance mumbled. "You should have called to let me know."

Chance's father Hugh pursed his lips. "Well, it wouldn't be a surprise then, would it, son?" He reached over to embrace Chance, as well. He let go quickly so Chance's sister also could hug her brother.

"Where were you?" Marybeth asked. "We got here almost an hour ago. I said to Dad, he can't have left for work already."

Before Chance could reply, he saw his mother, Ann, look over to Arlo and Charlie's house. "Were you in there? Is that the house where your gay neighbors live?"

Chance nodded with hesitance. "Arlo and Charlie…yeah. They're my friends, Mom. Remember, they helped me move in and they helped me when I got sick. And you don't need to identify them as my *gay* friends."

Ann patted Chance's arm. "Well, they are gay, aren't they? I'm glad they were nice to you when you were sick, providing they weren't doing it hoping for something else."

"Mom, don't start that again," Chance warned.

"Where were you last night?" Hugh questioned, ignoring Chance.

"Last night?" Chance repeated, wondering what triggered the question.

"We flew in late yesterday," Hugh explained. "So, we came by last night and rang the bell. There were no lights on in the house. We tried again later, and the same thing. I tried calling your landline and there was no answer. You weren't answering your cell either. Finally, we gave up and found a hotel to stay at. But we were worried."

"You didn't spend the night at…*their* place, did you?" Ann asked with concern, glancing toward the house next door.

"Whose place? Oh, you mean Arlo's and Charlie's? No," Chance lied. "I just came from there because I joined them for coffee. I do that sometimes before heading to work."

"That's nice." Marybeth smiled. "I want to meet them."

Ann shot her daughter an irritated glare, then returned her gaze to her son. "So, where were you that you couldn't answer the phone last night?" Ann pressed.

"Jesus," Chance spat. "I'm a grown man. What's with the interrogation? I…had a date."

Hugh smiled. "Ah. Well, is she someone we should meet?"

"No, Dad. It was a one-time thing."

Ann frowned and shook her head. "Spending the night with someone and never seeing them again isn't a date. Shame on her."

"Mom, get into the current century," Marybeth griped.

Ann huffed with her hands on her hips. "Are you trying to tell me you act like that—going out with a boy for one day and sleeping with him? Is that how I raised you?"

Marybeth didn't shrink from the attack. "Why would it be wrong for *me* to have a one-night stand, but you aren't shaming Chance for having one?"

"I do have a problem with him having casual sex," Ann replied. "Besides it being a disrespectful attitude towards women, it isn't safe."

"Ann, leave the boy alone," Hugh chastised. "He's just sowing his wild oats."

Ann rolled her eyes. "You and I both know this wasn't his first time doing that. The field should be plowed by now. He's thirty-three years old today." She returned her eyes to Chance. "You need to find a nice girl to settle down with before you're too old to have a family."

"Mom," Chance protested. "I need to go to the office."

"You won't work late, will you?" Hugh asked. "We flew all the way out here. We wanted to take you out for dinner to celebrate your birthday."

"Oh…um, I think Arlo and Charlie were planning something," Chance stated.

Chance could see the disappointed expressions on his father's and Marybeth's faces, and the disapproving one on his mother's.

"Chance, we came all the way from Missouri," Ann reminded him.

Hugh glanced at his wife with discomfort, then returned his gaze to his son. "Of course you made plans for your birthday. If they went through some trouble, then you should join them. But if they haven't, since we'll only be here for a couple of days, do you think your friends would mind celebrating with you after we return to Missouri? Or maybe they'd like to join us? My treat, of course."

Ann scowled. "I was hoping for a *family* dinner."

Chance felt cornered. "Uh, I'll call them about rescheduling. I need to get to work. Dad, the code for the front door is your two-digit birth month followed by Mom's. You can let yourselves in. The guest rooms are on the second floor. You'll see them."

"I'll be glad not to spend another night at a hotel," Ann muttered. "The prices in this city are ridiculous."

"It isn't like home," Hugh agreed, shaking his head. "Is it okay to use your personal laptop, son? I'm partially working while I'm out here. When you own a business, you can't really take vacation time. I didn't want to lug my computer along."

"Huh? Oh, yeah. Same PIN as the front door," Chance explained. "It's in my office on the third floor, across from my bedroom. Sorry I can't stay home with you. I didn't know you were coming."

"It's okay, Chance. I've never been to San Francisco. We can check out the city this morning." Marybeth smiled. "I'll take care of Mom and Dad."

Hugh grunted a laugh. "Yeah, okay. Does that mean you'll take care of paying for everything, too?"

"Dad!" Marybeth sighed.

"Go ahead to work," Ann commanded, shooing her son toward his garage door. "We'll manage fine. Knowing you, I'll want to get back here early enough to clean your place. I don't think you men know how to turn on a vacuum cleaner."

* * * *

When Chance arrived at the office, he gave a quick hello to colleagues and rushed to his office. The first order of business was to call Charlie to let him know that he couldn't join him and Arlo for dinner. He hoped Arlo hadn't yet gone out of his way to prepare birthday foods. Chance wondered if the two would be as disappointed as he was about delaying the next level of intimacy.

Just as Chance was lifting the phone, Maria entered his office, motioning for him to lower it. "Chance, would you please join me in my conference room for a few minutes?"

"Sure," he responded, wondering why they couldn't just meet in his office since they were both already there.

Chance followed Maria to the hallway. She still wasn't making small-talk with him. He found it disconcerting, but he was afraid confronting her about it would make relations worse between them. The best thing, in his mind, was to keep working hard, produce good marketing campaigns and be gracious to everyone.

When they arrived at the conference room, Maria motioned Chance to enter before her. He did and was startled to see Rakia, their HR director, already sitting at the table.

Chance shot a look between the two women, and he could tell from the serious countenance on each that the meeting was going to be unpleasant. "Good morning, Rakia," Chance greeted, hoping he didn't sound as nervous as he felt.

"Good morning, Chance," she responded with a tone that didn't hide her own discomfort.

Maria shut the door behind her and took a seat next to Rakia so that they were both facing Chance. He was keen enough to know the dynamics meant he was in trouble.

"What's this about?" he ventured. Chance's hand was shaking, so he put it under the table and on his lap.

Rakia cleared her throat, as if to muster the strength to be the hard-ass her role required her to be. "Chance, it has come to the attention of management that you are dating Dr. Kendall. As you might be aware, Dr. Kendall had communicated to Maria he would try to influence the Chamber of Commerce to send business the firm's way. When this conversation occurred between Dr. Kendall and Maria, Maria was unaware of your personal relationship with him. I'm sure you understand that if it were known in the industry or in the community that our firm was receiving special treatment because of your relationship, it would create ethical and potential legal issues for us."

"Oh," Chance uttered. This hadn't been what he was expecting, and the potential conflict of interest wasn't something he had even considered. "Charlie…Dr. Kendall…he made that call to Maria before he and I started dating. He didn't even like me at the time." Chance turned his gaze to Maria's constipated-looking face. "You remember. He suggested you replace me after I made a marketing pitch to him."

"So, what changed that, Chance? What made him not only call Maria to sing your praises, but then try to better position you with the firm by offering to send business our way?" Rakia pressed.

Chance knew he had to slow down his responses and think carefully about what he said. Rakia was taking notes and Chance's comments could be used as evidence against him. "He and I discovered we were next-door neighbors. We began to talk and I apologized to him that the presentation I had given him wasn't up to my usual standards. I believe that piqued his curiosity about me, and he researched some of my ad work. I guess he was impressed. Dr. Kendall acknowledged that he might have overreacted with Maria, and he wanted to let her know that his impression of me had changed."

"But you just said that at the time he made the call, he still disliked you. I don't understand why he would research your work, tell you he misjudged you and make that call on behalf of someone he didn't like. Are you sure he didn't reach out to Maria after you…slept with him?" Rakia pushed.

Chance's face blanched. "I'm sure! I had not slept with him at that point. There was nothing romantic between us at the time. I misspoke when I said he didn't like me at the time he made the call. He and I had smoothed things over once we met as neighbors."

Rakia's jaw tightened. "So, what you're saying is, he made the call, *then* you began sleeping with him."

"Yes," Chance replied. "Wait, no. I mean from a timing perspective, yes. I slept with him after he made the call, but it wasn't some quid pro quo thing like you're suggesting. He and I got to know each other as neighbors, like I said, and one thing led to another."

"Have you ever been in a same-sex relationship before, Chance?" Maria asked.

"What? I… How is that any of your business?"

Maria tapped her Christmas-red polished nails on the conference room table. "You've never mentioned having an attraction to men. Then suddenly Dr. Kendall makes a call that saves your job and lo and behold, you're gay and sleeping with him."

"I'm not gay," Chance snapped.

"That's not helping your argument," Rakia commented, writing down more notes.

"I'm bisexual," Chance clarified. "Not that I should have to divulge anything about my sexual orientation. Do I need a lawyer?"

Rakia frowned. "Whether you seek legal representation is up to you. No action is being taken today, though. We're investigating. We're trying to understand why a man that wanted you fired called Maria shortly thereafter with the intent of positioning you better with the firm. Then you and that man began dating. It raises concerns."

"I love him!" Chance blurted, hoping that would establish there wasn't a sex payoff. That wiped the smug looks from the women's faces as each registered surprise.

"You love him?" Rakia asked skeptically.

"Yes," Chance answered. He knew now it was true, and he was glad the fact might benefit him in the conversation. "I told you what happened. I appreciated his outreach to Maria. We talked more and got to know each other better. Then we started spending time with each other and my attraction to him grew. His to me, as well. We hit it off. That's the truth."

Maria frowned. "I'd really like to believe you, Chance. I'm sure you understand why I would have my doubts. It's still not clear to me what would have motivated his call just because he found out you were his neighbor. He had a lot of anger toward you the day of the presentation."

Chance wanted to explain it was because of Arlo, but he wasn't willing to share even more personal information. "I told you, I apologized to him. He felt guilty about being a jerk."

Maria waved a hand through the air to silence Chance. "Okay, Chance. I'm not enjoying this and I don't want to be doing this any more than you. If what you're saying is true, then I understand you may not have meant to cause harm to the firm. But didn't you think about the consequences of becoming involved with Dr. Kendall after he went on record saying he'd steer business from the charity board to us? Any campaigns the Chamber of Commerce sends our way might be scrutinized. Our competitors could complain that we have an unfair advantage. Frankly, they'd be correct. We and the city could get dragged into ugly lawsuits."

"I can ask him to make sure they don't send business our way," Chance reasoned.

"Then that makes you a liability to the firm," Maria replied. "The chamber is responsible for a good deal of business leads to firms like ours."

Chance swallowed hard, realizing that Maria's last point was hard to dispute. He glanced back and forth between their unwavering expressions and a bead of sweat began to trickle at his hairline. "So, what are you saying? Are you firing me?"

A bit of empathy cracked through Maria's tough exterior. "Chance, I hope it won't come to that, but…it's not my decision to make. I need to discuss this with the senior leadership team. Rakia will need to review the situation with our legal department. Until a determination is made, I think it's best you take a paid leave of absence."

"A leave of absence? Again?" Chance asked. "But I just got back…"

"We'll have a decision made within the next day or two," Rakia interjected.

Chance nodded weakly. "Is there anything I can say or do that would help me keep my job? If I left Charlie?" Chance hated himself for even considering it, but he was desperate and unsure which option would hurt him more in the long-run.

Rakia sighed. "Chance, I can't answer that for you. We don't tell employees who they can love."

"Really?" Chance shot back sarcastically. "Because it kind of feels like you do."

"Chance, we didn't create this problem. It's not appropriate to turn your anger on us," Maria chastised. "And if you really love Dr. Kendall as you claim, then you shouldn't leave him to try to save your job. The damage is done. It's a tight community, and I'm sure people will realize you two have or had a thing.

Business being sent our way would still be questioned even if you two broke up. And if you do split, and he takes the break-up badly and steers business away from us, you're still a liability to the firm."

Chance pinched the bridge of his nose. "So, you're saying I'm fucked! That's what you're saying, isn't it, Maria?"

Maria cleared her throat indignantly. "I'm saying you need to go home and wait a day or two for our decision. You should leave the premises now, Chance. Don't make a scene and force me to have security escort you out."

Chance's left eye watered, and he was angry with himself for letting the two women see his vulnerability. He pushed back from the table abruptly and stormed out of the conference room, taking the stairs to the lobby so he wouldn't be trapped by anyone while waiting for the elevator. When he made his way out to the street, he rushed to the parking garage, hoping he wouldn't shed tears in public and humiliate himself even more.

Chapter Fifteen

Chance made his way to his home street—Bayview Hill Avenue—and he remembered nothing about the drive there. His mind was muddled with replays of his conversations with HR and his boss, his parents and when Charlie had first told him about his call to Maria. It felt like everything about his life was teeter-tottering on a cliff's edge, and he wished he could fast-forward to his uncertain future just to know he had already dealt with whatever fallout might come from this day. He wanted to delay going home, knowing his parents would be there filled with questions about his early return from work.

"Happy birthday to me," he muttered to himself, flicking off the car radio when the song that was playing began grating on his already frayed nerves.

Chance considered leaving the BMW at one of the metered spots on the road and walking to Arlo and Charlie's house. It would be his best chance of being unobserved by his parents. As he contemplated the option, he noticed a small sign outside a Victorian home that read *Elijah Cummings, Attorney at Law*. There was also a rainbow flag hanging from the front porch. On a whim, Chance pulled into the visitor lot and parked.

After sitting in his car for ten minutes wondering if someone would ask him to remove his vehicle, he mustered the courage to step out and walk to the front double-doors of the house. They were old, beautiful and had inlaid glass panels which allowed him to see inside to what was once a foyer but had been converted to a reception area. He inhaled loudly and entered. The well-insulated home blocked out the street noise as soon as the doors closed behind him.

"Can I help you?" a very young, slightly built man asked from behind the reception desk.

"Um, does Mr. Cummings handle work-related issues?" Chance asked, assuming the youth before him couldn't be the attorney.

The young man paused for a second, and Chance mused that the receptionist's expression looked like he was trapping a goldfish in his mouth.

"Do you mean like work-related disputes, discrimination or wrongful termination kinds of things?" the young man asked.

Chance nodded. "Yeah. Maybe all those things."

The young man blinked. "Yes, he does. Do you have an appointment?"

Chance winced. "No. Of course, I need an appointment. I'm sorry. Shit just happened today, I saw the sign, and…never mind. I'll set something up."

"Hold on." The young man half-smiled. He turned his head toward an open door and peered at something that was out of Chance's view. "Dad? Would you be able to see a prospective client now? Some bad shit just happened to him at work."

If Chance weren't still upset, he might have chuckled at the kid's lack of professional decorum.

After a second, the young man returned his gaze to Chance with an impish smile. "He motioned that he's coming out."

Before Chance could thank the kid, a very handsome man similar in height and build to Chance, though likely around forty years old, emerged from what Chance imagined was his office. Since meeting Arlo and acknowledging his attraction to men, Chance had started noticing the physical appearance of many guys that were crossing his path.

"Timothy," the older man admonished. "Some *bad shit*?" Timothy blushed and the attorney directed his attention to Chance. "My apologies, Mr.…?"

"Findley," Chance responded, extending a hand to shake. "But call me Chance."

The lawyer shook Chance's hand and offered a wry smile. "Elijah Cummings. But call me Elijah. The young man who is *still learning the ropes* is my son, Timothy."

"Tim," the attorney's son corrected. Chance assumed from the sigh that Tim emitted it wasn't the first time he'd had to stress his preferred name to his father. Tim stood to shake Chance's hand, too, and Chance noticed the kid was appraising him with interest. He wasn't someone Chance found sexually attractive, but Tim had an adorable quality about him that would appeal to men who liked boyish types. Chance wondered if he'd liked his brain better when it had blocked thoughts of men as potential conquests.

"Come with me, please," Elijah requested, then returned to his office.

Chance shot Tim a small grin and mouthed a thank you before following the lawyer. Once in the office,

Elijah took a seat behind his desk and motioned for Chance to sit on the leather chair opposite.

"So, Chance…what *shit* happened that brought you here?" Elijah asked, unable to hide a small smile as he repeated his son's choice of words.

Chance huffed a laugh. "I promise he didn't offend me. After the day I had, it was a relief to be greeted by a cheerful face."

The tips of Elijah's mouth inched up and his pride was evident. "He's a good boy and he's a big help here."

Chance nodded. "So, this shit…I think I might be getting fired."

Chance provided background information on how he'd met Charlie and what led to Charlie's phone call to Maria as well as his offer of influence. He finished by detailing his conversation with Maria and Rakia.

Elijah frowned, tapping his pen on his desk blotter. "You were right to come here, Chance. Your firm handled this poorly. Their first mistake was when your supervisor told you that you needed to use your vacation time in that three-week period. A firm can decline the timing of your vacation request if it has a negative impact on their business, providing they allow you to use it in the year it's allotted. But they can't force you to use three of your weeks on the given dates of their choice unless it's a policy that they apply to everyone. Secondly, HR and your boss asking questions related to your sleeping situation with your boyfriend was out of bounds. The fact that they implied you might be exchanging sex for his endorsement was beyond the pale and could be grounds for defamation. And if they are concerned about a conflict of interest, they could simply restrict your involvement with any business referred to them by Chamber members. It is up to them to assign your projects to prevent the appearance of a conflict. Frankly, I'm amazed an HR person would be so careless as to open the door to a potential lawsuit. She sounds rather inept."

Chance sighed with some relief. "I think she's newly promoted to her role. She's nice, but I'll bet she feels pressured to make this happen for Maria. Maria might have other motives, like the high cost I am to the firm. So, you think I have a case if they fire me? You'd take this to court?"

Elijah shook his head. "I doubt this would ever make it to court. Arbitration, at most. Chance, most companies just want to settle in these situations. What you'd demand from them isn't worth countering with time from their lawyers, your boss, the HR person…as well as the legal fees that would mount for them. And, because there's a high risk they would lose, they could face reputational damage. This could look very much like you're being treated as you are because your relationship is with a man."

Chance frowned. "In all honesty, I don't think Maria is homophobic. I believe she'd be able to prove she isn't based on her friends and stuff."

Elijah was undeterred. "Doesn't matter. Their line of questioning was inappropriate, and it could be viewed by a jury as intrusive and insensitive resulting from a subconscious bias. I'll make that point with your firm's lawyers. It would be hard for them to prove otherwise."

"I'd rather not lose my job at all," Chance admitted.

Elijah scratched his neck like he was hesitating to respond. "Chance, maybe you won't. But based on what you've shared with me, I'd guess that's where they're heading. You need to be prepared."

Chance nodded. "The firm is having financial problems. Like I said, I'm expensive. If they let me go, not only will it save them money, but they won't lose my clients. I had to sign a non-compete when I was hired, promising not to poach business if I left the firm."

"That's helpful to know," Elijah said. "When you get home, document everything you can remember about conversations they've had about expense pressures. I can use that, if need be. In the meantime, don't communicate with them. If they fire you, call me right away. Even if they don't terminate your employment but take other punitive measures, let me know. Everything they've done is out of line. You've done nothing wrong."

Chance exhaled, slouching a little more in the chair to ease the tension he had been feeling. "Thank you, Elijah. I'm glad I came here. I was kind of in a state of shock about everything. I mean, so many things have happened in the last few weeks that I never believed would happen to me. Like I've never been with a man, let alone two at the same time…"

"Two?" Elijah interjected.

Chance could feel the heat rise to his cheeks. "Um…yeah. About that." He decided he'd better offer the truth about everything. If something leaked during an arbitration, he didn't want his own lawyer blindsided. When he finished his story about how he'd met Charlie and Arlo and how it had progressed into a three-way relationship, he waited for Elijah's reaction.

Elijah blinked a few times, his mouth slightly agape. Then he let out a small laugh. "Chance, you really dove right in, didn't you?"

Chance wiped a palm across his jaw. "Yeah, well…"

Elijah held up a hand. "It's okay. It has nothing to do with anything regarding their allegations or your predicament. It shouldn't come up, but thank you for telling me." He sat back in his chair, steepling his fingers under his chin. "May I ask, has it been difficult adjusting to your new lifestyle?" Elijah shook his head with embarrassment when Chance didn't answer. "Never mind. It's none of my business. I shouldn't have asked."

Chance looked down bashfully, but then returned his gaze. "Nah, it's okay. To answer your question, it feels like it was easy when I think of my time with Arlo and Charlie. I'm surprised how natural that has been for me. In most every other way, though, it's been hard. Like my family just popped in from Missouri this morning. What do I say to them? If I don't come clean with them, then I feel like I'm messaging that I'm ashamed of Charlie and Arlo. If I do tell them, my parents might shoot Charlie and Arlo. Maybe they'll kill me, too. They're from Missouri, after all."

"Do you keep a gun in the house, Chance?" Elijah asked.

"No. I was joking. They wouldn't murder anyone. But you know what I mean."

"I do." Elijah nodded. "Maybe let them get to know Charlie and Arlo. They could see the wonderful things you saw in them. Over time, once your parents are comfortable with them, it could make it easier for them to accept that they're more than friends with you."

"Ha," Chance shot back. "I doubt it. At least I don't see that happening with my mother."

"Well, I'm sure Charlie and Arlo can help you think it through. I'm probably not the best person to ask for advice," Elijah said.

"Oh yeah? Why's that?" Chance wondered. "Is it because you're straight? I noticed the rainbow flag on the house. Is someone close to you gay?" Chance didn't want to ask about Tim in case Elijah didn't suspect.

Elijah remained silent for a moment, then nodded. "The flag shows potential clients that I'm gay-friendly. But yes, there are gay people in my family. Timothy is gay. He's known since he was a boy. Lucky him because…I didn't really come to terms with my own sexuality until years into my marriage with Timothy's mother. It was Timothy who helped me face the truth once he'd matured. I'm lucky that my ex-wife was very understanding once she got over the shock. I think it helped that she loves our son for who he is. Listening to Timothy over the years helped her comprehend how people lie to themselves for so long out of shame and a desire to fit into society. Today, though, we're divorced and she and I remain friends. She's even encouraging me to meet someone."

"Oh," Chance mumbled. He wasn't expecting to hear Elijah was gay, too.

"People might wonder if it is hereditary, but the irony is, Timothy was adopted," Elijah elaborated.

Chance's eyes widened. "Wow. Maybe that was a stroke of good fortune? I mean, if it helped you."

"I hope we made things easier for each other," Elijah countered.

Chance nodded. "It's funny how once your mind opens to the truth, your eyes confirm it. I was just thinking earlier how I'm noticing men in ways I hadn't before. Not that I would do something with anyone other than Arlo and Charlie. But the fact that I'm seeing men as sexual beings is different than just a short while ago."

Elijah reacted with a slight smile. "That makes some sense. I'm pretty sure I prohibited myself from looking at men that way…until my brain rebelled."

Chance rose from the chair to shake Elijah's hand. "Thank you, Elijah. I hope I won't need you, but I'm glad you're here if I do."

"Me, too," Elijah replied.

As Chance made his way to the office door, he turned. "By the way, your ex-wife is right. You should try to meet someone. I'm sure there are lots of guys who'd be interested. For what it's worth, my brain and eyes noticed you right away."

The lawyer's face reddened before Chance turned and exited the office. He waved to Tim, who was on the phone, and made his way to his car. He was a little embarrassed that he'd told Elijah he was attractive, but he feared the guy might be alone because he blamed himself for his failed marriage.

Chance began the short drive down the street to his house, feeling better after seeking legal counsel. It made him think that he had options, at least regarding work. He wasn't sure what choices he had regarding his family. He was quite certain, however, he wanted Charlie's advice before deciding.

Chance pulled into his driveway and buzzed open the garage door, nosing in the BMW and parking it. He decided, for now, it was best not to worry his family about his job. He wasn't sure how he could explain anything without outing himself anyway. Chance planned to tell them he'd opted to take a half-day so he could spend time with them. That is, he would tell them once he finished speaking with Charlie.

Chance assumed Charlie was still at work and he would need to call him, then he saw Charlie's car parked in the road in front of his and Arlo's house. It was common for Charlie to return home for lunch, if he could, so his schedule must have allowed it this day. That was a stroke of luck.

Chance ran down the sidewalk to his neighbors' house when he saw Charlie and Arlo emerge from their front door.

"Chance? I thought I saw your car pull into your driveway," Arlo shouted. He turned to Charlie. "I told you I saw him…"

"Chance, what are you doing home so early?" Charlie asked. "You aren't sick, are you?"

The two men came down their steps to join Chance on the sidewalk. Even though they had just been in bed together hours earlier, each man pulled Chance into a quick embrace.

"I'm not sick," Chance mumbled. His eyes shot open wide when he remembered he had never called Charlie to let him know his family had flown into town. "Oh shit, I forgot to call you, Charlie. My parents and sister are here. They came to surprise me for my birthday."

"Oh," Charlie replied, clearly recognizing that it would ruin their plans.

Arlo was oblivious to the fact. "Hey, that's great! I can't wait to meet them. Chance, I might as well tell you now that I knew it was your birthday. Happy Birthday! I'm making a dinner that got raves from everyone when I've served it before. And I made a cake. I heard you like vanilla. You can bring your family."

Chance darted his eyes to Charlie and he could tell that Charlie was less optimistic. "Um, Arlo, I don't think we will be able to join you…"

Arlo's smile dropped. "What? Sure, you can. I made enough. It's not a problem."

"Arlo, they don't know about…me. About us," Chance explained.

Arlo shrugged. "I know that. Bring them over to our house and introduce us as your friends."

"Chance?" The voice came from behind Chance. His mother emerged from his front door. "Chance! I thought I heard you pull your car into the garage. I need to speak with you right now."

"Mom, I'm with my friends. I'll be home in a minute," Chance yelled back.

Chance's reply didn't land well with his mother. Ann charged down the front steps and fast-walked to where Chance and his companions were standing.

"Chance, I'm not asking. Get in your house now!" Ann snapped.

Charlie fidgeted at the scene and Arlo gasped with surprise, though he extended his hand to Chance's mother. "I'm Arlo…"

"I know who you are," Ann responded coldly, looking at Arlo's hand like it had just been used to wipe snot from his nose. "Or should I call you Chatter-butt-whatever?"

Chance felt his breath hitch. "Mom…"

"After your father typed in the PIN for your laptop, it brought up the name of the last site you were viewing. He came down to tell me that he was troubled that it sounded like a gay adult website. He told me not to snoop and to just drop it, but I couldn't. I needed to make sure there wasn't something to worry about. I pulled it up and couldn't believe what I was seeing. Then a pop-up box asked me to reconsider canceling my subscription so I didn't lose access to my favorite *model.*" Ann spun on Arlo. "Oh, and that would be when a picture of you appeared on the screen with that Chatter-butt something-or-other name."

"Jesus," Chance exclaimed, wiping a hand over his jaw.

Ann returned her anguished countenance to her son. "What is going on, Chance?"

"It's not what you think," Chance lied. He was floundering, worrying about both his mother's and Arlo's reactions.

Ann's expressions vacillated between fear and frustration. "Were you just curious what your neighbor does on that site? You weren't enjoying watching him, were you?"

"Chance? Did you log on to watch me perform?" Arlo asked.

Ann shot Arlo a chastising look. "*Perform*?"

"Chance?" Arlo pressed, ignoring Ann's sarcasm.

Chance's face twisted and his stomach lurched. "Arlo, I'm sorry…"

Arlo's eyes widened. "I've only done one show since I met you, Chance. It was the night I helped you unpack."

Chance re-wiped a hand over his sweating face. "Arlo, I don't know what to say. You gave me the information. It was like you wanted me to…"

"Bullshit," Arlo cut in. Though Arlo wasn't raising his voice, the tone was the first time Chance had sensed anger from his friend. "You knew how I felt about that. I told you it was dishonest for someone I knew to watch me and not tell me, and then you did it anyway." Arlo shoved his hands in his pockets and glared at the pavement before returning his gaze to Chance. "You heard all the things I confessed about the guy I had just met. God…"

"Will you answer my question, Chance?" Ann snapped.

"Mom…"

"And even after all this time, you never told me what you did," Arlo added.

"Chance, I can't believe you betrayed Arlo like that," Charlie admonished.

Chance felt it was getting harder to breathe. "Charlie, please listen."

"Listen to what, Chance? That you're sorry? Arlo and I were already with a guy who was sneaky and lied. You know how important honesty is to us. The one thing I won't tolerate is another relationship where someone is hurting Arlo."

"A relationship? What the hell is going on? Are you three in a relationship, Chance?" Ann gasped, holding her hand to her chest. When there was silence for a moment, Ann grabbed Chance's arm. "Answer me!"

"Mom…"

Ann looked as though she might cry. "Chance, go in your house now. I can't be talking to you about this out here."

Chance spun on his mother, clenching his fists at his side. "Mom, this isn't just about you, okay? Can you just go back inside so I can talk to Arlo and Charlie in private?"

Ann stared at her son as if she'd encountered an escaped mass murderer standing in her garden. She began to sob before stomping her way back to Chance's home. When Chance turned back to Charlie and Arlo, Arlo's expression had become flat.

"Why, Chance? You could have asked me. I would have let you. But sneaking on and watching me like that? Then you never even told me that you did it."

"I wanted to," Chance said, ready to explain how awful he had felt about what he'd done.

"Chance, I'm so disappointed," Charlie cut in with sadness.

Chance turned on him, annoyed at his lack of support. "You're disappointed that I wasn't forthcoming? Did you ever tell Arlo how we met…for real?"

Charlie's eyes narrowed in warning. "Chance, don't…"

Chance focused on Arlo. "Charlie is the one who suggested to my boss that she fire me. *He* was the guy you said must be a monster when I told you about my presentation the day we met."

Arlo looked to Charlie with confusion. "What?"

Charlie grimaced. "I…didn't think it was necessary to tell you."

Chance emitted a bitter laugh. "Yeah, because Arlo would have asked you why you were such a shit, and you would have had to tell him that it was because you were in a lousy mood since Wilson came to see you. That Wilson wanted to get back with you and Arlo."

Arlo's jaw dropped. "Charlie, is that true?"

Charlie grimaced and shot Chance a threatening glare before responding. "Arlo, I didn't tell you because I was trying to protect you."

"Protect me or protect yourself? You've been just as dishonest with me as Wilson and Chance," Arlo said, the hurt evident in his voice.

"Arlo, come on," Charlie pleaded. "You know everything I do is in your best interest."

Arlo shook his head. "Actually, Charlie, I don't know what's true anymore." He turned and made his way back to the stairs to his house. Charlie returned his gaze to Chance, and it had more sadness than fury.

"Thanks for that, Chance," Charlie mumbled. "Maybe you should go to your parents. It sounds like you have shit to deal with. I'll try to clean up the crap you just dumped on me."

Chance wanted Charlie to feel as guilty about what he'd done to Arlo as Chance felt about his own actions, but he wasn't sure Charlie deserved that. Most of all, he wanted to beg Charlie to forgive him and ask for his help navigating the mess he'd made, but he knew he wouldn't. So, instead, Chance remained silent and walked back to his house.

Chapter Sixteen

As Chance made his way to his steps, he half-heartedly contemplated making a run for it. He didn't even care where he ended up, as long as it wasn't facing his mother and father. He'd likely just lost Arlo and Charlie, and now he had to defend to his parents the reasons he had been with them before he could even grieve their absence.

When he entered his house, he heard his father just finish saying something to his mother that sounded like, "I told you to mind your own business, but you just don't listen." When he reached the top of the stairs to the main level, his mother was sitting in the living room with the side of her head resting in the palm of her hand. She had the look of someone who had just found out their child had been killed in a hit-and-run accident. It angered Chance. He had seen in the past how his mother would rage and act like she was the world's biggest victim, expecting everyone to acknowledge her grief and exude great effort to comfort her.

From the corner of his eye, Chance saw his father was in the adjoining kitchen, pouring himself what looked to be a glass of scotch. Chance wondered if it was the first of the day or if his father was already well on his way to numbing his feelings.

Chance walked to a chair opposite his mother and sat. "So, maybe we should talk."

Ann lifted her swollen, red eyes to meet his. "You told me to shut up and go inside. So, that's what I've done. Don't tell me to talk now like I'm a dog you expect to obey your commands."

"I did not tell you to shut up," Chance replied with an edge, trying hard to control his anger.

Hugh sighed as he entered the room, gulping a large quantity of his drink. "Ann, we need to talk if we want to understand what's going on." He turned to Chance. "Your mother is upset, son."

Chance couldn't squelch the irritation that was rising once more. "Oh, I'm aware of that, Dad. Mom makes sure that everyone knows when she's pissed off. Nice way to meet the guys I'm seeing."

Hugh clenched the glass tighter and grimaced. "You're seeing…*both of them*?" Chance could tell from his father's reaction that his mother had not yet disclosed that part of the revelation. Hugh shook his head like he was confused, then walked to an empty leather lounger and sat, placing the near-empty glass on a side table. "Chance…"

"Now do you understand, Hugh?" Ann asked with annoyance. "If I had listened to you, we wouldn't have found out any of this."

"Because we should be happy to know?" Hugh asked.

"Of course not," Ann responded, shaking her head. "I'm sick about it."

Marybeth, who had been sitting in the corner of the room with a worried expression, spoke up. "Mom, you don't have a right to be angry about Chance being…gay?"

"I'm not gay," Chance countered. "I'm surprised by my attraction to them, too. I guess I'm bisexual." He pursed his lips, mulling how to continue. When nobody said more, he wiped a hand along his jaw. "Anyway, why is there an issue? I get to choose who to be with."

Hugh interrupted with a bitter laugh. "Chance…it's two men! I mean, come on. If you said you were screwing *one* man, it would have been surprising enough. You'd never led us to believe you were anything but straight. Now, you're telling us you're sleeping with *two* men? What are you expecting from us? A congratulations and questions about a wedding?"

Chance heard his mother moan as tears spilled. He wanted to empathize, but somehow her histrionics annoyed him far more than his father's questions. "Nobody said anything about a wedding."

Marybeth rose from her chair and stood by Chance in support. "Why are the two of you upset? Because Chance is bisexual? I thought you two supported LGBTQ rights, or is that only when it's someone else's kid?"

Hugh rubbed his temple. "Marybeth, maybe give us a heartbeat to adjust to the news, will you? I get that your generation is all *let people live the way they want*, but let's be practical. This isn't a decision that sets up Chance for happiness. It's not about me thinking there's something wrong with him—it's about me not wanting a hard life for my son."

Ann removed her hand from her face long enough to chime in. "Just because I stand up to bullying and people being denied certain rights doesn't mean I want my son to be…bisexual." She focused on Chance. "You should be marrying a nice girl and starting a family. If you're bisexual, as you claim, then you're *making a choice* to be with men. Why? You must even doubt it's the right thing if you went on a date with a girl last night. Why don't you give her a chance?"

"The girl you slut-shamed for being a one-night stand?" Chance reminded her. "The one you couldn't even bring yourself to call a date? But she's sounding good to you now, huh? Well, sorry, Mom. She was fictitious. I was with Arlo and Charlie."

Ann narrowed her reddened eyes. "Just how many times have you lied to us, Chance? Even your boyfriend from the website called you out for being a liar."

Hugh coughed on a sip of the scotch, looking at Ann with wide eyes. "What? One of the neighbors was the guy you told me you saw…half-naked…on Chance's computer?"

Ann grimaced. "Yes, Hugh. Your son is dating a gay porn actor. It just keeps getting better, doesn't it?"

"Mom, stop," Marybeth pleaded. "Just because Chance's boyfriend does that, it doesn't mean he isn't nice."

"Marybeth, nice people don't do *that*. My God, am I so wrong to want my son to start a normal family?" Ann protested.

"I don't want a family, Mom," Chance answered. "That's *your* dream for me. It's never been mine."

"And what is your dream, Chance?" Hugh asked with enough of a sarcastic tone that Chance knew what would follow would annoy him. "To screw around with adult film stars? What's next? You quit your job and join your buddies on their site?"

Chance had to listen to his mother groan again, followed by sobs. "They're not porn actors, Dad. Charlie is a doctor. Arlo works in a nursing home..."

"*And* on a gay site," Hugh reiterated. "How can you be with someone like that?"

"You're beginning to sound as judgmental as Mom. You don't know his past. You don't know what he's had to endure. And he doesn't have sex with men on the site," Chance explained. "And even if he did, who is he hurting?"

"You," Ann snapped. "They preyed on you and now you're having sex with them."

"Is that how you see gay people, Mom? Sexual predators?" Chance shouted. "They didn't *prey* on me. I'm not some naïve child. I've been with a man before."

Ann re-hid her face with her hand.

"Chance, stop yelling." Hugh sighed. "You must see how shocking all of this is. It's like we don't even know you."

"He's still the same person," Marybeth countered. "What difference does it make who he loves?"

"Don't make it worse, Marybeth. He didn't say he loved them," Hugh responded before turning to his son. "You aren't in love with them, are you?"

"I don't know. Maybe..."

"Listen," Hugh interjected. "If you aren't sure, then break it off before you do fall in love. Your mother has a point. If you like women as well as men, you'll be better off dating girls. If you fall in love with these two guys, where will that leave you?"

"Lucky enough to have two men who care about him in return," Marybeth answered.

"I wasn't talking to you," Hugh admonished before returning his gaze to Chance. "Son…think about how hard you'd be making your life."

"My life already was difficult, Dad," Chance replied. "My job is stressful and…I was lonely. Arlo and Charlie make my life better."

Ann began to rise from the chair. "I've heard enough. It's obvious you don't *want* to change."

Hugh grimaced, wiping both hands over his face. "Ann, would you sit down? Everybody needs to take a breath." He gave Chance a conciliatory look. "Okay, so you're bisexual. It's unexpected, but son, you could have told us. Is that the reason you moved to San Francisco?"

Chance rolled his eyes. "Dad, there are LGBTQ people in Missouri, too. No, I didn't move here because of that. I came here for the job opportunity." Chance didn't want to mention how his relationship with his next-door neighbors was likely going to end said job.

Hugh nodded. "So, the city might have presented more opportunity to meet others like you. Is that fair to say? But, Chance, I'm sure the city has plenty of beautiful single women, too. You haven't addressed what I've been asking. Why make your life tougher by dating a man? Or worse, two men? I want to understand. I want to be supportive, but I'm baffled."

Ann glared at her husband. "Hugh, what are you doing? You're making it too easy for him to dig in his heels about being with men when you tell him you're supportive." She turned to Chance. "If you were gay, I would be heartbroken, but I would understand that there's nothing I could do. I'd tell you to at least find a nice man. But you aren't gay, and you aren't with *one nice man,* so I am not supportive." Ann retrieved a tissue from her pocket to wipe her nose. "This wasn't the surprise I wanted when we came here. I'm going to our room to pack our things. I'll leave your birthday present on the bureau. Open it when we're gone. I don't think I can bring myself to celebrate anything right now."

As she left the room in the direction of the stairs to the guest bedroom, Hugh exhaled, then finished off the scotch. He settled the glass on the table and stared at a wall for minutes while his children sat in silence. Finally, he returned his gaze to his son. "Chance, this isn't like you wanting a motorcycle when your mother is trying to convince you to buy a safe automobile. Are you ready to choose these two men over her?"

"Dad, that's so unfair of you to ask him that," Marybeth complained. "Maybe you should be asking Mom if she's willing to give up Chance if he wants to be with the men he loves." She pulled Chance into a protective half-embrace.

Chance's eyes stung with tears as his father's question registered, and he looked away from him so he wouldn't lose control of his emotions. "I don't know what will happen with Arlo and Charlie, but if they still want me after the cluster-fuck that happened outside, then I still want them. I don't want to lose you and Mom. Marybeth is right, though. It's you and Mom that have a choice to make…not me. I've tried to live the life you two wanted for the last thirty-three years. I want to start living for myself now."

Hugh went quiet for a few more moments before emitting a small laugh. "Interesting choice of words…cluster-fuck. Now, unfortunately, I have an image in my head."

"Jesus, Dad!" Chance grimaced.

Hugh held up a hand in apology. "Okay, son, I'm trying. I'm troubled…for all the reasons I stated. It's a lot to take in." He paused before proceeding. "Chance, I don't love it…but I love you. I don't want to push you away. That's something I wouldn't be able to bear. Please understand this is a hard adjustment for me, but I'll do my best to be supportive."

"Really?" Chance gasped.

Hugh nodded. "Son, I'm not giving you my blessing on this. I still fear this won't end well and you're going to get hurt. Forget that they're men—it's still *two* people, Chance. A relationship with one person is hard enough, believe me. But I'll be there for you when things fall apart." When Chance frowned, Hugh shot him an apologetic look. "*If* they fall apart."

Chance tried to ignore his father's pessimistic view of the situation and focus instead on his caring words. "And Mom?"

Hugh sighed. "I'll work on her. She doesn't deal well with change—especially when it doesn't conform to her ways of thinking. Don't expect her to feel better about this by tomorrow." Chance nodded with understanding. "Maybe Marybeth and I can get her on board by the holidays."

"That's months from now," Chance pointed out.

Hugh huffed a sarcastic laugh. "You're right. We shouldn't be optimistic." Chance frowned, not enjoying the joke.

Hugh rose from the chair, picking up the empty glass to take to the kitchen. "Chance, she *does* love you. Give me some time to help her realize what she's sacrificing if she can't reconcile herself to this."

Chance rose from his own seat and walked to his father, pulling him into an embrace. "Dad, I know this isn't easy for you. Thank you…for this."

Hugh gave three strong pats to his son's back. "Just be careful, son. Don't do anything…unsafe."

Chance barked a laugh. "Dad, you don't need to lecture me on that. And as I said, Charlie's a doctor. He wouldn't allow us to be unsafe."

"Okay, son," Hugh appeased, clapping his hand on Chance's shoulder before leaving to the kitchen, then to the guest room.

Chance walked back over to Marybeth to embrace her, as well. "Thanks, sis. It means everything that you had my back like you did."

Marybeth returned the hug and laughed. "Hey, you've had mine plenty of times with Mom. Glad to return the favor. And for what it's worth, I think it's amazing you're into men and that you're in a relationship with two of them. I'm so jealous. Are they cute?"

Chance grinned. "God, don't let Mom here you talk like that. And yeah…well, Charlie is super handsome. Arlo…he's *beautiful*. Yeah, cute, for sure."

"You're blushing," Marybeth teased. "I'm happy for you. In fact, maybe I should move to this city. If your ugly mug could land two hot men, then maybe I could give it a try."

Chance laughed with relief. "Uh, I think you've forgotten this is San Francisco. The odds are against it, sis."

Marybeth snickered at that. "Hmm, well, I'm bored with Missouri and you know me—telling me something is impossible just makes me want to prove people wrong."

Chance pulled her back to him. "That would be awesome, Marybeth. At least come back to visit. I want you to meet my guys."

As soon as he said it, Chance felt a sudden wave of sadness, remembering how he'd left things with Arlo and Charlie. Maybe they weren't his any longer.

* * * *

Chance could only feel depression the next morning as his family got in a cab for the airport. He had hoped that they would talk more over dinner the previous evening, but his mother had complained that she wasn't hungry and she'd stayed in the guest room the rest of the day. Marybeth and his father had joined him for sandwiches, but they said no more about Charlie and Arlo, focusing instead on safe topics like sports and the goings-on of extended family members.

Chance's mother had let him hug her goodbye, though she had stood somewhat motionless as he had done so. His father had pulled him into a farewell embrace, however, and given his son a parting glance that Chance knew was a reminder of his father's promise. Marybeth had kissed his cheek and asked him not to worry about them—to just focus on making things right with Arlo and Charlie. He'd thanked her again for her support and told her he loved her, and she'd repeated the sentiment before climbing into the taxi.

After the cab was out of his sight, Chance glanced over to Arlo and Charlie's house, hoping one or both would be outside and willing to talk to him. Instead, Chance saw an empty yard and couldn't make out activity behind the windows.

He dejectedly walked back up the stairs to his front door and crashed on his living room sofa as soon as he returned inside. Because he hadn't slept well the prior night, he drifted into sleep within minutes.

Chance was awakened a couple of hours later by the ping on his cell phone. When he looked to see the incoming text, he felt the blood rush from his head. The message was from his firm's HR department informing him that he would be receiving an overnight letter that would explain his official termination from the company and how they would pack and ship his personal belongings to him. The message elaborated that if he signed the letter waiving legal recourse, he would receive four weeks of severance even though he was being fired for cause. There was also a reminder that, upon hiring, Chance had signed a non-compete agreement, meaning he was forbidden from seeking employment with area marketing firms.

The news was the worst scenario Chance could have imagined, and his body shook as he re-read the text message. Chance knew he should contact Elijah, but he was too fragile to talk to anyone in that moment.

"How much do you expect me to bear right now?" he cried at nobody, since he didn't believe in a higher being. Tears streamed down his face. He shut down the phone and threw it over to another chair, not wanting to think about additional painful messages that might come his way. Even though it was still late morning, Chance went to the refrigerator and retrieved a six-pack of beer, fully intent on finishing every can before lunch time.

Hours passed and Chance never moved from the sofa. His only exercise was reaching down for another full can of liquor and popping the top. Even needing to urinate couldn't nudge him from the couch. It was easier to fight the urge than to will his body to an upright position. Everything was too much effort, and all was pointless now that he had no job and had likely lost the men he loved. He couldn't even look to his own parents for comfort. Although his father would try to be helpful, he would feel compelled to share his mother's views on the situation, and Chance didn't want to give her the satisfaction of seeing his life in shambles because of his relationship with Arlo and Charlie.

When the sun began to set, Chance couldn't fight the need to pee any longer, and he reluctantly made his way to the bathroom. Once he was finished with what had to be done, he traipsed back to the kitchen to retrieve a bottle of wine. He didn't bother with a glass as he wasn't intending to share the contents with anyone.

Several more hours passed before Chance passed out in the darkness. Fleetingly he wondered if he had set the security alarm, but decided he didn't care. He was going to lose everything anyway, and he wasn't particularly concerned about his safety either.

When Chance awoke the next day, he felt sick and groggy but figured more alcohol would fix the problem. Chance had never been a heavy drinker, but he had plenty of liquor stashed for the parties he sometimes threw for co-workers.

After another day and night passed, Chance awoke on the sofa smelling horrible. A three-day beard itched his face, and even the roots of his hair hurt as if complaining that his scalp needed to be washed. He felt an urgency to piss again, but ignored it and fell back to sleep.

As the sun began to set once more, Chance moaned with pain. His lower back was throbbing, probably from the days of lying on the couch. When he could no longer fight the need to urinate, he forced himself up and grimaced. His mind clouded and he felt dizzy. Chills like those he had experienced with his bout of appendicitis recurred, making him wonder if the surgeons had messed something up.

When he went into the bathroom, he noticed his reflection had the same ghastly white pallor as he had when his appendix nearly burst. This time, he looked even worse, as he was sweaty, dirty and unkempt. He walked over to the toilet to relieve his bladder, and he was shocked when his urine came out in little dribs and drabs, feeling like someone was slicing his urethra with razor blades with each passing drop.

"God! What the fuck now!" Chance yelled, grabbing the wall in front of him with his left hand, trying to stabilize his wobbly body.

He considered contacting Charlie, but he wasn't sure the man would care what happened to him anymore. This time, he needed to call for an ambulance.

When he exited the bathroom, he made his way to the landline phone, but a wave of nausea, pain and lightheadedness hit him. He just needed to lie down for a few minutes, then he would make the call. The last thing he remembered was falling toward the floor.

Chapter Seventeen

"Chance? Chance, can you hear me?" Charlie's voice was asking from nearby, but Chance felt confused and sick, and his vision was blurry.

"Charlie, what's wrong with him?" Arlo's voice followed, sounding fearful and panicked. "Did they lie about removing his appendix?"

"Of course not," Charlie's voice responded. "Chance, can you open your eyes?"

Chance forced himself to obey the request, though the light felt too bright and made his head spin. He was glad when Charlie's face leaned closer to his, blocking some of the glare. "What's happening?" Chance managed with a croak.

"I'm not sure," Charlie answered too loudly. "I think you took a fall. We found you lying sprawled on the floor. An ambulance is on the way. Don't move."

"Hurts," Chance complained weakly. "Sick of getting sick…" He ignored Charlie's command and rolled onto his back. "I'm cold again." His teeth chattered to emphasize the point. Arlo had pulled a throw blanket from Chance's sofa and handed it to Charlie who immediately swaddled Chance with it.

"You have another infection," Charlie explained. "Why, I'm not sure."

Charlie was glancing around the room disapprovingly, no doubt seeing empty beer cans and wine bottles strewn about. Chance grimaced. "I was drinking a little…"

Charlie ran a soothing hand over Chance's sweaty, unshaven jaw. "Yes. Maybe more than a little, huh?"

"How did you get in here?" Chance wondered.

Arlo's face came closer and he peered down at Chance, unable to hide his anxiety. "Do you remember that you gave me the code to your door-lock when you moved in? In case of an emergency?"

"Good thing you did, too," Charlie added. "We were getting worried. We'd been texting and calling for the last couple of days to no answer."

"I knew you were home," Arlo said. "I admit, I was watching the house, hoping I'd see you exit so I could pretend to run into you. But you never left, and the house was dark every night. Then we started calling and there was no answer…"

Chance's mind was still muddled. Trying to keep up with Arlo's rapid cadence was making his head hurt more. He was saved from responding by the sound of more individuals entering the house.

"What's his name?" one of the people in uniform asked Charlie and Arlo.

"Chance. Chance Findley," Charlie responded. "He's our neighbor and…friend. I'm Dr. Kendall."

Chance saw a very handsome, kind-faced man look to him with compassion. "Chance, my name is Pietro and I'm a paramedic. I'm going to help you. Did you have a fall?"

"I'm not sure. Was feeling sick..."

Pietro was helping a female paramedic place Chance on a gurney. "Okay, we're taking you to the hospital now. Everything will be fine." Pietro gave him an encouraging smile and a wink, and it made him more comfortable. He hoped he could ride in peace in the ambulance.

"Can I stop talking now?" Chance murmured.

There was a pause before he felt Charlie's hand wrap around his. "Sure, Chance."

* * * *

When Chance was brought into the emergency room, he was feeling better from whatever they had been pumping into him on the drive over. When he was led to the patient examining room, he could have sworn it was the same he had visited during his appendicitis. He mused that he should move some of his personal belongings in since he was there so often.

"The nurse will be here in a second to tend to you, Chance." Pietro smiled warmly, placing his big hand over Chance's. "And your friends are being allowed to stay in the room with you. It helps that one of them is a doctor." Pietro winked again. The man was like an angel that was making everything feel better.

"Thanks," Chance whispered. "You're really nice."

Chance heard Charlie chime in. "Thank you for everything, Pietro. What is your last name? I'd like to provide a commendation to your supervisor."

Chance had to resist warning Pietro that Charlie's commendations led to people losing their jobs. He heard Pietro respond with something and thank Charlie before leaning back over his patient. "I'll be checking on you, big guy. You get better."

Big guy? Chance found it to be an odd endearment, considering the paramedic was almost as big as Charlie. He watched Charlie and Arlo smile in Pietro's direction as he was leaving the room and he felt jealous.

"Are you thinking he can be your new third guy?" Chance muttered, remembering that the two might only view Chance as their neighbor and former lover now.

Charlie's and Arlo's heads swiveled in his direction, and each of their smiles turned to frowns.

"Chance, why would you say that?" Arlo asked.

Chance shrugged. Though he was feeling more alert since being pumped with antibiotics, his head still hurt, making it uncomfortable to have a discussion. "Never mind."

Charlie scooched closer to Chance and took his hand in his. "Chance Findley, I think your head is still a little wonky if you think we're looking to replace you."

Chance was using his left hand to grip the blanket they had laid over him, fidgeting with it. "After what happened…you both were angry and…"

"I overreacted," Arlo cut in, coming to the other side of the table on which Chance was lying. Arlo took Chance's other hand in his. "It was just that your sneakiness and being less than forthcoming reminded me of how Wilson treated me. But, Chance, you aren't Wilson. I had to remind myself of that."

Charlie ran a hand through Chance's greasy, unwashed hair. "And I shouldn't have compared you to him, either. There's a big difference between giving into the temptation to watch our beautiful Arlo naked versus repeatedly cheating on him and me."

Arlo brushed his thumb across the top of Chance's hand. "I would have done the same thing if it had been you that told me you had an account on that website. I would have felt guilty, but I wouldn't have been able to resist either. It makes me realize you were panting for me sooner than you let on."

Arlo had said the last sentence with a chuckle, but Chance didn't believe he deserved to be let off the hook so easily. "I *did* feel guilty. For so long. I wanted to tell you, Arlo. I really did, but I was afraid you wouldn't forgive me."

"I do forgive you," Arlo whispered, bending his neck so he could kiss Chance's forehead.

Chance glanced at Charlie sadly. "And I betrayed you by telling Arlo your secrets. I did it in anger, and it makes me a shit."

Charlie chuckled. "Yeah, I did think you were a little shit in that moment. But you were right. I was being a hypocrite, and since I was throwing you under the bus in front of Arlo, I can't blame you for what you did. I'm glad the truth is out there, to be honest. I don't want secrets between us. And we need to be better at cutting each other slack when we aren't perfect. You were already dealing with the drama of your mother, and it was a lousy time for us to add to your stress. It was insensitive of me and I'm sorry, too."

Chance nodded. "It's okay. I guess so much was happening, you know? Between thinking you guys wouldn't forgive me, my mother treating me like I'm some degenerate then losing my job…"

"What?" Charlie and Arlo shouted in unison.

"The firm knows we're dating," Chance explained, looking at Charlie. "They insinuated lots of shit about the motives for the commendation you gave me. The reason I had come home early on my birthday is because they told me to leave. I received the text the next day that they decided to can me."

"Oh God, Chance. Now I really feel bad about being so hard on you. So this is why you were drinking so much," Charlie said.

"I guess," Chance responded. "I knew I was being a melodramatic ass, self-indulging in my misery. I'm not proud of it. At the time, I didn't care. I wanted to stop thinking for a while."

"Jesus." Arlo exhaled. "You could have stopped thinking altogether if we hadn't checked up on you, Chance. Don't do stupid crap again, and don't deal with huge problems like that alone. It kills me that you were afraid to come to us after our argument. Chance Findley, unless I tell you I'm through with you, which I can't even imagine, you are one of the two most important people in my life. So, whether I'm angry with you or not, trust that I would never turn you away when you need me."

"Me either," Charlie added. "We'll get you a good lawyer, Chance. They can't fire you for dating me."

"I already have one," Chance replied. "Although I haven't called him yet. Too busy self-destructing."

"Hello?" A nurse announced herself, clearing a path to make her way to Chance's side, effectively pushing Arlo into a side-chair.

The nurse hurled a slew of questions at Chance until a doctor also made an appearance, asking most of the same questions again. Chance patiently answered each, embarrassed to what he was admitting, especially in front of Arlo and Charlie.

When more of the examination was completed and the doctor recorded his notes, he turned to Chance with a reprimanding expression. "Young man, you made quite a problem for yourself. Essentially, you had alcohol poisoning, dehydration from lack of water, weakness from not eating, a urinary tract infection from those poor decisions and not listening to your body when it was telling you it needed to release excess fluid—then that caused a backflow infection to your kidneys."

"Is that why my lower back hurt so much?" Chance asked.

"I'm certain." The doctor nodded. "Maybe that and not getting off a sofa for days. I don't mean to be rude, but have you even washed or brushed your teeth since you started this drinking binge?"

Chance wondered if the scruff hid the reddening of his face. "Um, no. I don't think so."

The doctor turned to Charlie. "Is there a pattern of excessive drinking?"

Charlie shook his head. "No, I can assure you. Chance just had a lot of terrible news hit him all at the same time. He's not an alcoholic."

The on-duty doctor frowned. "Your body is responding well to the antibiotics. I'll write you a prescription for more, and you need to follow the directions on the label until every last pill is gone. When you get home, take better care of yourself. There are healthy ways to manage stressful situations."

"Thanks, Doctor," Chance mumbled with shame as the doctor walked out to the hall.

Arlo placed a consoling hand on Chance's arm. "Okay, he was not as nice as Pietro. You don't smell *that* bad."

Charlie chuckled. "Um, actually, you do, Chance." Chance winced. "It's okay, baby. Come on. We'll take you back to our place and get you all fresh and pretty again."

Chance held up his hand in protest. "I...don't know. Charlie, I can't just go back to living with you guys. I have things I need to figure out. I don't know how I'm going to support myself or even pay for these hospital bills. I don't know what to say to my mother to make things right with her. I need to call the lawyer." He paused and wiped a hand over his oily face. "What I'm saying is, I'm nothing but a problem right now, and if you want me to feel good about myself, I need to fix more than just my hygiene. I can't move back in with you and feel like...a burden again."

Charlie and Arlo exchanged glances, then Charlie ran a hand along Chance's cheek. "Chance, you weren't a burden the first time you came to us. And what's great about having our relationship is the care we can give each other. Do you really think Arlo and I can be comfortable in our home knowing you're next door dealing with all of these things by yourself? Why would you need to? We want to help. We're a team. You know you'd be saying the same thing to me or Arlo if the tables were reversed."

"But they never are..."

"Chance, one day you will have that opportunity because we all need a little help sometimes," Charlie continued. "You're no problem—you're a blessing. You're a gift that we never expected to receive." He donned a mischievous grin. "Maybe a stinky one right now, but we love you all the same. And nothing will make you feel better about yourself than me and Arlo showing you how much we admire your beauty, and how much we love your company, and...how much we love *you*. Come on. Stop being stubborn. You've been enough of a pain today. Just come home with us."

Chance leaned his head into the crux of Charlie's arm and basked in the comfort of Arlo's hand stroking his back. "Okay, Charlie. Thank you."

Chapter Eighteen

Chance allowed Charlie to help him in the shower while Arlo busied himself making dinner. Once he was clean and a towel was wrapped around his waist, Chance told Charlie he didn't need more help. Charlie shook his head and insisted on shaving Chance's scruffy face.

"I know how to shave," Chance complained, wondering if Charlie viewed him as helpless now that he'd made so many serious errors in judgment.

"Just let me take care of you, will you?" Charlie asked. "Lean against the sink and I'll be quick."

Chance reminded himself that one of Charlie's pleasures was caring for the men he loved, and he didn't want to be like Wilson—pushing the man away because he misread his intentions.

Charlie lathered Chance's face and, like the surgeon he was, he skillfully and carefully began shaving Chance with an old-fashioned sharp razor. Chance focused on his reflection instead of Charlie's face—the man's adoring expression was arousing Chance, pushing the front of the towel he wore against the edge of the sink.

"There's my handsome Chance," Charlie cooed as he neared the end of his task.

"I'm glad you at least let me brush my own teeth," Chance pretended to gripe.

"Shh," Charlie soothed. "Don't move your face. I don't want to cut you."

Chance obeyed until Charlie grunted approval at his work, then pressed a hot washcloth over Chance's freshly exposed skin and wiped away the remnants of shaving cream. Chance smiled a bit, happy to look like his old self again.

After a few seconds, Chance narrowed his eyes with displeasure. "My face looks like I lost weight."

"Hmm," Charlie concurred. "You have lost weight. I could see that when you stripped down for the shower. It's just water-loss. You'll gain it right back. Don't worry. You're still the hottest guy in the room."

Chance blushed and shook his head. "I don't think so…"

Charlie leaned in to kiss Chance's cheek. "I *know* so, baby. You're a James Dean kind of handsome, and a few pounds more or less isn't going to change that."

"I have no idea who James Dean is. Wait, do you mean the guy who hawks breakfast sausage?" Chance worried.

Charlie chuckled. "Stop limiting your viewing to crappy television programs and watch some old classic movies. Maybe we can watch one together tonight."

"You mean, something starring the sausage-maker when he was younger?" Chance asked with bewilderment.

Charlie pursed his lips. "I'm not talking about the sausage maker! That's *Jimmy* Dean. I think he was an actor too, but *James* Dean was a very famous actor."

"He couldn't have been *that* famous," Chance muttered, turning his head away from Charlie, pretending he didn't want him to hear. "You and Arlo with your old movies…"

Charlie smirked before moving behind Chance and putting his arms around the man's frame. They both spent a moment looking at their reflections. It was the first time Chance had seen himself lovingly embraced by another man, and he found he liked it. Charlie's muscular, hairy arms pressed against his own sculpted chest looked artistic and erotic. Chance stiffened more at the sight.

Charlie brought his arms back to his sides then slid his hands up the back of Chance's thighs and under Chance's towel. He began to massage Chance's buttocks, occasionally spreading them, making Chance feel exposed even though he was covered by the cloth.

"I want to be inside you, Chance, if you'll let me," Charlie whispered. "I want to make you feel good."

Chance sighed in pleasure at the touch of Charlie's hands. If he had doubts before, they were quickly dissipating. Seeing the reflection of Charlie's want mirroring his own made him fully erect.

"But Arlo's downstairs…" Chance managed.

Charlie removed his hands and brought them to Chance's shoulders while kissing Chance's neck several times. "Chance, I didn't mean right now. And yes, with Arlo. When the three of us are physically in the same city, we include each other. That's the rule."

Chance nodded. He liked the rule.

Charlie smiled before lifting Chance's towel and lightly smacking his bum. "Get dressed. It smells like dinner is almost ready."

Chance saw in the mirror that his face flushed, probably the same soft pink of the palm print Charlie left on his ass. Charlie grinned smugly and exited the bathroom.

* * * *

Even though the three men were staying home to eat, Chance decided to wear one of his designer dress shirts that he had brought to the guest room of Arlo and Charlie's house. After they had endured seeing Chance at his worst, he wanted to look his best. He groomed his hair to its usual style, but it had never looked better. He figured not having washed it for days had brought back luster and smoothness. Chance left the first few buttons of his white shirt undone, letting some of his chest hair show. After indulging his momentary narcissism in front of the mirror, Chance retrieved his most expensive trousers from the closet. They were fine wool, and he knew they hugged his assets nicely.

When he entered the kitchen, both Charlie and Arlo ceased their discussion and gazed at him with awe and surprise.

"Chance! You look…wow." Arlo smiled.

"As always, Arlo finds the one word that says everything." Charlie grinned. "You are stunning, Chance."

Chance cast his eyes down, a little embarrassed by the praise, but happy that his efforts paid off. "Thanks. It's all relative. Anything would look better than I did earlier today."

Arlo bounded round the kitchen island and pulled Chance into an embrace. "Not true, Chance. You're always attractive, even when you smell like the guy who cleans the nursing home's bedpans."

Chance puffed a laugh. "Gee, thank you?"

"You're welcome," Arlo replied, unaware of Chance's sarcasm. He pulled his friend closer to give him a brief kiss. "I've missed being able to do that. I couldn't wait for you to brush your teeth. It teaches me a lesson for wasting time trying to show you I was angry with you. I love you."

There was the L-word again, and Chance didn't feel he needed to run. Despite his mother's words echoing in his head, being with Arlo and Charlie felt right.

The men avoided troubling topics during dinner, opting instead to enjoy each other's company. When the meal was over, Chance laughed as Arlo gave directions to him and Charlie on where to store the dishes.

"What's so funny?" Arlo wondered.

"You're bossy in the kitchen," Chance explained. "It's cute."

Arlo smiled happily. "Well, everyone should get to be boss somewhere. In the case of you and Charlie, you can boss me in the bedroom. I'm very obedient." He batted his eyelashes and bit his lower lip for comical emphasis.

Chance almost dropped the glass he was drying. His mind rushed to an image of Charlie and him directing orders to Arlo and watching the man comply.

"I think you just broke Chance." Charlie laughed, retrieving the goblet from Chance's hand and drying it before putting it away in the cabinet.

"Huh? Oh," Chance stammered, realizing he had been standing motionless for a moment. "Just started thinking about something."

"I'll bet." Arlo smirked. He turned to Charlie, feigning his submissive, childlike persona that he sometimes did with the man. "Is it too soon for us to play with Chance? He seems better now."

Charlie chuckled when both men watched him for a reaction, probably because Chance was mirroring Arlo's deferential behavior. "I think that's up to Chance."

Chance nodded emphatically. "I feel up to playing."

Charlie suppressed more laughter and donned a pretend, paternalistic expression of warning. "Are you sure? What I have in mind will require…stamina."

Chance wasn't certain what that meant, but he wasn't sure he cared. "My stamina is back."

Arlo let out a whoop, then ran over to Charlie and hugged him. "Thank you, Charlie. Can we do something right now?"

Charlie grabbed the back of Arlo's head and pulled him in for a kiss. "You're always such a horny little bunny." The corners of his mouth lifted. "You keep this old man young."

Arlo rolled his eyes. "Pfft. Yeah, so old."

Chance glanced between the two of them, unsure how to proceed. "Uh, should we go to the bedroom then?"

Charlie pursed his lips, shooting Chance a mysterious look. "I don't think so, Chance. I know you think you're ready, but as a physician, I have a responsibility to verify by thoroughly examining you." He turned to Arlo with a grin. "Would you be able to assist me, Arlo?"

Chance gasped as Arlo's eyes widened. "Yes, Dr. Kendall. I'd be happy to assist."

* * * *

Although Chance had been confident and eager, his will was beginning to falter as Charlie led him and Arlo down several stairs to the lowest level of the house. Chance had never ventured to that space while staying with his friends, assuming it was a storage room behind the garage, much like the layout of his own home. Now, in his mind, he conjured images from horror movies where unsuspecting victims were led to dark, basement places.

"Um, are we going to the garage?" Chance wondered.

Arlo turned his head back to smile at Chance. "Why would Charlie examine you in the garage?"

"You don't have a dungeon down there, do you?" Chance dared. They were near the bottom step, leaving minimal time to run.

Charlie's eyes widened in response. "Chance, you aren't afraid of us, are you?" He walked back up two steps to caress Chance's cheek. "Arlo and I would never, ever hurt you." He narrowed his eyes emphatically. "*Ever*. Trust me. There's nothing scary behind the door."

Chance nodded, sighing with relief. "I'm sorry. I do trust you. I was letting my imagination get the best of me."

They descended the final steps to the room that was behind the garage. When Charlie opened the door, Chance peered around the larger man's frame to see inside. He gasped when Arlo turned on the light switch. The room was set up like an OB-GYN's office, including the examining chair with attached stirrups.

"What the actual fuck?" Chance asked.

Charlie chuckled. "I have first-aid supplies in here in case I ever did have reason to administer emergency care to Arlo—and now you. But truthfully, Arlo and I use it for occasional role-play. Sometimes, it isn't a doctor's office at all. It's an interrogation room for a naughty spy or suspected drug smuggler."

Laughter poured from Arlo as he watched Chance wrap his mind around what he was seeing and hearing. "You're so cute, Chance. You should see yourself. I'm thinking you'd rather it had been that dungeon."

"What?" Chance stammered. "Uh, no. I'm just…wow. Where did you get the examination chair?"

Charlie shrugged. "I'm a doctor. It's pretty easy for me to order." He put a soothing hand on Chance's shoulder. "It's okay if this is too much for you. We can go back upstairs. It's just that Arlo told me about the conversations you had when you first met. How you'd like your sex to occasionally be less traditional. And you had said at the restaurant that you could get into some role-play…"

Chance looked to Arlo and he could see the man was hopeful, but he knew he would be supportive if Chance declined. The only reason he had doubts was the imaginary voices of others judging him that echoed in his brain. But those people weren't actually here—Charlie and Arlo were. And Chance would regret it if he became a coward and walked away.

"Okay," Chance whispered.

"Okay?" Charlie asked.

Chance half-grinned. "Okay, let's take advantage of your setup here."

Charlie put a comforting arm around Chance. "Listen, if at any point you want to stop, you just say so. This is about having fun. If at any time it isn't, tell me."

Chance nodded shakily. "Sure."

Charlie laughed. "You're a shy, good boy who wants to be dirty."

Arlo rubbed Chance's back. "Chance, would it be easier if I was naked too, so you don't feel all the attention is on you?"

"Yeah. Please," Chance agreed right away.

Charlie quirked an eyebrow. "Arlo, since you like us to get into character, what possible storyline has you—my assistant—also getting naked? Not that I object, mind you."

Arlo hummed as he contemplated. "Maybe, because your new patient is so shy, you encourage your assistant to take off his clothes, too. Chance just said that would make him more comfortable. It's plausible."

Even Chance laughed at the absurdity of that. "Only in an X-rated film."

Charlie lifted Chance's chin. "And you don't want this to turn into a graphic sex scene?"

Arlo snickered once more when Chance's mouth opened and closed. Arlo then outlined a story. "So, it's settled. Dr. Kendall has a new, shy patient who needs a very thorough exam. The poor boy hasn't been feeling much sensation when he ejaculates, and he wants to know what's wrong. Enter me—assistant Arlo—who agrees to drop his clothes to make the client more comfortable."

Charlie laughed. "Arlo, you have quite the imagination." He stroked Chance's cheek. "So, we'll get into character. It will be easier for you to pretend to be someone else when you're trying new things that might scare you a bit. But as I said, if at any point you want to stop, just say the word, and the real us will be right here supporting your decision."

Chance swallowed hard. A part of his brain was nixing the idea as silly, but it was losing a battle to his pumping heart and excitement below the waist. "Okay."

"So, Chance, I'm Dr. Kendall and this is my assistant, Arlo. What brings you here today?" Charlie asked.

Oh, the role-play is already starting. Chance gulped and shot glances between the two men, impressed that they had donned serious, clinical expressions. "Um, I'm having a little problem in the plumbing area?"

Charlie's expression remained neutral. "I'm sorry to hear that. What problem, specifically, are you having?"

Chance was embarrassed, even though the issue was fabricated. "Um, I can get it up, but when I come, it doesn't feel as good as it used to."

"I see," Charlie replied with feigned concern. "Well, a man your age shouldn't be experiencing diminished pleasure. Do you find this happens with partners, by yourself or both?"

Chance almost rolled his eyes. *Are they staging a medical documentary or getting to the sex?* "Uh, both."

Charlie pointed to the exam chair. "Why don't you undress, Chance? Then sit up there so we can figure out what's going on."

Chance glanced at Arlo, wondering if he was still planning to undress first. "Um, I'm kind of shy about just getting naked in front of...*two* people. It's..."

"Like playing the game 'one of these things is not like the other'?" Charlie mused.

Chance chuckled. "Yeah, I guess that's it."

Charlie turned to Arlo. "Arlo, we've had this situation before. It helped when you removed your clothing as well. Would you be kind enough to do that for Chance?"

Arlo blinked an assent, his expression remaining stoic. "Whatever is best for the patient, Dr. Kendall."

Charlie returned his gaze to Chance, who was now sitting on the edge of the chair. "Would that be better for you, Chance?"

Chance felt his mouth go dry and he licked his lips. "Um, yes. Thank you, Arlo. That would make me feel better."

"No problem, Chance," Arlo replied, revealing the slightest hint of a smile. He lifted the pullover from his hips and rode the shirt up over his torso and head, dropping it onto a nearby chair. Chance admired his chest as much as the first time he'd seen it.

"Thank you, Arlo," Charlie said, straight-faced. "I appreciate how you'll always…rise to the occasion."

Arlo smirked at the pathetic joke, unbuckled his belt, unzipped his trousers then pushed them down to his ankles. Since he hadn't been wearing shoes, it was easy for him to slide off the pants altogether. He hooked his thumbs into the waistband of his briefs and pushed them off as well. Arlo's hard cock bounced up, facing Chance.

"Sorry about the erection, Dr. Kendall," Arlo stated. "I can't deny that I'm aroused by being in the same room as two handsome men. I hope that's okay."

Charlie shook his head to indicate Arlo shouldn't worry. "Nothing to be embarrassed about, Arlo. You're a young man with a healthy sex drive." He turned to Chance. "Does it bother you, Chance?"

Chance was eyeing Arlo's body. "Huh? No. I'm good."

Charlie smiled. "Your turn, Chance. Would you undress, please? You can hand the garments to Arlo. He'll fold them and place them on the side-chair for you."

Chance didn't waste time unbuttoning his shirt, pulling it open and handing it to Arlo. Arlo did, in fact, fold the garment and place it on the nearby chair. Chance unbuckled and unzipped his trousers, pushing both them and the boxers down with one gesture. Charlie bent down to Chance's calves and slid them the rest of the way down Chance's legs and off his feet.

"Uh, sorry I have a boner too, Doc. I told you I didn't have a problem getting it up." Chance laughed.

Charlie gave him a warm smile. "It certainly appears that you don't, though I think it's not as rigid as a young man should be able to achieve."

Chance frowned. "Oh. Well, I don't think it's as hard as it can get…yet."

Charlie nodded. "Perhaps. If it doesn't get firmer, I'll try some stimulation techniques to see if that helps. In the meantime, I'm going to listen to your heart and lungs to make sure all is well." Charlie reached for a stethoscope that was set atop a wall-length counter.

Chance couldn't help but drop from character for a moment. "You're really going to examine me?"

Charlie raised his eyebrows in surprise. "Well, of course, Chance. Now, just sit still and I'll check your heartbeat." Charlie pressed the stethoscope to Chance's chest, using his free hand to graze Chance's right nipple. "Sounds normal. Now, I'm going to listen to your lungs. Take a deep breath each time I put the stethoscope to your chest or back, okay?"

"Sure," Chance mumbled, wondering why this was a kink for Charlie, but decided to go along with the game. It became clear that it gave Charlie multiple opportunities to brush his fingers against Chance's chest and back. When Chance calmed and let himself enjoy being touched, his erection stiffened.

Charlie noticed, glancing at Chance's lap with satisfaction. "Ah, that's what I would expect to see, Chance. Look at you. Your penis is fully engorged now." He reached his hand down to give it a light squeeze, causing Chance to buck his hips. "Very good. Now, Chance, lie back so I can examine your stomach." As Chance reclined, Charlie moved to one side of the table and motioned for Arlo to take a position on Chance's other side.

"What do you want me to do, Dr. Kendall?" Arlo asked.

"Mirror my hand movements on your side of Chance's abdomen. We're just going to press softly to make sure it doesn't cause Chance discomfort. According to his medical records, Chance has had some recent issues here," Charlie informed him.

Chance held back a laugh, thinking it still a bit odd that Charlie was performing a real examination. His levity turned to arousal, though, as he felt both men caressing his stomach and massaging their way over his pubic area and into the crevices of his groin.

"Everything feels nice," Arlo reported. "I mean, everything feels problem-free, Dr. Kendall."

"No pain, Chance?" Charlie asked, smiling when Chance shook his head no. "Great. Arlo, give gentle squeezes up and down Chance's thighs and calves, just to make sure Chance doesn't have any joint pain."

The two men used the ploy to massage and caress Chance's legs.

"He has good musculature, Dr. Kendall," Arlo stated. "I don't see any problems."

Charlie grinned. "Everything I'm seeing looks good, too. Chance, I'm going to examine your testicles now. If you don't do so yourself, you should start checking for a lump each morning after your shower. In the event there was something of concern, it's best to detect it early." He didn't wait for Chance to respond. Charlie rolled each of Chance's balls in his hand, rubbing his thumb over the soft skin of Chance's scrotum.

"May I examine them too, Dr. Kendall? I'm thinking of getting my medical degree in urology," Arlo stated.

"Of course," Charlie responded, removing his hand so Arlo could begin examining.

Chance sighed as Arlo pretended to concentrate on the health of his nuts, using the exam as an excuse to play with them.

"The skin of his scrotum isn't as soft as when I first started examining it," Arlo noted with a mischievous grin.

Charlie smiled in return. "The sensation of your fingers is triggering arousal." He glanced back to Chance's face. "Nothing to be embarrassed about, Chance. It's what I would expect from a healthy, fit man. I think we can move on to your prostate. If it is enlarged, it could be contributing to your minimized sexual pleasure."

Chance gulped. He hadn't had anything other than Arlo's or Charlie's fingers and tongues in his ass, to-date. He wondered if Charlie was planning to use something larger to probe him. "Um, okay."

"Arlo, put Chance's foot in the stirrup closest to you, please," Charlie instructed as he took Chance's other foot and strapped it into the stirrup on his side. Once Chance was secured in place, Charlie looked to Chance to ensure he was still comfortable. "Good boy, Chance. Slide down the chair a bit so I can better access your rectum."

Chance bit his lower lip, but shimmied down the table, feeling utterly exposed when his thighs were pressed toward his abdomen. Charlie pulled the stirrups farther apart, opening Chance more. He flushed when both Charlie and Arlo scrutinized his hole.

"Dr. Kendall, I usually need to hide my displeasure when seeing someone's anus. Is it just me, or is Chance's fucking sexy?" Arlo asked.

"I can understand your less-than-professional reaction, Arlo," Charlie replied. "Chance's anus is beautiful. Now, we'll need to be careful. He looks tight to the point of being virginal." He cast his gaze back to the patient. "Chance, do you ever use sex toys to stimulate yourself?"

Chance flushed, looking at the two curious faces peering over his ass. "Uh...no."

"As I suspected." Charlie nodded. "I'll take my time and examine you with care."

"Can I help?" Arlo inquired with enthusiasm, causing Chance to chuckle despite the circumstances.

Charlie reached for a box of latex gloves and lubricant. After snapping the latex over his hand, he handed the box to Arlo so he could do the same. Charlie squirted a generous amount of lubricant into Chance, then used the tip of his finger to push back into Chance what had dripped out. Chance sucked in his breath, and Charlie rubbed his ungloved thumb over Chance's opening. "It's cold, I know. It will warm once I begin to stimulate you."

After Charlie lubed his gloved index finger, he inserted it to the knuckle, causing Chance's breath to hitch. When Chance calmed, Charlie used his fingertip to stretch the opening, causing Chance to writhe in pleasure. Charlie pressed all the way in, poking Chance's prostate. "Jesus," Chance gasped.

"You're doing very well, Chance," Charlie soothed. "The size of your prostate is normal. That said, I think you could benefit from it being massaged. Done frequently, it can help you achieve firmer erections and more satisfying ejaculations. There are even studies that suggest it could be helpful in preventing prostate cancer."

Chance blanched a bit. "So, you're going to keep poking me with your finger?"

Charlie frowned. "Well, I don't think that would be enough to qualify as a massage." He slid his finger back and forth, causing Chance to squirm. "You see, even though the lining of your rectum is sensitive, once you're used to the intrusion of a single finger, it stops feeling adequate. You'll want something larger that can give you adequate friction as well as greater pressure on your organ."

"You sure about that?" Chance wondered.

Arlo laughed. "Dr. Kendall gives me prostate massages all the time. I promise, it feels amazing."

Charlie stroked Arlo's hair. "And I enjoy administering them, Arlo. Chance's rectum is no longer resisting. I think it's time to insert another finger. Arlo, perhaps you should put in yours along with mine, then we can stretch Chance to ready him for the procedure."

Before Chance could question the merits of Charlie's plan, Arlo had lubed his finger and poked the tip into Chance's hole.

"God," Chance whined.

Charlie placed a soothing hand on the back of Chance's thigh. "Shh, Chance. He'll move slow. You'll find it pleasurable once you get past the initial burn."

After a moment, Arlo was able to make his way inside, and both Charlie and Arlo waited for Chance to stop spasming and panting. When he had relaxed a bit, the two men began to work over Chance's entrance to prepare him for more. In a short time, Chance was writhing and enjoying the sensation, especially when one or both of their fingers met his prostate.

"Feels good," he whimpered.

"That's great, Chance," Charlie whispered. "I think you're ready for the massage. For your first time, we'll make it as easy for you as possible. Perhaps it would help to stimulate your penis simultaneously? Since Arlo enjoys a deep prostate massage, if you are open to it, he could lower himself on your erection while I complete your procedure."

Chance's eyes widened. "Um, I think that might help."

Arlo chuckled, removing his finger from Chance's ass, then climbed up onto the exam chair with Chance so that he was on his hands and knees above the man. He brought his face down to Chance's and asked him if he was still doing okay. When Chance nodded, Arlo kissed him while inserting his still slicked, gloved finger in his own ass to stretch himself.

"That's good, Arlo and Chance. I think this will work well for both of you. Chance, typically, I use a vibrator for this, but Arlo took it home with him the other day and has forgotten to return it. If you permit, I can administer to you the same way you'll help Arlo."

Chance pulled his lips from Arlo's. "Uh, do you think I'm ready for that? I mean, for real?"

He heard Charlie grunt. "If I didn't think so, I wouldn't suggest it. We can stop any time you wish, Chance."

"It will be great, Chance. I promise," Arlo whispered out of character, pressing his lips back to Chance's. "I want you inside me so bad. And I want you to feel what I'm feeling while you have me. You won't find a better, more careful person than Charlie to have your first experience."

Chance couldn't argue that he wanted to be inside Arlo. As for being penetrated, he had to admit the double-digit probing had been way more pleasurable than he had expected. He found himself nodding assent to the plan. "Okay, Charlie. I trust you."

Charlie laughed. "On a first-name basis now, are we? Okay, I guess if I'm going to be intimate with you, it's only fair."

Chance had forgotten the role-play aspect of their shenanigans, but before he could dwell on his faux pas, Arlo lined up his opening against the tip of Chance's cock.

"I have lots of experience with this, Chance. You won't need to take in Dr. Kendall as quickly as I can slide down on you." Arlo winked, already guiding the head of Chance's shaft into his ass.

"Jesus, Arlo," Chance cried, grabbing Arlo's hips to help steady him as the man descended on Chance.

When Arlo was completely seated on Chance's lap, he leaned forward to kiss Chance once more. He pulled back, giving Chance an encouraging smile. "You feel so incredible, Chance. I love that you're filling me. I've been wanting this since I met you."

For his part, Chance's eyes were wide with amazement, his mouth slightly agape. "Arlo, it's...wow. You're so tight. I'm not hurting you?"

"No, Chance," Arlo assured him, leaning in for another kiss.

Chance could hear Charlie unzip his trousers and begin lubing himself. Then, Charlie began to lubricate Chance more with his fingers.

The pulsing motion in his ass caused Chance to lurch up, and he was rewarded with Arlo pressing down simultaneously. He'd never felt anything like the double sensation. Arlo began lifting and lowering himself. When he leaned forward again for more kissing, Chance closed the distance between the base of his dick and Arlo's ass by thrusting.

"So hot, guys," Charlie murmured, retracting his fingers from Chance. Chance whimpered a bit, even though his mouth was covered by Arlo's lips. He looked to Charlie and saw that he was smiling. "Chance, relax your buttock muscles as much as possible."

"Huh?" Chance muttered, not wanting to still himself when Arlo was giving him glorious friction.

Charlie lined up the head of his cock to Chance's hole and pushed in until his crown was embedded. Charlie peered around Arlo. "Chance? Are you okay?"

"I think so," Chance gasped.

"Kiss me again," Arlo demanded. "Focus on me while he enters you. It's going to sting for about thirty seconds, being your first time and all. Stay with it. The discomfort will turn to pleasure, and you won't feel any more pain after that. Just bliss. Ready?"

Chance nodded, figuring he was just as strong as Arlo, so he could take what his boyfriend could handle. Charlie pushed in more, and Chance wondered if Charlie was already fully immersed based on the sting and his body's desire to reject the intrusion. Chance took a deep breath, then pulled Arlo back down for a kiss. Arlo ran his fingers over Chance's nipples while their tongues tangled, and Charlie kissed one of Chance's calves and massaged his sack. Chance felt his channel ease its death grip around Charlie's dick. Once that happened, he experienced the sensation of Charlie sliding his whole self into him.

"Fuck," Chance cried out. He felt stretched and full.

"Deep breaths, Chance," Arlo soothed.

"You're doing so well, Chance," Charlie added. "I promise, it's all good from here on out. I'm going to give you nice, long strokes. Just relax. When it starts to feel good, begin to do the same for Arlo."

After a few thrusts, Charlie's cock was like the relief of scratching an itch coupled with the tingling of every nerve in his rectum. When the tip of Charlie's manhood bumped against Chance's prostate, it was as if someone was flicking on a high-pleasure button that made Chance's body shake.

Arlo must have sensed the positive change in Chance and began sliding down more earnestly on his lover. Chance began to hump as much as he could, considering the assault on his own ass.

"Do you like it?" Arlo whispered in Chance's ear.

Chance almost didn't hear him. He was entranced by the wet sounds of fucking and the slapping of balls against asses. The pace was now frenetic. "Arlo…"

"Yeah, Chance. Fuck me hard," Arlo growled, nibbling Chance's neck while they continued to accelerate the pace.

"I'm going to come," Chance warned. "Arlo...are you sure?"

"We're tested," Arlo reminded him through his panting. "Mark me, Chance. You and Charlie are the only men who can."

Arlo's words pushed Chance over the edge and he spasmed. The intense pounding against his prostate gave his whole body an orgasm as he simultaneously felt the ecstasy of long, powerful spurts through his dick.

Charlie moaned, telling his lovers how hot they looked with Chance buried deep in Arlo, and cum oozing down the base of Chance's shaft and his balls. Charlie grabbed the sides of Chance's ass and slammed one last time into him, dumping his own seed.

Arlo, after hearing Charlie's yell, lost himself in his orgasm, shooting arcs of cum across Chance's belly and chest. When he finished, he bent forward to lay his face side-by-side with Chance's.

"Holy shit," Chance muttered as he began to soften inside Arlo. Charlie pulled away from him, leaving his butt feeling slightly sore and wet. Charlie reached for body wipes from the counter and began to clean himself and his men.

"Are you still okay, Chance?" Charlie asked. "By the way, role play is over. I'm asking as one of the men who loves you."

Arlo pulled off Chance and kissed his cheek. "I'm the other man, in case that wasn't clear."

Chance wiped a hand over Arlo's sweating face, then pulled him into a kiss. "It was mind-blowing. I never felt anything like it." He looked to Charlie. "Thank you for making it not so scary, Charlie. I wasn't sure about...bottoming. I can't believe my body could feel that amazing." He shot an affectionate look at Arlo. "And thank you for letting me inside you. I love you guys, too."

Charlie tweaked Chance's nose. "Come on. I have some robes hanging in the closet over here. Once I've had sex, I feel funny about walking around naked. Let's throw them on, go back upstairs and shower."

"Then cuddle," Arlo insisted.

Charlie chuckled. "Then cuddle."

Chapter Nineteen

Chance was finishing the potato salad he had volunteered to make. He wasn't much of a cook, but the online recipe's instructions had been easy enough to follow. He had figured since it was a side dish, the worst that would happen was everyone would take a bite and resume eating their burger, hot dog or grilled chicken.

Charlie approached Chance from behind and wrapped his arms around him, slipping a hand under the San Francisco 49ers chef apron to squeeze one of Chance's pectoral muscles. "Looks good," Charlie mused.

Chance quirked an eyebrow. "Yeah? It's kind of yellow. I hope I put in the right amount of mustard."

"I wasn't talking about the salad." Charlie smiled, nibbling Chance's earlobe.

Chance laughed. "Cut it out. Thanks to your invite, my father will be arriving any minute now and I don't need him walking in and seeing you groping me."

"Relax. He's cooler than you're giving him credit for. These last few weeks, you've said that he's been asking about me and Arlo, and he even sounded like he cared about the answer. And now he's agreed to come to a barbecue where he'll be the only straight person," Charlie reminded him.

Chance covered the salad with plastic wrap and walked it to the refrigerator. "I just don't know why you felt the need to call my parents to tell them I had been sick again. I've been fine for a long time now."

Charlie crossed his arms. "Because your parents should know that you had a setback and know it was, in large part, due to the emotional stress you were under. With your mother still barely saying two words to you every time you call, I felt she in particular should understand what it could do to you to keep laying on the guilt and judgment."

Chance nodded once he stored the food. "And there it is. So, it wasn't about keeping them in the loop. It was about you making them feel bad."

Charlie shrugged. "Maybe. Chance, I care about you. I don't ever again want to see you the way Arlo and I found you."

Chance sighed. "I told you before that you won't. I learned my lesson. I haven't even had a glass of wine or beer since that day. And I pee when I'm supposed to."

Arlo entered the kitchen, hearing Chance's last words. "Why are people talking about peeing?"

"Chance is annoyed that I called his parents about how he was sick," Charlie explained. "Chance, I know you didn't want to make them feel guilty, but I didn't have qualms about it after how your mother treated you. Sue me, but when I was on the phone with them, I was happy to hear their concern. Your mother wouldn't let me hang up until I assured her that you were doing well. And your father couldn't have been nicer. Even though he knew you'd been well for a while, he insisted on coming out to see you."

Chance rolled his eyes, removing the chef apron. "He's been good about it all along, so you shouldn't have made him worry. Bringing him back here could cause tension when he sees us together."

"I disagree," Arlo piped in. "I think it will make him even more comfortable when he sees how happy we are."

Chance curled his lip, less certain than his boyfriend. "Who is he even going to talk to at this cook-out you've invited him to? He'll be glued to my side because everyone else is gay and a stranger to him. You invited my lawyer, his son and the paramedic guy who called to check back on me. And what's up with that? I can't believe he accepted an invitation to this thing. He doesn't even know us. Is he that hard-up for barbecue?"

Arlo snorted. "Ha! He wants some meat for sure. What patient gets the kind of attention he gave you unless the paramedic has a hunkering for his man-sausage?"

"Jesus," Chance muttered. "Pass. He was nice and handsome, but I think three of us is enough, don't you?"

Arlo pulled Chance into an embrace. "I'd say the three of us together is perfect. Maybe he'll take a liking to Elijah."

Chance squinted. "Elijah? He's an attractive man, but I think his son is closer to Pietro's age."

Arlo shrugged. "I'm in my twenties, and I'm totally hot for you, even though you're a few years older. And I'm also in love with a thirty-nine-year-old man." He kissed Charlie for emphasis. "Some of us like a hot daddy."

Chance pursed his lips. "Don't talk kinky shit in front of my father, okay? I don't want him freaking out, learning about all of these subcultures you've been telling me about. He's making so much progress. Let's not ruin it by scaring him."

Charlie snickered. "Are you sure that's the best approach? He might enjoy hearing about the fun we've had role playing the last few weeks. I'm sure he'll be proud of how his son was such an able-bodied CIA agent, teasing information out of traitorous Arlo. That is, until I came to save him, and he and I took revenge by taking turns on your cute ass."

Chance's eyes widened. "Charlie, if you even dare…"

Arlo and Charlie burst out laughing, causing Chance to relax and blush.

"We'll be on our best behavior," Arlo promised when he became serious. "I still need to convince your dad I'm not a pervert for having done a fan site. I have a big hill to climb. I'm not about to throw more dirt on the mound. I'll be sure to drop into the conversation that I don't do the webcam stuff anymore."

"Good," Chance muttered. "I'm pretty sure me being with two guys is about all his heart can handle, and him knowing one of them isn't doing porn anymore will help."

Charlie shook his head. "Your father's heart is fine. He's still quite young. At least he looks it from all the pictures you've shared."

Chance shrugged. "He's older than you're guessing."

Charlie raised his eyebrows. "Well, he looks damn good for any age. I see where you get your handsomeness. If Pietro is into hot daddies, your father just might get lucky."

Chance lifted a spatula from the island counter and aimed it threateningly at Charlie. "Okay, gross. If anyone starts flirting with my dad…"

Arlo shrugged. "But he is attractive, Chance. I never envisioned a guy in his fifties so sexy."

As Chance stared down Arlo with horror, Charlie popped some grapes from a nearby bowl into his mouth. "Yeah, if he ever comes out as bi, he'll be hard to resist. I'm drawn to handsome Findley same-sex virgins."

Chance began to chase Charlie with the spatula, causing Charlie to whoop before hot-tailing it out the kitchen door to the patio. Just as the two men rounded the corner of the house with Chance ready to swat Charlie's arm with the utensil, they bumped into Chance's father, nearly landing him on his back in the alley-sized yard that separated the house from Chance's.

"Dad!" Chance greeted with alarm, lowering the spatula and wrapping a supportive arm around his father to steady him back on his feet.

"Chance," Hugh responded, his initial alarm turning to curiosity. "Is everything all right?"

Charlie put a protective hand on Hugh's elbow. "I'm sorry, Mr. Findley. Everything's fine. Chance and I were just horsing around. It's nice to meet you in person, sir."

Hugh nodded with uncertainty. "Likewise." He glanced at his son. "Horsing around? I hope that means you're back to feeling better, Chance?"

Chance blushed, scratching the back of his neck with his free hand. "Yeah. Dad, I don't know why Charlie called you about something that happened weeks ago.

He should have stressed that I've been fine. You didn't need to fly out here."

Hugh blinked, then pulled Chance into a hug. "He did stress that you were fine, Chance. I hated that you were in such rough shape—again—and I was so far away and not here to help you. I just wanted to come to see you."

Charlie cleared his throat. "Um, Chance, I'm going to check on how Arlo's doing with the marinating. Why don't you spend a few minutes alone with your father?" He turned to Hugh with a nervous smile. "I'm glad you're here, sir."

"Me, too." Hugh nodded.

As Charlie made his way back inside, Chance grabbed his father's upper arm and began to lead him toward the back patio. "Sorry about that, Dad."

"Well, I guess it's better than the other type of horsing around I could have walked in on," Hugh remarked, almost laughing when his son grimaced.

They rounded the house and took seats on the patio, then Chance put the spatula on a small side table by his chair. "I'm sorry you were worried, Dad. I hate that you felt the need to fly out here again so soon. I guess Mom didn't want to join you, huh?"

Hugh rested his elbow on the arm of his chair and leaned his chin on the palm of his hand. "You know, it's a long trip and we were just here…"

"Yeah. Sure." Chance nodded, unable to mask his disappointment.

Hugh sat silent for a moment before continuing. "I'm leaving your mom."

Chance's gaze shot up to his father's, his mouth opening but remaining wordless for several seconds. "What? Why?"

"How she's treating you…"

"No! Dad, I don't want to be the reason you two split," Chance protested.

Hugh held up his hand to silence his son. "Listen to me. I was going to say, how she's treating you reminds me of how she's treated me for years now. She's easy to disappoint and hard to appease. Frankly, I just don't care enough anymore to try."

"Oh." Chance gulped, still surprised.

"You're old enough to hear the truth now," Hugh continued. "Son, your mother and I struggled almost from the start. I'm sure she could give you a laundry list of reasons she finds me difficult. In fact, I think she has—many times—over the years, if my ears didn't deceive me."

"Jesus, I didn't agree with most of what she told me, Dad. It was just easier to let Mom vent, you know?" Chance explained.

Hugh chuckled. "Oh, believe me, I do. I never blamed you for sitting and listening without arguing. Besides, her perception is her reality, just as mine is. And my perception is that you need to work hard to earn and experience her love. That means being what she wants you to be, even if what she wants is impossible. If you didn't already know that, I'm sure you've learned it now."

Chance felt sad, reflecting on his father's words. "Are you saying she doesn't love me anymore?"

Hugh shook his head. "No, Chance. I said you need to work hard to *experience* her love—not to have it. Son, she loves you. If she didn't, she wouldn't be struggling so much with your situation. She truly fears for you—she's from a different place and era, just as I am. It's just that I recognize it and know that I should trust you to do what's best for you. She still thinks it's her role to guide you…and me and your sister. Your mother can't help herself. She tends to think she's always right."

That made Chance laugh. "No shit."

"She cares about you, Chance," Hugh reiterated. "She'll need evidence over a long time to convince her she's wrong. Until then, she's going to use the tactic on you that she's always used on me to get me to cave. She'll try to make you feel her disappointment. Don't let her. The worst thing you can do is lead her to believe that her actions are having an impact. In time, she'll give up because she'll miss you too much to continue the stalemate."

"Does Marybeth know you're leaving Mom?"

"She does," he replied. "Marybeth took it very well. She's siding with me one-hundred percent. I've asked her to go easy on her mom. I'm sure Ann doesn't understand why we don't see that she's just trying to make us better and help us avoid future disappointment. She's so busy worrying about what could happen that she's not enjoying the wonderful gifts she already has with you and Marybeth."

Chance swallowed hard, emotional about his father's sentiments, but also facing hard truths about his mother. "I appreciate that, Dad."

"Listen," Hugh continued, "I wish I had reacted better at learning you're bisexual. I've always prided myself on being the parent that you could come to and not be judged—just loved. In those first few moments, I failed you, Chance. I've reflected on how I wasn't listening, and it reminded me of my own father's reaction when I told him a long time ago that I had regrets about marrying your mother. Instead of supporting me, he reminded me of my responsibility to my family and that it was my obligation to stick it out, no matter what. Chance, what I should have said as soon as you told me about you and your friends is that you're my boy, I love you and I always will. There is no wrong decision if that choice makes you happy, isn't hurting others and is based on love. Don't live your life for your mother…or for me either. Live it for yourself because it isn't a dress rehearsal for a better one down the pike."

Chance bolted from his chair and hugged his father tight. "I love you, Dad. Thank you."

Hugh rubbed soothing circles over Chance's back before pulling away so they could face each other.

"Are you happy, Chance?"

"I am, Dad," Chance assured him. "And don't beat yourself up. When I reflect on that day, I just remember you were supportive much sooner than most other parents would have been. I get that it was a lot."

Hugh grinned a little. "It was. But hey, if you're content, why were you trying to beat one of your boyfriends to death?"

Chance chuckled. "Not to death. He made a comment about you looking hot. I wanted to give him a good welt to remind him that teasing me about you being attractive is forbidden. You're my father, for Christ's sake. He's only allowed to see you as a gross old geezer."

"Ouch." Hugh feigned a wounded expression. "That's a bit harsh of you. Anyway, I think my estimation of Charlie just rose."

"Of course, it did." Chance laughed. "You always were a narcissist."

Hugh smiled in return. "A genetic trait I passed on to you. And how's the other one?"

"Arlo," Chance corrected. "Please be nice to him, Dad. He's a good guy. He isn't doing the fan-site stuff anymore, not that it would have made me love him less if he did. You know, Arlo is so nice, he spent his entire last show just telling his viewers all the things he likes about them, why he'll miss them and encouraging them to see themselves as beautiful like he sees them. He told me that some of his longtime viewers were typing that they were crying, thanking him for everything and telling him they'd miss him, too. Dad, it wasn't just about sex. He cares about people. That's why he works in a nursing home. And Arlo has a way of making everyone love him in return. Well, except his parents, I guess. He doesn't have a cool father like I do who accepted him being gay. It bothers him more than he lets on. I know he wishes he still had his father in his life. Please don't make him feel like my dad dislikes him, too."

Hugh nodded. "Okay, son. I trust your judgment. And I'm sorry to hear about how his parents have treated him. But Charlie and Arlo—they're good to you?"

Chance kneeled next to his father's chair. "Dad, I never knew what I was missing until I met them. Yes, they're good to me. Very good."

"And what happens next, Chance? You stay with two guys for the rest of your life, living happily ever after? Is that possible?"

"I don't know," Chance replied honestly. "I *really* don't know. Yes? Maybe? Dad, I could have died a couple of times recently. It's like you said about your perspective versus Mom's. I'm focused on what I have now, and I want to hold onto it as long as I'm loving it."

* * * *

Hugh and Chance joined Arlo and Charlie in the kitchen to help them finish the meal preparations.

Chance appreciated that his father gave Arlo an awkward hug upon meeting him in-person, and he could see that the gesture meant a lot to his boyfriends. The three men made efforts to make pleasant conversation, even sharing lighthearted jabs. He chuckled when his father and Charlie began good-natured ribbing of each other's favorite baseball teams. Since his father was from Missouri, he was a Cardinals fan, which had him debating with Charlie whether his team or San Francisco's team would make the playoffs. Arlo finally interjected to stop the quarreling, asking which team's players had nicer butts. Chance was surprised that even his father laughed at that before cheekily responding that he was sure it was the hearty, corn-fed Cardinals.

Over the course of the hour, Chance's lawyer Elijah and his son Tim arrived. Because they had been engaged in so much conversation over the last few weeks, Chance felt he had gotten to know them much better. There were hugs exchanged by all, even though the two guests were unknown to the others personally. When Chance saw Arlo give Elijah appreciative scrutiny, he discreetly swatted Arlo's ass.

Arlo blushed, turning his gaze to Chance. "What? I can't look?"

"Is that what that was?" Chance chuckled. "I imagined you were summoning the spirits to make a stiff wind blow off his clothes."

Arlo lifted his eyebrows. "Hey, how awesome would that be?" Chance swatted his arm. "Ouch, stop hitting me. Chance, even if I had that power to blow off everyone's clothes, yours and Charlie's bodies would be the ones I'd end up ogling—for the most part. You know that."

Charlie was standing nearby and overheard the last of the conversation. "Good answer. Although, if you make that wind happen, I might spend a few minutes checking out Hugh's body."

Chance narrowed his eyes. "Don't you effing start…"

Charlie's laughter pealed through the air, lessening Chance's annoyance a bit.

"Hello?" a voice came from the open front door.

"Oh, that would be Pietro," Arlo noted to Charlie and Chance. "You remember him, Chance. The hunk that was hellbent on checking up on you once you were released from the hospital? I'll give him the benefit of the doubt and assume he thought we were just roommates."

Chance rolled his eyes, recognizing that even though he pretended to be jealous when Arlo or Charlie spoke of other men, Arlo really did harbor a beef with the handsome paramedic. It didn't bother him. He was pleased that Arlo was possessive of him.

"Come on in," Charlie shouted.

All heads turned to see the new arrival. Pietro shook Arlo's and Charlie's hands, then pulled Chance into a hug. "You look great, Chance."

"Well, it's amazing what a shave and a bath can do," Arlo quipped. "We had no choice really. The city was ready to cordon off our house for sheltering the homeless without a license."

"I volunteer at Support for the San Francisco Homeless," Tim piped in, somewhat offended.

"Shit, sorry," Arlo muttered. "I swear, I didn't mean…"

Chance leaned to Arlo's ear to rub it in. "Insensitivity backfire."

"Um, would you guys like a tour of the place?" Arlo asked the new guests, hoping to return to their good graces.

Pietro and Tim said they would and followed Arlo into the adjoining room. Elijah made his way to Chance to tell him he had an update on the case, asking if it was okay to discuss in front of Charlie and Hugh.

"Sure," Chance responded. "I told them everything. They can hear whatever you have to say."

Elijah nodded and gave a small smile. "Well, I have good news, Chance. Your old firm isn't acknowledging guilt, but my threats must have scared them. You're getting a *year's* severance, plus COBRA medical benefits for the next twelve months since the termination will be coded as a job elimination. Technically, that means you could even apply for unemployment should you choose. The firm also agreed to pay you five hundred thousand in punitive damages, and they're waiving the right to hold you to the non-compete clause you signed. As I pointed out to them, our position is that you were wrongfully terminated and, therefore, the agreement is null and void."

Chance beamed. "Wow! That's all way better than I expected. God!" He pulled Elijah into a hug. "Thank you, Elijah. You're amazing." Charlie hugged Elijah, too, then clapped Chance on the back.

"Congratulations, Chance." Hugh smiled. "That's great news. Now, whatever you decide, your former clients can come to you without repercussions."

Chance blinked, absorbing the implications. "And if I sell my house to move in here, I can use the money from that and the settlement to invest in my own firm."

Hugh arched an eyebrow. "You're moving in here?"

Chance gulped. "Oh. Uh, yeah. I meant to tell you. Charlie and Arlo asked me to since I'm always here anyway. I mean, it makes sense…financially."

Hugh tried to hide a wry smile. "Hmm, I suppose it does make sense…*financially*. You know, I might have a buyer for your house."

Chance was so happy that his father wasn't crapping on his moving plans that he almost didn't hear him say there was a potential buyer. "What was that now? Someone is interested in my house?"

"Me," Hugh replied.

"Huh?" Chance and Charlie exchanged surprised expressions.

Hugh looked around the room as if seeing the place for the first time. "I rather like San Francisco, despite the overrated sports teams. But there's always cable to watch St. Louis sports. And I could get used to this weather. Marybeth wants to move here, so both my kids would be close. And now that your mother and I are splitting…"

"What?" Charlie asked, reeling from the added-on surprise.

"Oh, I'm sorry to hear," Elijah interjected.

Hugh waved a dismissive hand. "Don't be. It's for the best. Anyway, Marybeth said she couldn't afford to move here without a job…unless she moves in with her dear old dad. When I mentioned to her that I was thinking of relocating here, she was very excited. She misses you, Chance. And she'd like to meet Arlo and Charlie in person instead of relying on your online chats. I just wasn't expecting a house to become available so fast."

Chance chewed on his lip. "That would be…next door."

"Didn't you say you have your own successful marketing firm in Missouri, Hugh?" Elijah questioned.

"I do," Hugh acknowledged. "But you know, I could run that from anywhere." He looked over to his son with hopeful eyes. "Chance, I know you've talked about opening your own firm, but what about working with me?"

"Huh?" said Chance.

Hugh returned his gaze to Elijah and Charlie. "I always wanted Chance to join my firm, but he was too talented to settle for a marketing rep role on my team. And he didn't want to stay in Missouri." He looked over to Chance once more. "Son, if I moved here and expanded my client base, I wouldn't want my firm competing with one you'd start up. You could be my partner. I'll be retiring in a decade or so. It would make me happy to know the firm would stay in your good hands. What do you think?"

Chance glanced back and forth between the three men, unsure how to answer. "I think I was too quick to give up drinking."

* * * *

After Chance's moment of panic at his father's proposal, Hugh gave his son space during the rest of the get-together. It forced him to spend more time talking to the other guests, and he found that he enjoyed their company. To his pleasant surprise, he particularly liked Charlie and Arlo.

It was obvious to Hugh how caring and protective Charlie was, and he took comfort in knowing the man would be in his sensitive son's corner, especially if others were cruel to him for his decisions. But it was Arlo who won his affection, with his childlike positivity and unabashed devotion to Chance and Charlie. Hugh also appreciated how Arlo went out of his way throughout the day to make sure he was doing well and feeling welcome.

When Hugh cornered Arlo alone in the kitchen, he asked questions about the website, and he admired how Arlo didn't become defensive or irritated. Hugh sensed that the stint addressed something Arlo's own parents had deprived him of as an adult—attention, admiration and support. He was glad Arlo could now feel those things from Charlie and Chance.

When Arlo spoke about his love for Chance, the man bordered on emotional. Arlo promised Hugh that he would always put Chance's needs above his own and that he would do his best to be deserving of him. Hugh smiled, as those were words that every father would want to hear said about their child.

By the time the sun set, the partygoers left, leaving the homeowners and Chance's father sitting around the backyard firepit. Hugh looked across the flames at his son. There was contentment on his boy's face. Hugh decided it was an okay time to address his earlier mistake of dropping so much on his son. He took a sip from the fifth wine he had indulged in during the day. "Chance, are you still speaking to me?"

Chance looked over the pit to meet his father's eyes. "What? Why wouldn't I be?"

"I blindsided you earlier," Hugh responded. "It wasn't how I should have told you that Marybeth and I were thinking of moving here. Then I got carried away with the idea of buying your house and making you a partner. It was just so exciting and I was feeling such joy thinking about it."

Chance nodded. "It's okay, Dad. It took me by surprise, is all." He turned to the encouraging expressions on Charlie's and Arlo's faces. "Actually, Dad—Charlie, Arlo and I spoke about it. When it comes to big life decisions, I want their opinions."

Hugh blinked with momentary surprise, but then cleared his throat. "Yes, of course. That's as it should be between partners."

"Charlie and Arlo helped me realize how sweet it was of you. I'm sorry I didn't recognize that right away. Maybe I've tended to keep people—even you—at a distance. I don't want to do that anymore, Dad. You've been awesome about everything, and I appreciate it…and I'm grateful for the offer. Charlie, Arlo and I agree that your proposal is generous and, if you haven't changed your mind, I'd like to accept it."

Hugh gasped. "You would? All of it? Working with me as well as me buying your house?"

Chance chuckled. "Yeah, well, having your dad living next door and working with him side-by-side every day…it took a bit for the idea to seep in. But it does make sense financially, and…I do want you and Marybeth here with me. I feel bad about everyone leaving Mom behind, but there's nothing stopping her from moving here, is there? She doesn't work. It just comes down to how much she wants me and Marybeth in her life."

Hugh nodded. "I'll suggest that she consider it. I can't promise she would leave her friends and the circle of acquaintances she's built…but you never know. Maybe in time?"

Charlie shot one of his intimidating looks at Hugh. "I think before anyone signs papers, we should clarify what you mean by working together as partners. Mr. Findley, your son is a talent and could easily start his own firm. I have no doubt he would give yours a real run for the money. I hope your proposal means a *full* partnership for Chance, with equal decision-making authority."

Hugh grinned. "I appreciate your directness, Charlie. And you continue to impress me with how you look out for my son. And yes, I meant what I said about Chance and me being equal partners and all that goes with that. Hell, I'd probably defer to him most of the time. I'm well aware that he's the town's Marketing Boy Wonder, and I could benefit from his up-to-date experience and the connections he has in the city. I recognize the value he brings beyond being my heir. And Charlie, I wouldn't screw over my son."

Arlo rubbed his hands along his denim-covered thighs. "This is great! Mr. Findley, we're happy that you'll be living next door." Chance shrugged as if to say the jury was out and Arlo waved a hand at him. "We are *all* happy about it. Don't let him fool you. And I can't wait to hang out with Marybeth. She's a hoot."

"Yeah, Arlo and Marybeth hog all the time during our chats," Chance pretended to grumble.

"Sorry." Arlo blushed. "But, Chance, after meeting you, you completed my family. You, me, Charlie and Grams. But you come with a great dad and sister, too. I miss all of that." Arlo turned to Hugh, dropping his smile. "I mean, if you wanted to consider me part of your family, Mr. Findley."

"Hugh," Chance's father corrected. "No…wait. I've changed my mind. I don't think you and Charlie should call me that."

Chance's jaw dropped. "Dad!"

"Yes, that's the word I want you boys to call me," Hugh clarified. "If you're accepting me as part of *your family*."

Chance, Charlie and Arlo remained quiet for a moment, overwhelmed with surprise. Arlo's eyes misted. "My own father doesn't let me call him that anymore. He told me not to call him anything."

Hugh grimaced. After spending the day with Arlo, he couldn't understand how the man's parents wouldn't embrace someone so loveable just because of his sexual orientation. He rose from his chair and walked over to the man, pulling him into a half-hug. "Well, I insist you call me Dad. Okay, son?"

Arlo leaned his face into the side of Hugh's trousers while hugging the man's legs. When he pulled back, he wiped a tear from his eye. Hugh looked to Chance—he mouthed a 'thank you' Hugh's way.

Arlo pulled up his shirt to wipe follow-up tears. "Sorry about that...Dad."

Hugh tousled Arlo's hair. "Don't be. Nothing wrong with a man shedding a tear on occasion. And now that I see that six-pack you have, I understand how you got hundreds of online viewers."

Chance blanched. "Dad...Jesus."

Arlo chuckled. "Oh, they were looking at my stomach all that time? Here I was taking off my pants for nothing."

It was clear Chance was about to shush Arlo, but Hugh roared a laugh, pulling Arlo back into a half-hug. "Well, you don't need to do that anymore to feel loved, Arlo. It's obvious to me Charlie and my son are happy to give you all you need. I understand why after getting to know you better." He looked to Charlie with a small smile. "And same for you, son."

After a couple of moments of sappy silence, Charlie got a teasing twinkle in his eye. He turned to Chance. "Your father is something else...and I don't just mean his smoldering good looks."

Chance's eyes bugged before he donned a murderous expression. "You fucker." He grabbed a stick they had been using to stoke the firepit logs and ran after a laughing Charlie who had dashed around the corner of the house.

"Yeah, and there's that," Arlo deadpanned. "You're sure you want to sign up for this?"

Hugh laughed. "Yeah, I'm sure. I wouldn't have pictured saying this a few months ago. But you three…I can see that it's special. I'm becoming quite okay with it. Maybe more than okay." Then Hugh chuckled. "And it's the first time in a very long time I've seen Chance having fun. I have you two to thank for that. But hey, do me another favor, will you?"

"What's that?" Arlo asked.

"Make sure those two idiots don't kill each other."

Arlo smirked when they heard Charlie trying to call off Chance, promising that he'd stop his teasing as the two men continued to run around the house. "It sounds like they're reaching a truce for the night."

Hugh clapped Arlo's shoulder. "Good. Let's get them inside. We have lots of planning to do…a whole new life for this crazy little family."

Want to see more from this author? Here's a taster for you to enjoy!

Oh, Baby!: He Doesn't Know Jack

Gareth Chris

Excerpt

It wasn't the kind of day I expected to be life-changing. Then again, when did I, Benjamin Bailey—a thirty-four-year-old librarian working in a quiet corner of New York City—ever anticipate such things? My job was uneventful, sometimes mundane, and required little interaction. There were library patrons, of course, but with each passing year, there were fewer. Books were no longer the main draw. Most people visited to search the internet, read a periodical or to use the public restrooms. I sometimes wished the stereotype about library bathrooms was true and I could watch some good-looking men share knowing looks before they headed to the john. While I would never participate and risk my career, it would be a titillating distraction envisioning what was happening behind the lavatory door. But no, our little public service building only attracted men and women seeking intellectual stimulation or bladder relief.

I was typing a response to an angry patron who was demanding we remove a book about transgender studies from the library, rewriting my note multiple times to remove words and phrases that might be deemed unprofessional. What I wanted to communicate was that she was a bigoted Neanderthal who didn't have the right to dictate what others could read. I forced myself to hold back—I needed to be diplomatic. That meant I also needed to refrain from calling her a pot-stirrer, considering how determined she must have been to find a book that was on one of two shelves labeled 'LGBTQ Studies.'

"Excuse me," a female voice from the other side of my reception desk wall echoed.

An attractive older woman who stood more than six feet in height was looking my way. Tall women always made me self-conscious of my own height, which was a mere five-foot-nine. I was glad I was seated. "Yes, may I help you?"

She smiled and her expression struck me as mischievous. "Yes, you may. I've come here many times. I love this library. It's large enough to find amazing stuff, but small enough to be charming and accessible. I'm Andrea, by the way." Andrea reached a long arm over the dark mahogany wood partition to shake my hand. The many bracelets on her wrist clinked together as she did so.

In all my years of employment at the library, it was the first time a patron had introduced themselves, let alone shaken my hand.

"Hi," I responded. When she remained quiet for a moment with an expectant expression, I added, "I'm Benjamin."

She clasped her hands together. "Oh, it's so nice when someone uses their longer given name. My daughter's name is Alexandra, but she insists on being called Allie or Alex. If I had wanted to name her Allie or Alex, that's what I would have done."

"Um, sure. So, you said you needed my assistance?"

Her smile dipped for a second. "Well, this is going to seem weird...but here goes. When I've come here, I've noticed you. I mean that in a good way. You're such a nice-looking man, and I'm sure you're smart because whenever I see you, your nose is buried in a book or you're staring at a computer screen. Also, I have this theory that a man who works as a librarian must be a gentle soul, and I think that's very becoming in a world full of insecure alpha males."

Whatever flattery I was feeling was eclipsed by anxiousness that Andrea was about to ask for a date. Considering she looked to be seventy or older, I at least had to admire her confidence. "Oh, um, I'm not..."

Andrea's eyes went wide and her mouth opened a bit with horror. "Benjamin, I wasn't hitting on you."

"Oh..."

"I mean, trust me, in my day, I would have. I never believed a woman needs to wait to be asked. Then again, I was a bit of a rebel and a fierce fighter for women's rights. Well, I still am. But one thing I've never been is an idiot. I know I'm well past the age of a woman who'd interest you. Besides, I'm married." She paused. "I may be a nonconformist, but I'm not an adulteress. What about you?"

"Huh? Am I an adulterer?"

"No...are you married?" Andrea asked.

I shook my head. "Uh...I'm divorced."

"Ah!" she exclaimed. "Everyone from your generation is divorced! Alexandra is divorced, too. You know what the problem is, don't you? Young people today focus too much on the physical. You think you're in love because you see a nice pair of tits."

"Andrea, you...we're in a library," I stammered, unsure what I had done to invite this woman's crazy observations. I slid my black-framed glasses up my nose, unsure of what else to say.

Andrea remained oblivious to my discomfort. "Of course, we hooked up back in my day, too. Free love and all that." Andrea smiled at the recollection. "But hell, I didn't marry a guy because he was good on a mattress. People back then married someone who had common interests and values."

When I had married, I had thought my husband and I had similar interests and values, too. I wondered if my generation was just better at deceit and hidden agendas.

"I'm glad your marriage worked for you," I stated, uncertain if my tone was patronizing. "Anyway, I need to finish this response to someone who complained, so…"

"About you? Why? What did you do?" Andrea asked. The way she leaned in and grinned, I could tell she was hoping for juicy gossip.

I flushed. "I didn't do anything! Some woman complained about a book we have on transgender studies and is threatening a campaign against the library if we don't remove it."

"Twat," Andrea spat. I opened my mouth with surprise. "Oh, not you…the hag with the stick up her ass."

I still found Andrea peculiar, but I also found myself laughing. "Well, I should get back to it…"

"Wait," she interjected. "I haven't told you yet why I was buttering you up with compliments."

"Okay…"

"I told Alexandra about you during one of my visits with her. And don't worry, I understand that physical attraction is important. Take my word for it, she's very beautiful because she's the spitting image of me at that age. People mistook me for Audrey Hepburn. I know that you and she would have similar interests. Alexandra is a liberal, as I can tell you are from your reaction to the hag. She's very successful and her townhouse is filled with books. Imagine how you'd be able to bond over the interesting things you two read."

I hadn't exhaled during Andrea's description because I had been trying to interrupt. I took advantage when Andrea paused. "Andrea, I'm flattered but I'm not interested in dating."

Andrea pouted. "Too soon after your divorce? Don't become a hater of women because of one bad experience, Benjamin."

"I don't hate women," I countered. "I just like…men." I glanced down at the desk, causing my glasses to slip back down my nose a bit.

When I looked back up, I noticed Andrea's face had gone white. "But you told me you were divorced." Then her pallor changed to red. "Oh, you're divorced from a man, aren't you? Look at me, falling into generational assumptions. God, just wrap me in a Confederate flag and ship me to a Klan cookout because that's where I belong for my backward thinking. I'm sorry, Benjamin."

I smiled. Andrea was beginning to grow on me. "It's okay."

Once Andrea collected herself, she leaned over the partition, her many bangles sliding down to her wrist. "Okay, so Alexandra's out. Darn! I was so hopeful for the two of you. Well, is there a nice boy in the picture then?"

I didn't have the heart to shut her down, even though I wasn't keen on sharing personal information. I could tell that Andrea was harmless enough and had taken a liking to me. I swiveled my chair to face her head-on. "No. I meant it when I said I'm not looking to date anyone."

"Your ex crushed you that bad, huh?" she pressed.

I pursed my lips. "He disappointed me. Contrary to what you think about my generation, I married him thinking we had a lot in common. I thought we had the same goals. I wish I had realized we didn't before we tied the knot. Anyway, he's been out of my life for several months now, and I'm surprised how little I miss him."

Andrea smiled. "That's a good thing. It's like I say to Alexandra, life is too short to wallow in the past. Create new happiness. But why can't that involve a man? I'm sure there are nice guys out there. In this city, it might be easier for you to find one of them than it will be for my daughter."

"It's complicated," I replied. Expanding on the reasons with Andrea would be too much. Friendly as she might be, she still wasn't a friend. I wasn't about to babble my rationale and history to a stranger. "Listen, maybe someday...but that day isn't today."

I saw the corner of her mouth quirk up. "Well, if marriage is off the table, then you can just hook up. Free love and all that still works in modern times, too." She winked. "You do still have sex, don't you?"

My eyes flew open. "Andrea, this isn't the place...."

"Don't be a prude like old Miss Twat who soiled her adult diapers when she saw a book," Andrea warned.

I snickered at the image. "Okay, speaking of her, I should get back to typing my response."

"I can take a hint." She smirked, backing away from the partition. I wanted to tell her that she couldn't, considering I had dropped hints a few times already. "But I'm here a lot if you ever want to chat. And even though you shouldn't need my assistance, I can scout

out the attractive men that come here and send them your way."

"What? No, don't do that," I implored. "I'll get fired if my boss thinks you're pimping me out at work."

Andrea was unphased. "Please. I'm not an amateur at discretion. I had a closeted homosexual friend in college, and I found him all his hook-ups and his secret never came out. Listen, if I strike up a conversation here in the library with a nice-looking man, and I can tell that he leans a certain way, I'll suggest to him that he check out the cute librarian. I'll let him know that I have it on good authority that you play for the same team. Easy-peasy."

"Please don't," I begged, pushing my glasses up my nose. "I don't think I should..."

Andrea held up a hand to silence me. "You can turn anyone away, Benjamin. No harm, no foul." Before I could protest, she waved a hand good-bye, jangling the many bracelets again. "I'm going to scan the place to see if there's someone else who'd be good for my daughter. Ta-ta."

True to her word, she hustled toward the rear of the building with eyes darting, using the library as a brick-and-mortar version of Tinder and Grindr.

About the Author

Gareth Chris has a degree in English and a minor in Theater / Playwriting. When he isn't writing stories about dashing men overcoming challenging situations, he provides consultative organizational design and executive coaching to international clients. He volunteers his time to local charitable organizations that focus on helping the less fortunate—particularly those needing food and shelter.

Gareth makes his home in the lovely New England area of the United States, where he, family, and friends enjoy the proximity to beaches, mountains, and numerous historical cities and sites.

Gareth loves to hear from readers. You can find his contact information, website details and author profile page at https://www.firstforromance.com/

Sign up for our newsletter and find out about all our romance book releases, eBook sales and promotions, sneak peeks and FREE romance books!

www.ingramcontent.com/pod-product-compliance
Lightning Source LLC
Chambersburg PA
CBHW020817260626
47169CB00003B/708

9781802507478